Sensorama

Edited by

Allen Ashley

www.eibonvalepress.co.uk

Contents:

Blinding a Few Dogs
Gary Budgen

He thinks, as a consequence of this, that it may be possible to live visually in one part of the world, while one lives bodily in another. He has even made some experiments in support of his views; but so far, he has simply succeeded in blinding a few dogs.
"The Remarkable Case of Davidson's Eyes" by H. G. Wells

Across the dual carriageway the advertising billboard had been vandalised again. The poster, made up of six rectangular sections, never stayed intact for very long because the local kids would tear at it, pull away pieces. Now, the upper portion was for a Hollywood movie and a woman with ice blonde hair in a low cut white dress stared out; just where her cleavage plunged the poster had been ripped off to show the bright yellow sands of a tropical island from some holiday dream of months ago.

Avery stared at the poster. There was a problem with his left eye. His vision had become partially obscured by an obstruction shaped like a curved diamond, a little smudge filled with ambient colour. Around this his sight was unaffected; it was just this small area that had gone wrong. The diagnosis was macular degeneration. The cells of his macula had become damaged and the condition would get gradually worse so that eventually it would affect both eyes although the rate of decay could vary between them.

The day Avery came back from the doctors with the diagnosis he knew he would have to make the most of his time left because soon he might no longer be able to see Jennifer.

At the window he sat in his armchair and looked out over the dual carriageway. Apart from the smudge he could still see everything clearly. There was the billboard and the endless succession of mostly silver-grey cars under the gaze of the speed cameras. And beyond the dual carriageway was a row of houses, almost identical to the row this side where his own house was. Many had doors and windows boarded up and even those houses still inhabited were dilapidated with the paint flaking off their badly clad fronts. Cheap rents for those with nowhere else to go. There was nothing beautiful here at all. Only Jennifer was beautiful.

He sat this way until dusk watching the car headlights come on with their drowsy distant glow. When he woke, still in the armchair, the traffic had dwindled. Avery looked around the room and knew that he should clear up. Soon he might be blind and didn't want to trip over the boxes of returned packages that Jennifer had sent back, the soft toys, the chocolates and lingerie. On the coffee table a stack of letters from the police and the court had slid into an untidy pile. Perhaps, after all, not seeing all of this might actually be a relief.

In bed he thought, as always, of Jennifer. The first time he had seen her had been in the newsagent in one of the little streets beyond the dual carriageway. He often went to that newsagent because it wasn't too close to his house and was usually empty. He would be in and out quick, grabbing one of the magazines and paying for it without really checking it was one that he would like.

This time *she* had come in and Avery knew there was an instant attraction. He had stood by the little carousel of birthday cards and watched as she'd gone to the counter.

"Hello, Jennifer," the shopkeeper had said.

She'd bought cigarettes while Avery took in her back, her black hair, the shape of her body in the track suit.

He'd followed her home that day.

*

In the morning the smudge in his eye had changed. In shape and size it was the same but there was something about the light and colour that was different. He lay back on his bed and tried to examine it.

It had become darker, yet not quite black. The light had changed and what had been an obstruction was now a crack that he could see into. Then the crack darkened with shadow; then lightened again. This happened again without any regular interval. The shadow sometimes covered the whole of the crack and sometimes only part of it, making odd darker shapes against the grey.

Avery lay and watched and at last realised that the flittering shadow was in fact something moving. He tried to focus as though his own eye might look through that part of itself that was this crack. But then the moving shadow was gone and the crack became what it had before, coloured the same dull magnolia as his bedroom walls and ceiling.

By the time Avery got up it was mid-morning; too late to see Jennifer on her way to work. But he could make it for when she came out to lunch. As he left the house he found it easier to close his left eye as much as possible rather than being distracted by the crack there. He got a few strange glances on the bus but soon it had dropped him further up the dual carriageway at the edge of the industrial estate where Jennifer worked as a receptionist in a print firm. Avery wasn't allowed into the estate anymore but if he stood at the entrance, over 100 yards away from the print firm entrance, he might see Jennifer when she came out to go to the little caravan that sold tea and snacks.

But today she did not emerge even though he stood there for over an hour, the wind picking up and blowing grit onto his skin, making him close both eyes against it. Once he saw one of the other girls who worked with Jennifer. She knew who he was but she ignored him.

For the afternoon he retreated via a foot tunnel to the other side of the dual carriageway where there was a row of shops and a café.

As he sipped tea the image in the crack in his eye came to life with a wavering of flickering shadow that moved from side to side and then, adding for the first time depth, seemed to move inwards away from him. And unmistakeably, for a moment, the shapes became the silhouette of a human being.

"Are you all right?"

Avery must have cried out because the old waitress was stood next to his table, speaking to him.

"I'm fine," he said looking at her only for a second.

"Well, you can't just sit there all afternoon with one cup of tea again."

He ordered another and screwed his left eye closed. As long as he could see Jennifer later it didn't matter.

After three or so hours he went over and waited again by the entrance to the industrial estate. Mercifully the crack in his left eye had become dim and grey, devoid of movement. He saw the staff come from the print firm but Jennifer wasn't with them. As they passed him one of the men – the one called Frank – came over.

"Why don't you just fuck off?" he said to Avery.

"Where's Jennifer?" Avery asked.

The woman he had seen earlier came over; she was red-faced and when she spoke she spat the words: "You've done it now, you freak. She's gone somewhere you'll never find her."

"Where?"

"Just fuck off," said Frank.

"No," said Avery, "she wouldn't do that. She wouldn't leave me."

On the bus home he shook as he wondered what might have happened to Jennifer. He knew she had a difficult life, that she couldn't express what she felt about him. Avery had always suspected some man in the background, some bully. Probably Frank at the print firm. Poor Jennifer. At first she had replied to his letters and presents but then she'd begun to send them back. There had been a message: *Please. I really don't want you to bother me anymore.* But Avery had not been deceived. He knew there was some kind of duress involved.

In his armchair again he looked out over the cars as the evening came. He would have to make sure that she was gone, to go and see the house even if it meant going against the court order. The crack in his eye was dark, hardly seen but when he stood to go out a jabbing pain poked at his eye. It became so intense that he fell to his knees; but even with his eye screwed shut he could feel the crack changing, growing.

He looked.

What was there was a room. The view was larger now, the crack became a hole in which he could see objects made up of grey: a bed and a wardrobe; near the foot of the bed a chest of drawers with a chair in front of it. Beyond the bed, straight ahead, was a square of mud-coloured light contrasting with the greys of the furniture. It was a window. He was looking into a room at night.

There was still the pain and, carefully, Avery touched the surface of his eye. But this only made him flinch. He needed water so he stumbled towards the bathroom, his foot catching on one of the returned packages. The pain was getting worse even as the scene he could see became more distinct so that he could make out the two columns of furled up curtains either side of the window. Now the room was both light and dark, like creased silver foil. The moon was coming up outside the window. It began to burn away, searing the surface of his eye.

Hurrying, Avery threw the toothbrush out of its plastic beaker and filled this with water. He tipped his head back and poured the water into his eye. For a moment, as the water dribbled down his neck, the pain lessened. The room in his eye was drenched, as though beyond a wet car window screen.

The first time he had really looked at Jennifer he had been waiting across the street from her house. It was morning, before eight o'clock, but he had got there early in case she left for work. It had been before he found out where she worked.

She was smartly dressed in a dark trousers suit, her hair pinned up. Yes. He approved; she should dress like this rather than the track suit she had been wearing in the newsagent. He crossed the street to get behind her, noting with delight that a strand of her hair had come loose. It began to rain and she started to trot. Because the sun was still bright the rain drops sparkled on the pavement. Her hair, tightly held except for the loose strand, shone with wet light. It was one of those moments he wanted to fix. To keep forever.

At the bus stop on the dual carriageway he spoke to her.

"Hi," he said.

She nodded at him and looked away. Then she shuffled down to the other end of the shelter.

Perhaps she was pretending not to remember him. Perhaps she was playing hard to get.

He sat two rows behind her on the bus and when she got off at the industrial estate he said goodbye. She ignored him but he noted the time and place.

With his eye still soaked and screwed shut, he left the house and began to walk towards the dual carriageway. There was a hospital not far away. He passed the billboard lit up for the evening. The advert had changed again to one for a brand of commercial vans. The van, a smart white box, stood proudly above the lesser vehicles that passed on the road beneath it. As he reached the grounds of the hospital he dared to open his eye. The moonlight silvered the room. It hurt for a moment as he tried to make out the features: the bed in the foreground where a shape stirred. Then the pain again and he stumbled through the plastic doors of the casualty department.

They irrigated his eye and eventually the pain subsided. He kept it closed as they led him to a bed in some kind of transit room.

He would be outside the print firm most days, walking with her to the caravan where she got her lunch, usually some sort of sandwich, occasionally a burger.

After the first time she was never on her own, always some gaggle of other women or – worse – men in overalls. The women glared at him. The men abused him. Jennifer said nothing. He realised that everyone was trying to keep them apart, to keep her from him. It was as though she were being held captive in plain sight.

Then, one day, one of the men attacked him, punching him and pushing him to the ground.

"Don't, Frank," Jennifer pleaded for the man to stop; trying to protect Avery.

"It's all right, Jennifer," Avery said. His head throbbed from the punch. "I'm okay."

She bent low, pushing her face towards him as though she were some long-necked beast.

"Don't you fucking see?" she said. "I hate you."

When the police came as he waited outside the print works Avery was confused. Weren't they here because Jennifer had called them after Avery had been hit? But they put him in a cell and questioned him and the whole process that led to the court order began. The relentless interviews; the making him watch the CCTV footage of himself on the industrial estate, his fuzzy edged figure shifting his weight from foot to foot as he waited to see Jennifer.

It seemed that Jennifer's false friends had conspired to ruin everything.

"Mr Avery," some young man, possibly a doctor, said to him. "We're going to have to keep you in hospital. We think the condition of your eye has deteriorated rapidly."

"I can't see very well." This wasn't really true but he did not know what else to say.

"It's all right," said this doctor or whatever he was, "we have your notes. The consultant will see you in the morning."

Avery tried to focus on where he was as they led him through the hospital to a ward. There were beds with their white sheets and heads of men poking out the top. Most were sleeping in the dimmed light from the nurses' station. His left eye felt a little better and he ventured to open it. In the room inside it was night and, just like the ward, there was a shape asleep on the bed.

In the morning the consultant came. Within his eye, now painless, calm, what had once been the rounded diamond crack was now a much wider opening. Avery could see the room there clearly: a bedroom with someone asleep in the bed, their form hidden by blankets.

"Good morning, Mr…. Avery," said the consultant.

Avery tried to take him in, closing off the interior room for a moment and focusing on the hospital ward. He saw a tall man in a purple bow-tie, grey and with glasses.

"I've got your notes here. I understand your vision has taken a sudden decline. You've had some pain as well?"

"They said it would become steadily cloudier, but…"

The consultant came closer and Avery just wanted him to *do* something, examine him, but he just seemed to want to ask questions.

"Yes, please go on Mr Avery."

"There's a room…" Avery didn't know how to explain it, "and other things. I'm not going blind…. I can see. Just not here. Or not only here."

"Hmm." The consultant rubbed his chin. "If I could just examine your eye."

He leant towards Avery with his ophthalmoscope. The room was still there inside, touched by the light from the instrument as though the sun had come down too close to the Earth. On the bed the covers were stirring, being thrown back. Two slender feet and legs slid out.

"There's certainly damaged cells in the macular…"

In the morning light of the bedroom that only Avery could see Jennifer sat on the edge of the bed yawning. She wore a ragged tee-shirt and her hair was messy but it was undoubtedly Jennifer. Avery had found her again.

"Have you had any injuries lately," the consultant was saying, "I mean head injuries?"

"What's that got to do with my eye?" Avery said.

It was hard to pay attention; he was watching Jennifer.

"Certain neurological injuries…"

In the bedroom the edges of her legs were lined with the touch of light from outside. As she put her feet to the floor, the light flowed across her as she turned. Avery watched her walk towards the window.

"We can tell from the examination that the cells in your left eye have degenerated. But what I'm referring to is you saying you can see still. Is that correct, Mr Avery?"

She stood at the window. The curtains were already open and she looked out over the vast expanse of sky. She was up high somewhere. Not her old house. All the objects in the bedroom were clear, the wardrobe, the chest of drawers and chair. Mirror light played on her back where the tee-shirt just reached to the top of her legs. Then she went over to the chest of drawers and began to search for something.

"Anton-Babinski syndrome. Rather rare condition as a matter of fact. The illusion of sight in a blind person. The brain supplying the images…. That's why I asked if you'd had a head injury."

Avery was disappointed that her underwear was plain, boring. But he quickly dismissed this and focused on her, on her presence as she sat, now dressed, at the mirror and began to put on make-up.

"What I'd really like to do is keep you in for observation. There's a man… a colleague, who I think would like to talk to you. Mr Avery? You understand what I'm saying, don't you?"

Avery ate the meals when they were brought and struggled somehow to the toilet, trying for a few minutes to remember where he was, to look at the other beds, the stands with their drip bags, the other patients. But he couldn't not look at Jennifer. He followed her from room to room and she was completely unaware of her desirability; and this made him greedier for her. If only he could zoom in. If only he could taste her with his eye. The eyes were nervous tissue after all, wasn't that what some doctor or other had told him?

Although she had dressed in work clothes she never left the flat. For a while she watched daytime TV. She made a phone call in the evening but Avery couldn't hear what she said. Afterwards she lay on her bed and cried, great sobs that shook her whole body as she curled her arms around her head.

"Mr Avery, I've brought someone to see you."

It was the consultant speaking. He stood there again, twiddling his silly bow-tie. Beside him was another man, a tall, broad man in a dark suit that matched his close cropped dark hair. He might have been in his sixties but he was still tough looking. He smiled for a moment at the consultant then stepped ahead of him, right up next to Avery's bed.

"Hello, Mr Avery," he said, "pleased to meet you. I'm Danes."

There was a quiver in his voice as though this Danes had found something slightly funny.

Jennifer was watching TV. Some old film. Avery had often thought about how their evenings might be spent when they were together. Sat close on the sofa watching something sentimental. Something she would like.

Then Danes said: "Can you see Jennifer, Mr Avery?"

"What are you talking about?" the consultant said.

"Oh," said Danes, "I think this is best left between myself and Mr Avery. Why don't you go and rustle us up a cup of tea and a biscuit? There's a good man."

For a moment the consultant hesitated, looked at Avery as though for an answer and then turned and walked away.

"Who are you?" Avery asked.

"I'm the man hospitals call when they get people like you."

"You're an eye specialist?"

Danes sat on the edge of the bed, his bulk making it sag.

"We know all about you, Mr Avery," he said. "We know all about your little brush with the law. The stalking."

Avery didn't like that word. Other people had used it. But stalkers were weirdoes. Dirty old men.

"I never did anything…"

"It's fine," said Danes, "don't be concerned. We understand perfectly. Be reassured, there's a place for you. It's going to be all right."

*

On the drive to the country Avery was only half aware of where they were going. They were in a large black car and Danes was seated in the front next to the driver. They went along the dual carriageway near to his house. The billboard had been vandalised again, the side of the white van ripped away to reveal a piece of beach, or perhaps the folds of a dress of an extremely glamorous woman from a movie. He couldn't tell if it was a person or a landscape.

He watched Jennifer as she settled down in bed, her body once again beneath the sheets as night fell. At some point, after motorways and smaller roads, the car bumped along a lane. There were lights, a gate in a high chain link fence. After the entrance buzz the driver showed a pass and a torch shone into the car.

"Sorry, Mr Danes," someone said and the car crunched down on gravel.

Jennifer slept on.

"Welcome to my domain," said Danes.

Avery was given a small room with a bed, and a bedside table. A male warder came back after a while with a bedside light. There were bars on the windows.

Avery didn't mind. He was content to peer into his own inner darkness, the darkness of Jennifer's room, never truly dark because the curtains were left open. He studied her silhouette on the bed.

When he woke in the morning he watched as she got up and dressed. Once again she put on her smart work suit with a skirt and tights. She applied make-up carefully, slowly. She walked to the front door of the flat and Avery was suddenly alarmed. If she left would he be able to follow her? She opened the front door. Outside was a lobby and the door to another flat opposite. Jennifer stood there holding the door jamb. Stood in the open door. She seemed to be there for a great length of time before she closed the door and went into the sitting room and slumped down on the sofa, kicking her shoes off. She held her head in her hands and cried.

"Mr Avery," said a different male warder who had come into the room, "come along. Mr Danes is going to show you round personally."

"I'm hungry." Avery realised this as he said it.

"Mr Danes will take you to the resting room. You'll be able to get some food there."

Avery followed in the pyjamas they had given him in the hospital. Danes appeared and took his elbow but Avery shook him off.

"Oh, yes," said Danes, "forgive me. I'm so used to having to help the inmates here."

"What is this place?"

"This is the Davidson Institute. We help people like you. That's why I had to get you away from those fools in the hospital. They think you're imagining your inner sight. But we know better, don't we?"

Jennifer was still crying.

"Yes," said Avery, "I know what I'm seeing is real."

"The girl?" said Danes. "Sad really. I'm given to understand she was somewhat traumatised. Moved towns. Agoraphobic."

"I need to go to her."

"Yes," said Danes, "amazing, isn't it? And soon you'll see so much more."

Avery stopped in the corridor. He wanted to go back to his room, to watch Jennifer but this Danes might be able to help him.

"What is it? What's happening to me?"

"Well," said Danes, "we have no more real idea of how it works than we did when the Institute opened. Quantum entanglement. Sympathetic Magic. Who knows?" He laughed for a moment. "But in the end we don't worry too much about that. This is not a theoretical research facility. Our work is primarily practical."

"Practical?"

"Oh don't worry. We don't torture dogs anymore."

"Sorry?"

"Just an in-joke. I mean we gave up long ago trying to create the effect. We just have to find the right sort of people. People like you."

And he led Avery ahead through some double doors into a large open room, done out like a series of little lounges with sofas and armchairs. Warders moved about the room and Avery saw people, mostly men but a few women, sat on sofas and armchairs staring into nothing. The warders delivered trays to their laps and placed drinks in hands.

"Looks like you're just in time for breakfast," said Danes. "You see how fortunate you are. All the others here, with similar abilities to you, have gone blind in both eyes."

Danes led him over to one of the little arrangements of armchairs around a coffee table. One of the chairs was occupied by a man of perhaps Avery's age. It was difficult to tell because he was bald.

"Tom," said Danes addressing the man, "I'd like you to meet Avery. Sam Avery, isn't it? He's new here."

The man turned his head slowly towards Danes's voice and sighed as though coming out of a sleep.

"Oh," he said, "sit down. Danes always brings the new ones to me. I suspect he thinks I'm understanding or something."

"Well I'll leave you to get acquainted then."

After Danes left Avery hovered for a while and eventually settled in an armchair.

"I'm not staying," said Avery, "there's someone I want to see."

"Your focus?" said Tom.

"What?"

"The one you stalked. The one who set all this off."

"How do you know? What have people been saying?"

Tom raised his arms and indicated the room.

"Who do you think we all are?" he said.

"What do they do here? Don't they help you?"

But they were all blind. All blind.

"They get to us while we can still see a little. I went to a doctor when I could just see a tiny bit of where…she was called Sally, where Sally was. I thought I was just going crazy. Well it doesn't matter. No-one missed me when they brought me here. No-one misses people like us. They show you endless photos and videos of someone they're interested in. Someone they want to keep tabs on. They give you drugs. As you begin to lose your real sight your focus shifts. You can't help it. The one I see now is a politician in the Pakistan. I can't stop watching him. Watch him take a shit. Fuck his wife. But I shouldn't complain, at least he's still alive…"

Avery stood up. He had to get out of here.

"I've still got one good eye," he said, "I'm not like you."

"Oh," said Tom, "they'll find you ever so useful". He looked up at Avery with his blank dead eyes.

From the corner of the room warders were approaching, big men with heavy arms. And somewhere Jennifer was putting on her shoes, was brushing down her skirt and heading once again to the front door of the flat.

Stone
Richard Mosses

Stone. Stone has a life of its own. A pulse. Dare I say, a heartbeat? It may seem cold, crude, sullen. But beneath there is breath, pneuma, spirit. The sensual susurration under the tips of my fingers, as I explore its surfaces and contours, arouses me. I adore the way it can seem to surround me, the way it enters me, the way it completes me.

Many up here resemble hard granite, perhaps pink or grey, flecked with shiny shards of mica, forged in the heat of the earth. Occasionally I meet someone of sandstone, blonde like the buildings, formed by the metamorphosis of one substance into another. Rarely, there is a something more unusual, jasper, tiger's eye, or jade. I've never met a diamond, cut or in the rough.

It took me a week to find a gallery. I walked the streets and was surprised that so few people looked at me. Perhaps my appearance was tolerated?

I finally found a reasonable sized space – what appeared to be a barn reborn as a gallery. The exhibition space was wide and open. The glass doors let in the changing light. This would be perfect for showing my work.

A woman had been watching me from a desk overflowing with papers at the back of the gallery. She was slate – slippery, layered, brittle and treacherous. Her grey eyes caught mine and a smile was engraved into her face.

The woman left her small laptop and approached me while I looked at the photographs on the wall. "Such a strong collection of work."

"Yes," I said. "It would have been better for her face to have been more in focus than the activity around her. She's at the centre of it all, but she seems to be shying away from the attention."

"Interesting that you should say that – they're all self-portraits."

"I'm looking for a space for my own installation. I love the light here. And unlike some studios on the Left Bank, you can actually swing a cat or two."

"I'm Jacqueline. But most people call me Jacque." I took her offered hand, which, like most flesh, was limp and lifeless. "Tell me what you had in mind."

I was just about to finish my latest piece when the doorbell rang. Irritated, I arranged myself, put on my veil, and hesitated over dark glasses. The doorbell rang again. "Just a minute." As I walked down the hall I could see two figures silhouetted through the frosted glass of the front door.

"Hello?" I said. The security chain kept the door from being opened more than a crack.

"Detective Inspector Crane and DC Blackwood, CID." Two warrant cards were thrust at me. "We're looking for Media Eurinaes."

"My name is Medea."

"We'd like to ask you a few questions," said DI Crane. He had rough features. It was difficult to tell if he had shaved or not. I thought he had a moustache, but it might have been lichen growing in the shadow of his nose. DI Crane was short and his assistant towered over him, a sarsen and a menhir. "May we come in?"

"Certainly." I resented the intrusion, but this would be the easiest way to get rid of them. I took the door off the chain. "Please excuse the mess. Can I get you some tea, or coffee, perhaps?"

"Tea would be great," said DC Blackwood.

They both seemed bewildered as I led them past my works – I have nowhere else to store them but in my hall and home. I could feel their eyes on my arse as I walked barefoot across the floor boards.

While I put together a tray of tea and biscuits in the kitchen, I could hear them poking around in the living room. Soon we were all seated, tea in the pot, mugs brimming, certainly not my best china.

"Very life like." DC Blackwood nodded at the slender woman behind my shoulder. Was it the silver ring in her right nipple that caught his eye?

"Thank you."

The Inspector half-emptied his mug in one draught. "How long have you been living here?"

"Only a couple of months."

"And before that?"

"Liverpool."

"Why did you move to Glasgow?" DI Crane took another drink while DC Blackwood helped himself to another chocolate digestive.

"I like to move around, Inspector. I can exhibit my work in different places and also find new inspiration."

The Inspector's eyes flickered to the plate of biscuits then returned to mine. "Eurinaes is an unusual surname. Where are you from, originally?" he said.

"I'm British, but my mother was Libyan and my father was Greek, before he took British citizenship."

"Why are you wearing a veil? Are you a Muslim?" DC Blackwood was reliable – he could weather any storm and stand for a thousand years – and remain blunt.

"I choose to wear it. I don't wish my face to be seen."

"Do you know Peter Bain?" the Inspector said.

My opening nights always leave me restless. I can't settle until I swallow that first glass of wine. I'm never sure if it is simple stage fright or a deeper fear that I might be exposed as an untalented fraud. I finished fretting over my clothes and left the flat.

I walked to the gallery. The cool night air helped me to calm myself. Jacque greeted me at the front door with a glass of exquisite French red. The evening was off to a good start. We had laboured for several days to ensure the internal lighting brought each piece to life. I was proud of our work and pleased to see a number of guests had already begun trickling in.

I finished my first drink quickly and set to small talking my way into a few sales. Half way through my second glass, I was getting into my stride and the gallery was warmed by the mass of bodies. I turned too quickly and bumped into an unusual man.

"I'm so sorry," I said.

"Don't worry about it." The wine bloomed on his shirt. "The artist, I presume?"

"Yes. Medea."

"Peter. Peter Bain." He shook my hand – a proper grip, free from an attempt at dominance. "You won't try to cut me into small pieces, will you?"

"Only if I need to escape in a hurry." I laughed.

As Jacque's orbit coincided with mine I grabbed another glass from her while Peter was studying the nearest piece.

"How do you get such...such ferocity? Such fear? I don't know what that is on their faces."

"You know what they say, use what you know."

A woman, naked, was reaching forward with her left hand to lift up something delicate. While her repose suggested she should be lying on her back, I had decided, as much to save space as any aesthetic consideration, to put her on her feet, and prop her up against a wall. Her long hair fanned out around her. The cool, green marble was unusual amongst the other pieces. A prominent white vein ran through it with darker, black veins emerging in places. The final touch was the silver nipple ring. I had been quite surprised how well it had worked out.

"Do you have an agent?"

I laughed again. "I didn't realise sculptors had agents."

"Don't all great artists require someone to look after their work?"

*

"We met at my opening a few months ago," I said.

"His wife has reported him missing. We're following up with known colleagues and associates." The Inspector took another drink of tea.

The news that he had a wife surprised me, but not much. I had already seen that he had a hidden side. "It's been two weeks since I last saw him. He came round to model for my latest piece."

"Can we see it?" DI Crane watched as DC Blackwood helped himself to the last digestive.

"Certainly. Please, follow me." I took them through to my studio in the spare bedroom. More silent figures stood, crouched, or lay, formed from a variety of materials.

Peter's sculpture was made from bright green porphyry. He was on all fours, well threes, as his right hand reached out, fingers holding the edge of something and lifting it, like a table cloth. Like many of my sculptures he was naked and erect. Like all of them, those in this room being no different, the same look was on his face.

This unsettled my guests.

"Very...life like." DC Blackwood said.

"Thank you."

"When did he leave?" the Inspector said.

"I don't recall exactly. Maybe 2 a.m.?" I looked directly at the Inspector.

"And you haven't seen him since?"

"No."

"Are you having an affair with him?"

"I didn't know he was married until just now. I thought we had the beginnings of a relationship." I sighed and sat down on the bare back of Peter's sculpture. Despite being beneath me, it felt like the stone was crushing down on me. I really had thought it would be something special, but like all the others, it seemed the mystery just had to be solved.

"I'm sorry, Ms Eurinaes."

At that moment I felt judged. His tone implied that this was all my fault. Like some Jezebel I had led a man from the straight and narrow into sin. I could see, now, that DI Crane was made of the same rock as Wee Free kirks. I resisted as my hand rose up towards my face.

"We have all we need for now. If anything else occurs to you, please give me a call." The Inspector took a small business card from out of a wallet.

"I will. Thank you."

Having ushered both policemen from my flat, my composure melted and I slumped onto the floor behind the door.

I lay beside Peter, idly running my fingers through his chest hair. I felt like I had finally been able to really touch someone rather than their carved facsimile.

"Now will you let me see?" Peter exhaled – his smoke was an alien, heavy fragrance in my flat. The discarded blindfold lay coiled on the floor like a snake.

"No." I stopped playing and turned onto my back.

Peter stabbed out his cigarette in a scavenged saucer. "It doesn't matter to me what you look like."

"Why do you have to see?"

"I want to see all of you." He climbed over me, his knees between my legs, his right hand trapping my left, an angry throbbing erection between his legs.

"Don't, Peter."

"I want to see you."

His penis brushed against me. He lifted my veil. His expression changed.

With great effort, I rolled the sculpture onto its side and slid out from underneath it. I longed to feel flesh once more, but all I had was stone.

Stain

Ian Hunter

I've been licking the bathroom ceiling again.

You would have thought I would have learned after last time. I almost slipped again. One foot on the rim around the bath, the other on a ladder step, stretching too far. I toppled to the side, almost smashing through the shower screen. That would have been something to explain to the kids. Crying for help as I lay bleeding to death in the bath, covered by shards of broken plastic. A really big one embedded in my thigh where the blood was pumping out.

The stain is just too dammed hard to reach, right next to the light fitting and above the crazy shade that Jan put up. Dangling silvery disk things that make a chiming sound when they collide. Then it comes to me, like a light bulb moment. Take the shade down.

Today the taste is different, better. Sharper. Fizzy.

*

How to explain what it looks like? The stain. The main stain. Stain prime. Mother stain.

Imagine an obese person's legs, thick like an elephants, the flesh white, and greying, with veins running through them. There's some necrosis working there, loosening all the toenails. They are a mess, those legs. Horrible, really, but you can't take your eyes off them. You have to keep looking. Sometimes I think the main stain looks like a negative picture of some distant galaxy. Dark space is the white of my ceiling against which something is seeping through from the other side.

Different.

Diseased.

It is getting bigger, but somehow stays in proportion, not like the other marks on the ceiling which appear as black dots before growing. Furry and fungal, creeping along the sides of the coving and spreading out across the ceiling. Dots appear on the grout. Stains on the tiles. Watermarks beneath the glaze.

I often wonder where the stain came from. Could there be something dead lying in the attic right above the bathroom ceiling? Right above the light fitting? Surely not. It would have to be in some state of decay to seep through the wooden flooring and the insulation, as well as the ceiling itself. There would be other signs, wouldn't there? Smells. Birds were always getting into our attic at the old house. Some of them broke their necks flying into the skylight trying to get out. One died in the water tank. There was a stink every time we turned a hot tap on. I had to fish it out. This white, slimy, slippery thing.

*

It gnaws at me. What might be in the attic, lying above the bathroom. Dead, spreading, seeping. Glorious. I only have a wind-up torch bought from a discount supermarket. I turn the handle faster and faster and switch it on. The light is pathetic, but grows stronger when I turn the handle again. I place the ladder under the attic hatch, and start climbing, reaching up to push the hatch back and over. A black square waits for me. The light of the torch illuminates motes of dust. I climb all the way, holding on to a wooden beam to pull myself up. Hot air clings to me, snatching at my breath. In the autumn and winter months the attic is cold and there is a damp smell, but now everything smells stale. I pick my way across joists, around piles of old records, suitcases full of clothes, mainly Jan's, forgotten now. I should bin them, or take them to a charity shop. I wind the torch up, powering the light, training it on space above the bathroom which shows some paperbacks that have slid off the top of a box, and are now wreathed in cobwebs. There is nothing that oozes darkness.

The children are to blame, of course. My wonderful children. Without them none of this would have happened. I can take a shower in minutes flat, using a bar of soap or some gel, followed by a splash of shampoo into my palm, but they seem to stand under the water for half an hour at a time. Stand as if they are dissolving themselves, dissolving a layer of skin away as well as all the dirt. If it wasn't impossible I would say they are listening to the some music under the jets, or texting. Open the window, I used to tell them, but they never did, and the extractor fan connected to the light switch is busted. That bastard plumber who charged us an arm and a leg for our great bathroom, put the cheapest fan in he could find. I used to lie back with a book in my hand, or read some magazines that were balancing on the end of the sink, stretching back occasionally to take another one down. Now I just lie back and watch the stains. Imagine I can see them creeping towards me. Try to make sense of the patterns they make. What they are trying to tell me.

*

The sealant around the bath is turning black in places. Once, I used some folded toilet paper to try to wipe some of it away, but the paper got soaked and fell apart and only managed to smear black specks everywhere, like a disease, a plague. The dark stains are starting to get furry and eating into the sealant, moving downwards through it and disappearing behind the bath. I look at my fingers. Pieces like blackcurrant jelly cover them. I wonder what they taste like.

Jan ran off with Phil from the mountaineering club. Tanned. Slim. Fit. Everything I'm not. She texted me to say she wasn't coming back. That she had met someone else. That I had changed, become "sum 1 elz" and didn't want "2 chng bck 4 me". She did come back when I wasn't here. Took her clothes, books, CDs, DVDs. Nothing of mine. She said she would "B n tuch". She never has. I've heard she goes off on climbing trips with Phil. Nepal, Argentina. I never knew they had mountains there. The kids miss her. So do I, even though I lost my temper once and told them to stop talking about her. Lost it big time at the dinner table and sent everything crashing to the floor with a sweeping arm after they went on and on and on asking when mum was coming back.

I used to think it was a mistake tiling the bathroom. The floor and walls, but it wasn't, although I'm glad we didn't go the whole hog and tile the ceiling. There would be no stain if we had done that. The tiles make everything wet and slippery. Water runs down the walls after a shower or a bath, gathering under the glaze. The plants in the corner seem to be thriving in the heat. They are tall and sharp-looking. Lottie is scared of them, and refuses to take a bath and lie with her head close to the leaves. I like the plants. They make the bathroom seem wild, different, other.

*

I first licked the ceiling when I was trying to paint it. The plumber wouldn't replace the busted fan. Quoted us eighty quid for a new one. I called round a few other plumbers and electricians, hoping it might be just a blown fuse. Jan berated me for not even being able to change that. She got fed up having to paint the ceiling to cover the stains and asked me to do it for a change. I bought special stuff, anti-fungal, and was supposed to have rubbed or scraped off the stains before painting, like Jan always did, but couldn't be bothered. That's you all over, I could imagine her saying. I stood on the ladder, arm moving backwards and forwards with the roller, head cocked to the side because I was so close to the ceiling. Even then some of my hair still stuck to the paint. The stain was there, less than an inch from my face. I wanted to touch it. Almost did, then took the plunge and licked those dark tendrils. I've done it every day since.

I shouldn't blame the kids, not really. Without their long showers – their steam, prime stain would never have appeared. It is their gift to me, and my gift to them. I know it now. I am the opener of the way. The guardian. The keeper. Preparing the bathroom for others. The way the children must go through first.

This is blasphemy, but it has to be done. I need it. I stroke the mother stain, feel its warmth, then gently scratch its surface, getting some beneath my fingernails. A dark edge that I can gnaw anytime, suck anytime. Get the taste, the fizz. I won't be brushing my teeth anytime soon, and will hardly eat anything from now on, especially anything highly flavoured that can interfere with my taste buds. This way the taste will always be with me when I need it, even when I wake in the night, although more and more often I'm thinking about sleeping in the bath, below the stain, and when it is ready it will break free from the ceiling and land on my face to feed.

I've put a hook up on the ceiling, rawl plugs and everything to hold it in place. A rope goes through the hook and there is a noose on the other end of the rope. Lottie's head is through the noose. I'm holding a Stanley knife to encourage her. Not that I'll use it, or the noose, but she doesn't need to know that. I told her that it's a game, but can tell she doesn't believe me. She looks scared, I suppose. I hold the ladder firm. I just want her to lick the stain. It's bigger now. Denser. Parts of it seem to pulse, like blood rushing through veins. Something is living in it. In me now, and Andy. I played this game with him earlier. Made him eat the furry pieces of sealant then lick the stain until his tongue was black. He's in the other room. I had to tie him down to stop the thrashing. I couldn't believe the black froth oozing out of his mouth. He's changing, I expect Lottie will too. Just one more step, I tell her, then stick your tongue out.

Little Fingers
Christine Morgan

Touching her.

Tentative.

Little fingers.

Soft and tiny. Warm.

Sticky.

Oh God, sticky with what?

Warm, soft, pudgy, sticky little fingers. Touching her. Touching her hand. Poking. Quick pokes, hastily withdrawn.

Tapping at her knuckles. Flicking at her fingertips.

A pat. A pinch. A fast squeeze-and-release.

God, the touching, touching her hand, prodding her palm. Leaving residue. Moist, sticky, tacky residue. Fingerprints. Smears and smudges.

Candy? Melted chocolate, licorice, taffy? Cupcake frosting? Ice cream?

Greasy-gritty… the salt and butter of popcorn? French fries?

Touching her!

All over her hand, tickling and creeping fleshy pads like warm damp animal noses like mouse paws –

God make it stop!

Why couldn't she scream? Why couldn't she move? Or see? Or anything?

Just… just feel… the little fingers exploring her hand…

Only the one. The left. Never moving past the wrist.

Sticky little fingers with scratchy little fingernails.

She tried to pull away and couldn't. Tried to clench her fist, couldn't. Tried to grab the next squirming worming thing; once she got it, she'd hold on tight, refuse to let go, twist, crush it to a pulp –

Couldn't do that, either.

Couldn't *move*!

God, what was this? why? where? how?

Another set of little fingers touched her, these ones not tentative, not hasty. These ones eager. Greedy. Fat, stubby little fingers, little sausage fingers.

They curled around her pinkie. Gripped hard. Bent it back in a sudden savage jerk. Pain exploded like a pine knot bursting in a campfire. She couldn't hear the crack, but she felt it. She thought of chicken drumsticks, the wrenching crackle of gristle, the brittle splintering snap of bone.

Again, she tried to scream and couldn't. Her hand throbbed with red-hot flares. Her pinkie seemed to jut up and lean out, at a stiffly crooked but loosely wiggling askew angle.

What was this, what *was* this? If it was a dream why didn't she wake?

Couldn't scream, couldn't move, couldn't cry.

Then the pain ended. It didn't dwindle or fade. It was just, abruptly, *gone*.

Or her hand was gone. She couldn't feel her hand anymore. Not at all. She felt no more little fingers groping hers, felt nothing at all.

Something touched her hair.

Her hair?

A fleeting touch. The barest sense of pressure against her head. The briefest stirring rustle of disturbed strands.

Followed by another. A hesitant pat, the way a child might – with coaxing – touch a strange dog.

She could no more move her head than she'd been able to move her hand. Still couldn't see, couldn't hear, couldn't speak or call out to demand answers, ask who was there.

The little fingers stroked her hair, messed with it, fiddled the locks this way and that. Ruffled it. Snared it and tugged, bringing stinging snags and prickles to her scalp. Her eyes should have watered but didn't.

Little fingers twined in her hair, coiling it. Little fingers combed through her hair and worked loose a tangle. Little fingers seized a handful with a vicious yank… hideous peeling and ripping sensation… follicles popping out by the roots.

They wormed into her mouth next.

Except, they didn't.

Her mouth was shut. Wasn't it?

Or open?

She felt no little fingers prying against her lips. She couldn't feel her lips at all… not her jaw… when she attempted to bite down, her teeth met on nothing because her teeth weren't there, her teeth didn't exist… but the little fingers were in her mouth.

How?

Not bumping the roof of her mouth, not at her gum line or gagging her throat.

But they were in her *mouth*!

On her *tongue*!

Those sticky little fingers and yes she tasted them now, tasted the sugary-sweet cotton-candy / taffy stickiness and chocolate and cake and butter-popcorn-salt and syrupy artificial coloring/flavoring in fruit punch and berry blue.

Which also made her want to gag but she couldn't.

Couldn't gag, couldn't bite; she would have bitten oh yes bitten chomped down hard chomped the damn little fingers off!

They rubbed weirdly along the top of her tongue. She tasted dirt as well, and sweat, and soap. With a million sensitive nerve endings, she felt their skin texture, even felt the whorled ridges of fingerprints – if she knew fingerprints, she could identify them!

Fingernails. Sharp and scratchy. Uneven, ragged, rough as if gnawed on… digging into her tongue, little fingers with little fingernails cutting little fingernail grooves into the soft and spongy meat and she couldn't bite, couldn't scream, couldn't spit them out, couldn't do anything!

The little fingers caught her tongue-tip between them and waggled it. The little fingers raked along its underside.

No saliva flooded her mouth, bitter and sour-metallic with that dentist's-office tang. She tasted no blood, felt no blood well up or flow in coppery trickles.

But she felt the pain in precise and vivid clarity.

And when the little fingernails gouged out a chunk –

She thought she did taste blood then but it was pizza caked in the fingernails instead, pizza-grease, tomato sauce and pepperoni.

Why couldn't she *move?* Why couldn't she *do* anything?

Dream nightmare drugged madness.

She wanted to collapse, sobbing, weeping.

Couldn't.

Was she paralyzed? Anesthetized? In a coma?

Had something happened?

An accident? A car crash, a bad fall? Down the stairs, maybe? That damned throw rug at the top of the stairs, hadn't she said time and again they should get rid of it before someone tripped and broke their neck?

Was that why she couldn't feel anything?

Except the little fingers…

And when they weren't touching her…

Nothing.

Like this.

Like now.

Nothing.

Dear God, was she dead?

Was this Hell?

It couldn't be Hell, she didn't deserve Hell, she wasn't a wicked person!

Yet it certainly couldn't be Heaven. The little fingers couldn't be those of angels or cherubs. Angels or cherubs wouldn't scratch, wouldn't pinch, wouldn't taste of grime and pizza and sticky candy and artificial flavoring and popcorn.

Demons, maybe… tiny capering devil-imps with evil little fingers that –

– that sank into her midsection with a slippery, squelching push.

The scream she couldn't scream!

It hurt oh God it hurt! A revolting, gross invasion! Pressure and pain, like gas, like bowel cramps, like menstrual cramps, like labor and nausea and ruptured appendix all at once!

The little fingers plunged and delved and slopped about. They pulled on long wet loops of intestine, stretching and stretching. They wallowed and churned with slow, awful, slurping and sucking sensations.

Nothing in the world had ever been so agonizing.

Maybe it *was* Hell.

It almost had to be!

Devil-imps burrowing into her guts, rolling her kidneys and ovaries in their evil little fingers, turning her stomach inside-out, fumbling at her liver… what else could it be *but* Hell?

She didn't deserve Hell!

She was a good person!

Wasn't she active enough with the church? With charities and school committees and the community center? Wasn't she a faithful, loyal wife? Not to mention forgiving!

Yet the little fingers squirmed deeper, almost seemed to be scooping up loose dribbling handfuls of viscera, playing with her innards and entrails, and she imagined the devil-imps cackling, chortling, fiendish eyes shining in their horned, misshapen heads as they crouch-squatted over her, halfway up to their elbows.

What had she done – what possibly *could* she have done – to earn this torture and torment? It was a mistake, it had to be a mistake!

As if she'd somehow shrieked the words aloud, despite being unable to move or make any sound, the little fingers slid back out. Parts of her insides clung to them, clasping like clammy quicksand, an unbearable feeling of hideous disarrangement.

Then she felt nothing again.

Nothing, and she welcomed it.

Nothing, and she embraced it.

Nothing, and she surrendered to it with what would have been convulsing wails of relief… if she'd had limbs and body to convulse… throat and lungs and voice to wail.

It was over, please God, let it be over, whatever it was, let it be over, no more, please God no more.

*

Bethie didn't like this game very much. She was surprised Miss Margot had been allowed to do it in the first place, that Mr. and Mrs. Phelps would let her. They didn't approve of that kind of thing. Usually, there were only silly baby games and activities. Nothing really gross or scary.

Most of the games still *were* the silly baby kind. Bean-bag tosses and one where you hooked goodie bags with a toy fishing pole and a wading-pool ball pit with some of the balls marked with stickers for prizes. The prizes weren't all that great, really, but they were okay. Better than nothing.

There were high-schoolers doing face-painting, and a not-too-creepy clown making balloon animals. There was a crafts table with construction paper and glitter and glue. There were refreshments. Later, there'd even be a puppet show.

And there was Miss Margot, who'd talked the carnival committee into letting her do this witch thing.

Miss Margot sure looked extra pretty in her costume, Bethie thought. Not like Snow White in the cartoon, but a more grown-up and curvy Snow White with red-red-*red* lipstick and a ruffly short skirt.

Bethie's own costume was of a butterfly. She wore her fuzzy footie pajamas with wonderful big sparkly cellophane wings, and a headband with antenna-deelie-boppers. The high-schooler at the face-painting had done a butterfly on one cheek and a flower on the other.

She didn't really want to stick her hand in another box.

They bothered her, those boxes. Well, not so much the boxes themselves, but the way each was set on the point of a star in a circle, marked on the big round table in thick lines of different-colored chalk.

Last year, Jacob got sent home just for dressing up as Harry Potter.

This year, they had this chalk circle-star.

Maybe it was because Mr. and Mrs. Phelps weren't here to disapprove or say no, and nobody else figured it was their place to interfere. Just like nobody else figured it was their place to lecture Miss Margot about her skirt, which really *was* short. And her lipstick, which really *was* red.

Besides, Bethie had heard the other grown-ups saying, Miss Margot *had* volunteered to help finish organizing everything when the Phelpses had to go out of town. She'd done lots of work. It would have been ungrateful and not very fair to not let her do this one thing she wanted.

So, here they were with these sheet-walls hung up around the table, forming a sort of tent in the corner of the community center's rec. room, in which Miss Margot had gathered the kids to hear the story of the Mean Old Witch.

The Mean Old Witch, according to the story, had been this awful, ugly, spiteful hag who magic-tricked a handsome king into marrying her instead of the beautiful princess he really loved. But the princess found the way to break the spell, and the king's soldiers caught the Mean Old Witch.

"Then they chopped her into pieces," Miss Margot had said, widening her big blue eyes at them. "Most of the pieces, they fed to the dogs. But some pieces, they kept."

And she'd led them to the first of the boxes, lifting aside the cloth draping its front to reveal a dark opening, a hole in the box.

"Here," she'd said, with a smile that didn't look very much like Snow White at all, "is the witch's hand!"

One by one, the children had – with varying degrees of courage – reached into the hole to feel what was inside.

"Eeew!" went most of the girls.

The boys laughed and joked, teasing the girls, daring each other.

Bethie hadn't wanted to, but her best friend Deena told her not to be a scaredy-cat. It wasn't like it was a *real* hand, Deena said… just a stuffed rubber glove with maybe some chicken bones in it to make it seem less fake.

Cringing, Bethie had gone ahead and reached into the box. There, resting in a shallow dish, had been a hand-shaped thing. She poked it a couple of times with tentative little fingers. It felt all rubbery and cold. Deena was right.

When it was Mikey's turn, he, being a brat, said, "I'm gonna break the witch's finger off!"

"Gross!" said some of the girls.

"Heh, yeah, do it!" urged the boys.

"Don't," Bethie had said. "Please, Mikey, don't."

"What? It's not like she'd feel it!"

Miss Margot smiled that not-Snow-White smile again. "Well, she might. Who knows what a witch can do?"

Taking this as permission, Mikey stuck his hand in the box. There was a muffled but terrible cracking noise. Several girls jumped, squealing. So did a few of the boys.

He didn't get in trouble, either. Mikey, who wore a superhero costume bought at the store, and whose parents had lots of money, hardly ever got in trouble no matter what he did.

They'd moved to the second box, where Miss Margot said, "And this, children, this is the witch's hair!"

"It's fine," Deena said to Bethie, who hung back. "It'll just be some stringy mop-head or somebody's ratty old wig or something."

Bethie knew about wigs. Her grandma wore them. They felt like a doll's hair, curled and styled and stiffened with hairspray. Nothing scary about that. So she reached into the second box. It wasn't so bad. Maybe not exactly the same as her grandma's wigs, but not so bad.

Then, though, Miss Margot brought them to the third box and told them the witch's *tongue* was in it. The girls went, "Eew!" again while the boys went, "Nice!"

"I feel it!"

"It *is* a tongue!"

"It licked me! Yuck!"

"Oh it did not."

"It did! It totally licked my fingers!"

"Deena, I don't want to," Bethie had said, but Deena was getting way impatient with her by then. Deena was a tiger, complete with furry ears and a tail, and wasn't afraid of anything.

"Why are you such a baby?"

"I'm not!"

"Then do it!" Deena poked her hand into the box. "Jeepers, it's only a sponge."

"A… sponge?"

"Yeah." She'd squinched half her face, her concentrating look like when she was trying to give the right answer in class, as she groped around. "Or a chunk of that foam stuff for mattresses, cut in a tongue shape."

"Is it all cold and wet?"

"Not *all* wet. A little."

"Is something the matter, Bethie?" Miss Margot asked.

"No… I… no." Bethie steeled herself and reached in to touch the damp, clammy, spongy object in the dish.

"Careful," said Mikey. "It… might… *lick ya!*" He tickle-grabbed her sides, just below her butterfly wings.

Bethie jumped, yipped, spun, and whacked him on the arm. "That wasn't funny!"

Everybody else thought so, giggling and laughing.

"If you got frosting on me —" Bethie added, twisting to check. He'd been pigging out on chocolate cupcakes, and, sure enough, there were dark smudges on her fuzzy footie pajamas.

"Behave, Michael," Miss Margot had said, in an absent-stern voice that made it seem like she personally thought so too but had to be the authority person. "Has everyone felt the witch's tongue? Are we ready to move on to the next box?"

"I haven't," Ryan said, though Bethie was pretty sure he already had.

He stuck his hand in the box anyway, his grubby-grabby scraped-up hand with pizza stains on it. Ryan was biggish for his age and dressed like a hobo, which wasn't very different from the way he usually dressed because his family was poor.

"See?" He'd turned to Bethie, showing her a ragged scrap of sponge or foam rubber or whatever, pinched off in his chewed-on fingernails. "Nothing to be scared of."

"Ryan!" No absent-stern voice from Miss Margot now; it was a whipcrack. "Did you tear a piece out of the witch's tongue?"

"I was only showing Bethie —"

"Any further mischief from you, young man, and you'll be spending the rest of the carnival sitting in the office."

"Sorry, ma'am," he mumbled, looking at his hobo-shoes.

"Good." Miss Margot clapped briskly. "Now let's come over here to the fourth box…"

Deena elbowed Bethie on the sly. "Ryyyyy-an liiiiikes you," she singsong-whispered.

"Shut up!" Bethie said, blushing.

"Girls?"

"Here, Miss Margot," they'd chorused, quickly joining the group.

"In *this box…*" Miss Margot did a dramatic pause and gazed around at them. "In *this* box, boys and girls… are the witch's *guts!*"

The other kids made various noises of ghoulish delight and squeamish disgust. Bethie hung back again, shivering with goosebumps, as her braver friends crowded up to take their turns.

"That's right," said Miss Margot, doing another of those not-Snow-White grins. "They cut open her tummy and scooped out her guts into a big bowl."

Were the other grown-ups *that* thankful for her stepping up to help with the carnival on short notice? Enough to let her tell little kids a story like this, with tummies cut open and guts scooped out? Maybe they didn't know. Maybe they didn't think the Phelpses would care. Bethie had a hard time believing it, though. This was no different from those bad video games where people got shot, or black-magic devil music.

"Ohh gross!" Mikey cried, cackling gleefully, his arm through the hole up to the elbow. "It's all slippery and slimy!"

Horrible squishing noises came from inside the box as the others took their turns and stated their opinions.

"Feels like… noodles, a bowl full of cold noodles!"

"Gummy worms in Jell-O!"

"Like oatmeal with lumps and stuff!"

"I got gunk on meeeee! Eeew!"

"Is it the insides from a pumpkin? I don't feel any seeds though."

"What is it, Miss Margot? What's really in the bowl?"

"I told you, children… those are the witch's guts."

"No, really."

She'd tutted at them and shaken her head, teeth twinkling in a smile. "There's paper towels right here if you want to wipe your hands."

"I bet it is guts," Deena said, squelching experimentally. "Turkey giblets or something."

"Dis-*guss*-ting!" some of the other girls squealed.

"Come on, Bethie. You try."

"Deena —"

With an exasperated sigh, Deena turned away and went to wipe her hands. She didn't say anything. Didn't even look at Bethie.

The thought of Deena mad at her, of Deena maybe not wanting to be her friend anymore, pushed Bethie past her apprehension. She shoved her arm into the hole and her hand plunged into a gooshy mound of cold glop.

Her chin quivered, her lower lip wobbled, and for a second or two she was positive she'd cry, or throw up, or maybe even faint. It was awful, worse than anything, worse than having to use her little fingers to dredge the soapy hair clogs out of the tub drain or the time she'd stepped right square into a pile of cat barf.

"There, okay?" Yanking her hand out of the box, she'd shaken it and flung bits of glop onto Ryan, who'd been standing too close like he wanted to protect or comfort her. "There, I did it!"

"Very good, Bethie." Miss Margot patted her on the head in a way that made Bethie's cheeks flame. "Aren't you brave? Now, only one more box to go."

One more box to go.

They'd come four-fifths of the way around the star in the circle, and the last thing in the world Bethie wanted to do was reach into that last box.

But what could she do? If she threatened to tell, if she said she was going straight to Mr. and Mrs. Phelps as soon as they got back, then everyone would say she was a tattle-tale, a scaredy-cat, a cry-baby and a spoil-sport. This was the only kind of Halloween party they were allowed to *have;* nobody in town did tricks-or-treats or haunted houses like on television. Only this, and they couldn't even actually call it a Halloween party; they had to *call* it the Fall Festival or Harvest Carnival or something safe and sane and stupid like that.

What if she ruined it?

They'd hate her forever!

"And here," said Miss Margot, leading them to the next and final box with a black cloth drape hanging down over the hole in its front, "last but not least… are the witch's *eyes!*"

"Eeewww!" went several kids.

Ryan leaned close to Bethie's ear. "Olives or grapes, I bet," he murmured. "Come on. It's a game, a dumb party game."

She nodded.

Miss Margot stopped Mikey. "Why don't we let Bethie be first this time?" she said, sweet as could be.

"Yeah, okay!" Mikey took a sideways step and bowed, doing a waving flourish thing with his arm. "After you, Baby Bethie."

She moved into place before Ryan, who bristled, had a chance to say anything back to Mikey. If they started fighting, she knew who'd be in trouble and who wouldn't.

"Tell us what you feel," Miss Margot said.

Shutting her own eyes tight, Bethie tentatively crept her hand into the hole in the box. If finger-walking could be tippy-toe, that's what she did. First, she found the rim of another shallow dish, then dipped her little fingers into it and inched them, flinching, toward the center.

A low, miserable whimper escaped from her lips as she touched two cool, slick, rounded objects.

Olives or grapes, Ryan had said, but these felt way bigger.

"What do you feel?" urged Miss Margot.

"Um… like…"

"Like what? Tell us."

"Like eyeballs?" suggested Mikey, snickering.

"Um…" Gulping, Bethie sort of rolled them under her fingertips. "Like… boiled eggs, maybe… or tomatoes, the peeled kind from the can… am I done now? Can I be done?"

"Don't you want to pick one up?" Miss Margot asked.

"No! I touched them, okay? Please."

Mikey crowded close up beside her then and crammed his arm through the hole too, wedging them both so that Bethie couldn't pull hers back out. The cutout's cardboard edge dug in.

"Ow! Mikey!"

"Pick up an eyeball!" Inside the box, his hand grabbed hers, not in any holding-hands way but in a way that covered hers. He forced it over one of the slick round things.

"Mikey! Quit it!"

He made her fingers curl around the eye – it wasn't an eye! it was a tomato or egg! – and lift it. Then he squeezed, like it was one of those exercise stress balls.

It didn't pop.

It *smooshed*.

*

Her eye!

She still couldn't scream.

The touches had been bad, bad and disturbing, the little fingers gliding over the surface of each apparently disembodied orb… tracing odd blurs of light and color when faint pressure was applied… the only visual stimuli in this otherwise black, silent, engulfing nothingness.

Couldn't scream, couldn't move, couldn't see.

Could only feel.

Only feel the little fingertips, and see but not-see the brief blurs of light and color.

But then…

Oh God but then!

The sudden rough grab, one of her eyes crudely cradled in far too many little fingers! Dazzles of color like fireworks! A chewed nail scratching her cornea! Salt! Grit!

No eyelids to blink. No tear ducts to flood away the irritants.

Then the brutal, relentless squeeze.

Her eye… crushing against a soft palm. A single all-encompassing flash, a blinding white nova, snuffed in a darkness more utter and complete than before.

She still felt it. Felt everything.

The rupturing distortion, the sudden surrendering sense of *give* and *burst*. Ocular tissue squirting in thick, chunky ribbons between the knuckles of the little fingers. Dribbles oozing down the back of a hand, along a tender wrist. The plop and squish and splatter. The unbelievable pain.

And she still could not scream.

Bethie's hysterics put a quick end to the game. The obnoxious child refused to be placated, refused to be bribed even with another sundae or her choice of the carnival prizes. She only insisted that she wanted to go home, making such a scene that it nearly brought the festivities to a close.

The other carnival committee members were rather less than pleased. They wasted no time, as soon as the various families and attendees had left the community center, in expressing their opinions to Margot.

They'd had doubts all along about this suggestion of hers, they said. They'd felt it smacked too much of the wrong influences, the occult and paranormal. Even if it was only a story, there was no need to be filling impressionable young minds with anything to do with witches or witchcraft. Furthermore, they said, it was morbid and grotesque.

Margot took the appropriate stance of contrition, apologizing, swearing she had never meant for a harmless party activity to get so out of hand, expressing her deep and utmost remorse, insisting that the last thing she'd wanted was to frighten or distress any of the children. She promised she would apologize again to Bethie, and Bethie's parents, once the girl had a chance to calm down. If the rest of the committee no longer thought she was a good fit, she'd understand and resign with no hard feelings.

Well, they weren't willing to go *that* far, not on their own. Anything so drastic would need to wait for a full and proper committee meeting, a discussion, possibly a vote. None of which, of course, could happen while Steven and Janice Phelps were out of town.

Eventually, the ruffled feathers were sufficiently soothed for the evening. They cleared away the craft tables and carnival games, they took down the autumnal-themed decorations, they cleaned up the various messes – popcorn, taffy wrappers, spilled punch and melted ice cream, pizza crusts, cupcake crumbs.

Some of them helped Margot dismantle the sheet-curtains around the Mean Old Witch booth, but when it came time to deal with the boxes themselves and the pentacle chalked onto the tabletop, she was on her own.

As a parting shot, one of the committee-biddies informed her, lips pursed into a nest of wrinkles, that in the future, Margot might want to reconsider her choice of costumes. That skirt of hers was, well, very short. And all that make-up, well, you know what they say about women who use too much make-up. It was just as well, concluded the biddy, that Janice and Steven hadn't been here to see it.

Thanking her for her concern and sage advice, Margot began opening the boxes that sat at each point of the pentacle. In the first was a glove, stuffed with chicken bones and cotton batting. The pinkie finger of the glove stuck out sideways, the cloth torn, fluffs of cotton leaking out around jagged ends of bone. In the second was a thrift-store wig, mussed and tangled, originally ash-blonde but now dyed a few shades darker, more mousy-brown. In the third box, a shallow dish held a moistened piece of foam rubber cut to the size and shape of a tongue; a puddle had seeped to surround it. The fourth box contained a mixing bowl of overcooked pasta wallowing in a clear jelly. In the fifth, one soft-boiled egg slid around like an oblong enormous pearl, while the other was a pulped mess of runny yolk and wiggly white semi-solid chunks.

Everyone else had already gone. Nobody saw Margot's smile as she finished cleaning up. Nobody heard her humming, or saw the bouncy spring in her step as she went to her car.

Even if someone had, so what? She didn't care. They would never throw her off the committee without the agreement of Mr. and Mrs. Phelps, who ran the whole damn show around here.

And that, well, that simply just wasn't going to happen.

She went home. Without bothering to change out of her sexy Snow White costume, she headed downstairs to the basement.

"Hello, Janice," she said to the woman tied upright to a post in the middle of a chalk-drawn pentacle. "How are you feeling? Oh, wait. You can't answer me, can you? Can't speak, can't move, can't scream."

The flickering light from many black candles was less than flattering to Janice Phelps in her nakedness. In her doughy, dumpy, forty-something nakedness, all sag and cellulite and varicose veins.

What a man like Steven — handsome, distinguished, so athletic and fit for his age! — had ever seen in someone like that… why he'd go back to her, stay with her… when he deserved… when he could have, and *would* have, so much better…

"Ugly cow," Margot said. Her smile widened into a cruel curve as sharp as a blade. "Mean old witch."

Janice's mouse-brown hair was a rat's nest of tangles and snarls. Some clumps looked like they'd nearly been torn out by the roots. On her left hand, the pinkie jutted sideways, slivers of bone sticking through the mangled flesh. Blood trickled down her chin as if she'd bitten her tongue — though she hadn't.

No one would by no means go so far as to say the skin of Janice's belly was unblemished, not with those stretch marks and that puckered surgical scar. But it was unbroken. Unbroken, if bruised and swollen from the gut-wrenching damage done within.

"They did a real number on you, didn't they? Wanting to touch. Wanting to feel and pinch and poke."

As for her eyes …

Margot brushed aside a lank, knotted tangle of hair. She surveyed the blank, glassy stare of one eyeball and the deflated ruins of the other.

"All those little fingers," she said in smug satisfaction. "All those little, little fingers."

Then, leaving Janice, Margot went back upstairs to where Steven Phelps slept a potion-drugged sleep, like an enspelled king in a fairy tale.

Good Old Dirt

Aliya Whiteley

Sam ate dirt. He licked it from the potatoes he grew, in the raised bed he erected in his roof garden, next to the chimney. The plants were leafy, with white flowers that had no particular smell, as I recall. I've read that smell is the best way to provoke a memory, but none of my memories rely on my nose.

Did Sam sweat, once upon a time? I can remember a time that he came to my flat instead of going home after football practice, and he was shiny and slick with the moisture of his body. I slid my tongue along his neck, and the taste was tangy, salty, prickling. I couldn't have cared less about anything but the taste of him, and so when I'd saved up enough money, it was the Tasterama that was bound to win out.

I think about it for a long time, straining for details, letting the mask soak up the bumps of his upper vertebrae, the merging of his dark hairline into the fine white hairs across his shoulder blades. The feeling of those hairs on my tongue, mingling with the water from the shower head – my thirst for him never diminishes. Not for the words, deeds, or look of him. Just the taste.

The mask is an exact fit, made of a thin, rubbery material that moulds so closely to my face that at first I fight claustrophobia. But the first words that swim out of the darkness once it is in place are:

BREATHE NORMALLY
The mask will not impede your breathing.

Difficult to do – but once I have control of my initial reaction and my hands are no longer gripping the exterior of the mask, another message swims up:

OPEN YOUR MOUTH
when you are ready to begin the Tasterama experience.

It's a strange feeling, sitting there with your tongue hanging out and a light pressure upon it, rather like going to the doctor's. My immediate urge is to say *Aaaaaaaahhhhh*.

My mind has wandered. I'm off topic. I never was good at meditation. But the mask gives a soft chime and tells me the immediate input is over, so it must have received enough data. It will begin synthesis. This stage takes anywhere from ten minutes to an hour.

I didn't think I would be this excited. I'm not ready to put the Tasterama down, so I return to the main menu.

EAT WITHOUT COST.
ENJOY WITHOUT TRAVEL.
SAVOUR WITHOUT WEIGHT GAIN.

1. RECREATE A TASTE
Upload your memories to the cloud for others to enjoy.

2. EXPERIENCE A TASTE
Choose from a range of uploaded tastes.

I select option two. There are so many memories here, sorted into sub-menus, each one placed there by a person who cherished those mouthfuls. I select:

HAPPY TIMES
A night in Morocco. Lamb, couscous. She said yes!

There is darkness once more. My face feels fresh, as if it has been sprayed by a mist, and then there is taste. My tongue registers lamb. Grilled, or perhaps barbecued? There's a smoky edge to it, and then a light touch of apricot, and the heat of many spices, stirred through the heaviness of the couscous. How can there be texture? There's nothing here to be chewed. But my brain tells me there is meatiness. It fills my mouth, but then the sensation is gone again, a moment later, like water, and there is nothing to chew on after all.

In the aftermath of the memory meal, I realise that my flat is so very quiet this Friday night. Manny, who lives downstairs, will be back late, no doubt, and will put on his music and sing along, not caring who he wakes. He's a big man, late twenties I think; he likes the sound of his own voice and talks over me in our conversations when he catches me on the stairs. The way he leans in is threatening, but I'm fairly certain he's unaware of it. His devotion to one particular song is scary too. He gets stuck on it, and plays it over and over again. Soft Cell's *Tainted Love* is his current obsession. He leaves it on repeat for hours. It floats up through the floorboards and gives my flat a spiky, melancholic air.

Why has the lamb triggered thoughts of Manny in me? Perhaps the man who uploaded that meal is similar to Manny. I can picture Manny in Morocco, eating great mouthfuls of couscous with a spoon, browbeating some poor woman into giving him an affirmative answer. Yes, I can taste the overbearing nature of the man in the food now. I usually like lamb, but suddenly the thought of it is unpleasant.

I return to the main menu, select option two again, and browse through until I find:

THE BEST MEALS
Noma, Copenhagen
Reindeer Moss & Cep

Is this an advertisement? That makes sense, I suppose. How better to attract clientele? Noma is famous. It's meant to be the best restaurant in the world, available only to the rich few. The chance to taste its fine dining is too tempting for me. I select it, and wait.

The tingle on my face leads to a coldness in my mouth, almost icy, that passes and seems to heighten my taste buds, so that the earthiness of the dish is almost unpleasant. Mushroom is such a unique taste, and it is also slimy in this dish. If I hadn't read the description I could mistake it for snails, oyster, something from the mollusc family. The moss is soft and fills the mouth like wet cotton wool. And yet, together, the cep and the moss make something strange and new that I find I want to explore again. As the taste disappears, I'm left with the feeling of clarity to my palette that I have not experienced before. It's like standing under a very clear blue sky.

I can picture Noma now. Square plates and long glass windows, not far from Copenhagen harbour where the yellow and red boats bob, and cheaper tables for tourists line the quay. The quality of light there is breathtaking. It would hurt my eyes. I would have to screw up my face against that wall of blue sky, and the power of the sun within it, making long broken shadows of the masts upon the sparkling sea.

It's too intense for me. Maybe the adverts are ramped up to a higher setting, to make a stronger impression. That would make sense. It's true; I do now fancy a trip to Copenhagen. If I hadn't spent all my money on the Tasterama I might even consider booking a trip.

I disconnect the mask, and it peels away from my face. It feels strange to close my mouth now. It's funny how quickly we get used to things. My flat is murky, and the photo of Sam, nearly lost amidst the detritus of instant food packaging on the coffee table, has smears on the glass frame. My fingers – how did they get so greasy? I've left marks on his smiling face, on the smartness of his uniform. His image doesn't console me in the least. It's become a daily part of my background, like the mess of the flat, like *Tainted Love*.

There's the happy melody of my mobile. I check my watch – is it really that time already? Nine o'clock, and yes, it's Sam calling. I made a list of things to say today, compiled at my desk while I was meant to be working on a presentation about the new living opportunities out in the black beyond, but I can't remember where I put it, or what I put on it for that matter. I know I don't want to mention the Tasterama, because I don't want to tell him that I'm trying to recreate him, but what else is there to talk about? It gets so difficult to think of a fresh topic every day.

There's no video, as usual, so I don't worry about composing my face for him.

'Tay?' he says.

'Hey baby.'

'Hey, hi, hi. Having a good day today?'

'Fine. The usual. Work's good.'

'Great. It's good here too. We finished stage two today. They'll turn it on tomorrow for a trial run.'

'That's brilliant!' Stage two of a twelve stage process, none of which I understand. Sam has an engineer's brain, capable of making, calculating, completing. I wonder if I've ever completed anything in the way he does. He finishes it, puts it down, and leaves it behind without a thought.

'They might move up the delivery time at this rate,' he says.

'Really?' I can't let myself sound too hopeful. I need him back, yes, but we haven't been together that long. If work hadn't got in the way we might be at the living together stage by now, but this time apart has arrested our development. And so I watch every word I say for fear of ripping the delicate patterns we've tentatively put in place.

'Tell me about you,' he says.

Every day, he asks me this. I do the usual. The weather, the office. The shows I've streamed. He's entrusted me with reminding him of what home really is. This time the words come easily to me, and seem sharper than usual. Maybe it's the after-effects of the Tasterama, bringing a deeper dimension to my senses. As I describe my day, I am filled with the need to taste him again. It makes me brave, and I ask him a question that I've not risked before.

'Do you miss your potatoes?'

What's that sound? It's a soft laugh. I haven't heard it since we were in the same room together, and the intimacy of it is so good. I'm a starving cat presented with a bowlful of cream; I want to purr down the phone to him. 'I miss them every day.'

'Is it the taste of the dirt?'

'What?'

'The dirt. You licked off the dirt. You said you liked the taste, remember?'

'Yeah, I got that from my granddad. He used to do that too. Right now I'd give anything for some good old dirt.'

'Good old dirt,' I repeat.

And in this closeness, this wallowing, I find him again, without the aid of the Tasterama after all. He's so far away, and he's in this mouldy old flat with me. He's on the tip of my tongue.

Time is up. Our allotted ten minutes is over, and he is gone. I get up and make a cup of something sweet, and wander around under the halogen lights of the kitchen, eating biscuits from the packet.

When I return to the living room, the mask is chiming. I pick it up, settle myself on the sofa once more, and place it over my face. It moulds to me, but this time I don't find it so cloying. I open my mouth before I need to be told, and the main menu pops up from the darkness.

YOUR MEMORY IS READY
Name   Save   Upload

I think of a name. Sam, I think. Sam in the shower. I can't be the only person to have done this, to want to make a meal of something that can't be eaten.

I select it, and the sensation of cool mist hits my skin, then warms, gets hot, hotter. There is the tang of salt, of soap, the soft bristling of fine hairs, the muscular contours sliding over my tongue. Is this the taste of a man? Is this Sam?

It fades. It has no aftertaste.

I return to the main menu. Option two. I scroll through the submenu, and find:

A TASTE OF THE EXOTIC
Catering for the adventurous. Age 18 and over.

The list is long, and strange. If I ever wanted to taste somebody else's bodily fluids I would be in heaven. I wonder if the original inventor of the Tasterama had this in mind for their creation. I'm guessing not, but it has an inevitability to it. Of course it would be adopted by businesses of all kinds. I'm not so innocent myself in this department. Will I upload Sam in the Shower to this collection of oddities? No, I don't think so. It didn't capture him at all, and even if it had, I want him to myself.

I realise that I'm looking for something in particular. I scroll through the list, thinking about what policing might be involved here, and what uploads have been removed. But my needs are innocuous enough, if a little strange. Yes, there it is.

PICA.
Soil. From my garden.

I select it, and the words fade away. I wait for the taste to take me over, and I think about those potato plants, poking up through the soil of the raised bed with such ease, all the while burrowing roots deep down below into the dirt.

Good old dirt.

Graft
Adam Craig

Born in anger, those last moments were spent flying.

The sound of the impact fell away from Russell as if he were soaring upwards. Not travelling in a low arc over the top of the 4x4, his motorcycle still being shredded into a cloud of twisted pieces. Wind, coldest thing ever, knifed through his thin hoodie and squeezed his sweatpants around his dangling legs. One foot was completely bare, trainer and sock ripped away in the collision. Only his face seemed warm, head cocooned in the helmet.

One instant: fall never-ending. Next: road rushing towards him. No time to think. Road rising. No time for fear. Road rising to catch Russell.

The harsh, unforgiving road.

They kept Mia away until Russell was almost whole.

"Oh Christ, Russell." Mia stood frozen at the edge of the room. "I am so sorry. If I hadn't, if we –"

Dr Stern had him strapped down beneath a tent of gauze, only his head uncovered. All Russell could do to soothe her tears was say, "It wasn't your fault, it was mine," over and over.

"I wanted to come."

"I know. Best you didn't."

"Everybody said that, but —" Mia stared at the tent. Russell's body naked beneath. All of it a fresh-made pink. Her gaze touched monitors, bags dangling from stands. Tubes and cables snaking beneath the gauze. "All this, it's so…"

"Frightening? Yeah, it is a first. You get used to it." Russell had to admit this was true.

"All the same." Mia pulled up a chair, attention constantly snagged by the tent and the pink shape beneath.

Stern and his team had barred all but Russell's parents and sister from visiting until quite recently, when secondary infection had become less of a threat. Subtle changes in temperature or air movement no longer set Russell cringing with pain, and he had been able to move out of intensive care into this side room yesterday.

"Best not to think about it," he told her. "Like they keep telling me, concentrate on the future."

"But this is all my fault."

"If it's anyone's, it's mine for riding off like that. Getting angry." Russell had almost no memory of their argument, little idea what had started it. He smiled up at Mia, wanting to reassure.

After a time, she asked, "What's it like? Feeling all your skin grow back?"

"Itchy. Weird." There was no describing it. A million-million crawling sensations. Threads knitting, tingling. Like being wrapped from neck to toe in coarse wool, each strand flexing. Only it was nothing like that. "I don't know."

"Is that why you're strapped down?" She leaned forward, hand outstretched but not touching the tent.

"Yeah. Just in case I scratch or break the skin accidentally. It's only for a bit longer."

"Oh." Mia frowned. Hand still hovering. "I'm so sorry."

"Forget it."

Itching… Flexing…

*

Every few minutes, Russell looked at his hands again. Studying them. Pinkness beginning to fade, skin looking normal. Except there was not one blemish. And his tattoos had vanished. New-grown flesh smooth and hairless. Russell stared at his palms, fingers exploring each in turn. Every scar and mark gone. Gone even the deep groove along the pad of the third finger of his right hand, made by the edge of a broken jar when he was nine.

Each hand flawless. No fingerprints. No lines.

"A policeman told me that lack of fingerprints would be even more telling than a dozen characteristic scars." Dr Stern smiled warmly as he came into the small examining room. Dropping back-to-front into an office chair and wheeling across the space separating them. "Not that I imagine you're thinking of a life of crime, Russell."

Rolling up the sleeves of his smock, Russell looked at the equally unmarked skin of his arms, gently plucking the flesh of one forearm. It springing back instantly. Like the skin of a two-year-old, not a man in his mid-twenties. "Hadn't thought of it, no." He held out his arms towards Stern. "How am I doing?"

"I was hoping you'd tell me." Resting his elbows on the back of the office chair, Dr Stern gently manipulated the skin of Russell's arms. "How're the new clothes?"

His old clothes seemed to chafe against the new skin, although there was no inflammation or sign of allergy. Finally, Stern's team found some baggy, well-worn surgical scrubs for Russell to wear. "Okay. Better."

"And the irritation's gone?" Stern checked the line at the base of Russell's neck where the old skin of his face met the newly-regenerated skin covering the rest of his body.

"Yeah. Well, mostly." It still itched faintly. Except *itched* was the wrong word.

Russell said nothing else until the doctor had almost finished his examination.

"I was just wondering. I mean, you explained about all the trials, but –" Not an itch, more like a draught, restless and humid, playing over him. "I was wondering..."

"The process hasn't failed." Stern waited while Russell pulled the smock on again. Turning the office chair around and sitting down again. "You're not rejecting, Russell."

"My clothes… and the bed sheets. Yesterday…" The physiotherapist had suggested walking widths across the swimming pool to strengthen Russell's legs, trying to ease the leg injuries that were sometimes forgotten in all the fuss about the graft. Russell barely managed two laps before having to be pulled out. The pool water had seemed painfully hot at first, before abruptly turning icy against his skin. But it had been the sensation of the water as Russell had struggled through the last width that had brought him to the edge of panic.

It had felt like wading through abrasive, arid sand.

"It's no more than your brain adjusting to the new nerves." Dr Stern looked directly into Russell's eyes as he spoke. "That's all, Russell. In the trials, we didn't see anything quite as extreme as this. But it's nothing to worry about. Nothing."

Stern patted Russell gently on the shoulder. Russell closed his eyes, nodding. Trying not to flinch at the unexpected texture of the other man's hand.

Russell heard his mum calling from the other room. Ignored her, focusing on the work surface.

"Russell?" Mia stuck her head around the kitchen door.

"Huh?"

She held out his mobile. "Another interview."

"Oh." Russell managed to turn away from the counter, forcing himself to think. "Can you," he whispered, not looking at the phone, "put them off?"

"You don't…?"

Russell pulled a face, shaking his head. Being a minor celebrity had been okay. Appearing on TV, in newspapers and magazines. But the headlines were idiotic – *The Boy They REGREW… Vatman* – and always the same questions in every interview, the same assumptions, until it began to blur. Since leaving hospital, coming back to his own flat, it had been hard to see the sense of any of it. Believe the attention was real.

"No."

Mia nodded, disappearing into the other room, her half of the conversation sounding disjoint: *... wants some space... back home, he's doing... needs...* reminding him of a film with the wrong voices dubbed on.

Russell looked at the work surface again. Hesitantly stretching out his fingers.

"How are you getting on with those sandwiches, Russ?" Mum was standing beside him. Russell had not noticed her come in. "Oh, you've spilled the coleslaw. Let me –"

"I can manage, Mum."

"I know. I just want to help you tidy up."

"*Mum.*" Russell slammed top slices down on each sandwich.

"Sorry. I'm just..."

The look on Mum's face made Russell guilty. Unable to form an apology, he fidgeted with the sandwiches. Stammered: "Can you get the plates? That cupboard –"

As Mum got the crockery, Russell looked at the spillage. Resisting the urge to run his hand through the mess again, he quickly licked each finger clean.

The clash of impressions almost made him grunt. The texture of finger over tongue was as he remembered. But the sensation of his tongue against his fingers was shocking. Not like he was touching his tongue. More like pressing against something hard. Its surface brittle, like crystal. Bristling with splintered jags. Only slick, moving with a life of its own. Not a part of him at all.

"Russ?"

Mum was looking at him, worry badly hidden.

"Nothing. Another flash, that's all." Dr Stern promised they would dwindle, stop completely after a while. Sometimes it seemed like they were lessening. At least he could bear normal clothes again. Not his old clothes – they had all been thrown out, the memory of them against his new skin still troubling – but normal enough. "It's nothing."

Mum nodded. Finding a smile before frowning. "How are you, really?"

"I'm fine." He snatched a wad of kitchen towel off the roll, mopping the spillage without touching it. "Great."

*

"So what's it like being a replicant?" one of his workmates asked first day back. "A clone?"

"I'm not a clone." Russell pretended to be interested in a spreadsheet full of docket codes and consignment numbers.

"Something like that, in'it?" His mate waved a hand vaguely. "They hacked into your DNA, got it to grow skin and that?"

"It's not cloning." Russell refused to look away from the screen, sick of questions.

"It in't? You a sodding expert all of a sudden?"

Russell did look then.

"Oh." His mate blinked. "Right. Yeah. S'pose you would be, yeah. Right."

They worked in silence for almost five minutes before his mate could not stand it any longer.

"So, what is it like, Russ?"

Russell was not going to answer. After a few seconds, though, he snapped:

"Like being inside someone else's skin."

They were watching TV, Russell having said he was too tired to go out that evening. He could see Mia from the corner of his eye. Glancing towards him every few minutes. Look, look away. Gaze lingering when she thought he was lost in the images shuffling across the screen. Russell leaning against the arm of the sofa, fist pressed against the side of his face.

Without thought, he flattened out his hand. Palm cupping cheekbone. Fingers splaying. Exploring.

"Russell?"

His face was the only original part left.

"Russell?" Mia's weight shifted, sofa frame giving a soft creak.

Although the old skin was integrated with the new, it felt a little strange as each fingertip brushed against the fold of his ear or rasped across the stubble appearing despite the excessive closeness of each shave.

"Russell, are you really interested in this show?"

The heat from her hand made him flinch before Mia could touch him.

"What is it?" She gripped his arm.

"Nothing. You made me jump is –"

Russell stared at Mia's hand. Positive he could feel the ridges and whorls of her skin. The bone beneath.

"It's okay." She pulled gently, other hand cupping the side of his face as he had done. Guiding him closer. "It's okay." Lips touching. Her mouth moving across his face. Mia's hands –

Russell jerked back. "Sorry. I – can't."

"What –? Why?" Mia's eyes teared in the silence after her question, widening. "You blame me, don't you?"

"No. It's –"

"You think this is my fault. That's why you're cold, keeping distant."

"No. I don't." Stammering, so even to Russell it sounded as though he was lying when he was not. "It's..." His mind refusing to turn over, too preoccupied to form an explanation.

"You know, what you need is counselling." Mia did not look back as she flung herself out of the room. "Get over it," she screamed as the front door slammed.

Russell knew he should go after her. And sat touching the places Mia had kissed. Trying to name the sensations fading from the skin of his face.

He sent flowers to where she worked. An *"I Am Sorry"* e-card to her phone. A simple voice message.

They talked over coffee, made up.

"A flash," he explained, as if this explained everything.

"Another?" Mia leaned across the table, took his hand and let go immediately, face stricken. Russell held her hand instead.

"I thought Dr Stern said they would go?"

"They are." He smiled. Releasing her hand to sip from his cup. Ignoring the taste of the latte as he added, "Probably a one-off."

But he could not make love that night. Forced himself to relax as they kissed, as Mia's hands moved over him. Gasped at her kisses leaving trails across his face. At the sensations awakening there, even there, gasping although they were muted like distant echoes from the graft but not echoes. Gasping at sensation invading his face under her lips and hands; gasping in surprise and that surprise sounding like passion, encouraging Mia to kiss and explore and caress, textures and impressions strengthening, layering, building – Until he stopped things going further. Claimed it was the pain from his legs, a bone-deep fatigue from a day of worry. Asked for patience, understanding.

Afterwards, after Mia had gone home to her own house, Russell stood in the apartment's small bathroom. Scrubbing with harsh soap and a nailbrush until his skin, old face and new graft, no longer echoed to Mia's touch.

Next day after work, he stopped at the retail park. Wandering through the motor spares shop, the DIY store opposite. Circling the unisex boutique once before going into the sports shop, a shoe franchise, mother and baby centre. Ending up in the supermarket. Slowly turning over the fresh fruit and vegetables. Prodding and snatching his hand away from shrink-wrapped cuts of beef and turkey. Brushing a cheese grater against an ear; flicking across a display of duffle coats with the tip of his tongue. Comparing. Judging. Trying to find descriptions for what he was feeling throughout his body.

He began pausing before almost every new action. Wondering: what is this going to feel like? Familiar things could be made to feel as they had, but only with concentration. A moment's distraction and those memories were swamped. It was easy to become disoriented. Eyes and ears clashing with the range of new sensations he was discovering.

"Russell?"

It was like one of those augmented reality headsets presenting sights and sounds he remembered while his body experienced something...

"Russell!"

...different. "Huh? What?"

Mia was staring at him. So was the gang of kids in the booth across the aisle, a woman hushing her six-year-old on the other side of the burger bar. "But that man's washing his hands in sauce, mummy."

"Jesus, Russell..." Mia's eyes wide, mouth sagging.

"Oh... Oops. Spilled..." Russell took a napkin. Smearing away ketchup. Smooth and sticky.

Ketchup: *firmyielding-slightnap-thrum.*

Mia sat on the edge of the sofa, watching closely as he came in and out of the kitchen. Plate of biccies. Steaming mugs. Back to fetch milk.

"You always have yours black."

Russell sat on the floor, leaning against the wall. Ignoring the sensation of carpet pressing against his legs. Peripheral friction from the wall, the paint on the wall.

"Black?"

Despite all his other senses told him, the apartment felt wrong. Had changed.

Mia knelt in front of him. "Always."

"Oh." Russell looked at the mug that was more milk than coffee. "Got into the habit—" because the texture of black coffee inside his mouth made him uncomfortable, was at odds enough with memory and taste to force a break with old preferences – "in rehab. The physios and nurses always forgetting, giving you milk, it's a bind always complaining, so..."

He trailed off. Mia said nothing. Simply looking into his eyes or at the new flesh left exposed by his T-shirt.

"What?" Squirming self-consciously.

"The ketchup."

"Told you, I was miles away."

"I'm –" Mia held out her hand. Not touching. "Could it be stress? PTSD?"

"It's nothing." Unconsciously trying to create more distance between them.

"Call Dr Stern."

"I've a check-up in a –"

"Call him now, Russell. This isn't right. You're not –" Mia bit her lip. Slowly, she stretched out her hand again. "We haven't – don't –"

Making contact.

Russell spilled his coffee. "Sod it."

Pretending it was an accident. Asking Mia to get kitchen towel. Kneeling. Looking at the spreading puddle. Remembering her touch:

Brittlepointknife-slicknessfervid-envelop...

A warm wind skimmed across the flat roof of the block of flats. Moon a hazy ghost behind the sodium glow, night reducing the city to chequer patterns of window-lights, traffic drone, its breath stale exhaust fumes and steam from takeaways.

Russell stood by the parapet and felt cold threads coil through his stomach. Under the pressure of the wind, his scalp tightened. Hesitating, he wiped his palms against his thighs.

Each day was worse than the previous.

Each day more frightening.

Each more intense.

More mesmerising.

He had tried to resist. Not repeat the ketchup incident. Easier to keep Mia at a distance. Keep telling Mum and his friends he never felt better.

Never felt... this.

It was there. Always. In every glancing contact. Any time he held out a hand, moved. A little less defined across face, head, mouth. But there, always to the touch. As if he was deaf and blind, able to explore the world only through touch.

Not the world he felt he knew before the accident.

New. Alien. Revolting.

Yet beguiling. Pulling him deeper. Invading his dreams, images finally marrying with sensation.

Tears streamed down his face (*tallowcrawl-nipgrateburn*) as he stripped naked and basked under the pale moon's glow.

Two days later:

A ringing on the doorbell becomes a knocking on the door becomes a rattling letterbox becomes a voice becomes words becomes a name becomes a name becomes a name a name becomes sounds. Becomes silence.

Perhaps to begin all over again.

Perhaps not.

He sits. In semidarkness. Blinds drawn. Across the window here in the front room, in every room in the flat. Phone off. TV black. Sitting. On the floor. Naked and still. Very still. Any movement too much movement. Breath shallow. Each blink slow-deliberate.

Footsteps heading away. Giving up for now. Perhaps to try again later.

Perhaps not.

Russell sat very still. Looking at sofa and chair draped in semidarkness, what little light escaping through the blinds golden with another sunset.

Russell sat very still and felt an invisible room become more solid the darker it got.

When he woke to himself again, it was day. He had no idea how much time had passed. Knew he was ravenous, knew he was exhausted, muscles and joints aching stiff. Russell lay on his back, blinking at a ceiling. That was about all he was sure of.

Very slowly, he sat up. Dizziness made floors and walls teeter. Russell closed his eyes. Tasting bile, skin turning clammy.

His skin felt almost normal.

Surprise made his eyes snap open. Dizziness forced them closed again. Not before he glimpsed the state of the kitchen, himself.

Russell clutched a cupboard door, deep breaths threatening to become hyperventilation.

His hands still shook by the time he found the phone.

"Mia...? Please..."

She said very little when she came in, nothing that registered. Russell had managed to wrap himself in a sheet, unlock the door. Otherwise the apartment was as he left it.

Mia half-carried him to the shower. Washed him clean. Let hot water fall on him until the shivering stopped. Towelling him dry, new skin glowing red.

"I've been frantic," she said as she helped him into the sitting room. "It'll be okay now."

Wrapped in dry towels and blankets, Russell listened to Mia cleaning up the kitchen. Remembering: broken crockery, soup and milk and yoghurt spattered over the walls, contents of the fridge strewn across the floor, all of it pulped into a sludge, much of which had covered him, together with blood, scraps of flesh from a piece of steak, a bag of liver. Most of the cupboards had been tipped out. Churned together into a riot of textures. A mad clashing of liquid, abrasive, sharp, prickled, slick. As if he had been experimenting. Searching for something that did not normally exist.

Russell looked at his hands, the hairless flesh of his arms. Both seemed normal. Tingling from being scrubbed as they should. Maybe he had burned it out. Overloaded it, so the nerves and whatever could only register human sensations now.

He fell asleep, feeling only terry towelling and fleece next to his skin.

*

He woke at Mia's touch. An instant of bliss: because he remembered nothing; thinking this was some time past and normal. Focusing on Mia, and feeling the pressure of her hand on his arm. That pressure unleashing memories of the sensations it had once spawned.

It all came out then. A choking flood of explanation. Tongue stumbling when it came to describing just what his grafted skin made him feel. A void where there had been word-combinations for the new feel of sour yoghurt, or raw liver, or the caustic touch of mould remover.

Russell examined his all-too-smooth flesh, seeing not one mark despite all he had done to himself. Revelation leaving his mind blank. As if it meant nothing.

And still the words came.

"Hush." Mia clasped him, rocking. "Hush."

Russell tensed.

Mia's hands moved as she rocked him. "Hush."

Russell, feeling nothing strange, tried to let go.

Her hands soothing. Pats becoming caresses. It had been so long...

"Relax."

Mia's lips trailing, ear to neck. Tongue leaving dabs of wetness. Russell unwinding, beginning to respond.

It had been so long.

Breath juddering.

Skin bared.

Mia rubbed against him. Palms. Fingers. Tongue darting, lingering.

Russell unwinding, responding. Moving. Bare skin against bare skin. Palms. Fingers. Tongue. Russell responding. Unwinding. Hidden away. Beginning to open out.

Again.

The graft prickled. A wave of *tingleflex* enveloping his whole body.

"God –"

"Mmm... oh, yeah..."

Mia's saliva was frost burning his flesh. Her tongue emery deliquescing into vapour that tingled as it dissipated. Too many fingers stroking, rippling. Russell squirmed, trying to get on top. But there was no sense of where Mia ended, he began.

Revulsion. Welling, its copper taste filling his mouth. Sensation (*spinetips-slickgripping*) crawled. Clenched (*velvetangles-gratesliding*). Touch becoming an image as before. Hidden world made flesh.

"Oh. Christ."

"Harder –"

The images the graft was spinning through his head were appalling. Everything he had been searching for in the kitchen. More. Russell opened his eyes. Seeing fleshsight and eyesight overlay. Merge.

He yelled. Body rigid under the graft. Bucking.

Mia rolled away. Unable to speak. Only pant. Grin.

Yes, inside there was still revulsion. Russell clung to that, about all he had left. It was that or admit he wanted – needed – to do this again.

The street appeared solid. Until the exhaust of a bus wrapped a hand around his *mouth (twinedigitprobe-palpitatecaress)*, a kid barring any escape as he tried to thrust a leaflet into Russell's hands (the jarring contact sending a wave of *brittleedgesheat* through the graft to conjure an image of something crystalline and sharp). Fleshsight rising, sensations threatening to override everything his other senses told him. Russell lurched away, eyes wide in the hope this would keep off what the graft was feeling. Or discovering. It was hard not to think that, when every step brought a new combination of flesh against clothing, wind or exhaust or shadow against skin.

Russell's reflection stared back at him from the window of a vacant shop. His face looked wrong. Misshapen.

Skin. Wrong.

Turning sharply away (clothes leaving *slithertingle* across shoulders, trousers clasping legs as the slight breeze effervesced with a dull *bitesmear* through the fabric), he tried to think of something else. Latched on to Mia. Slamming the apartment door shut without looking back at her. Clattering downstairs. Desperate to get away. Not wanting to find out where fleshsight ended, other senses began.

Russell tried not to remember, to think, after that.

Walked fast for a time.

Walked slow after.

Got on a bus. Got off.

Walked. Stood, not seeing the junction he stood beside.

Not exactly.

Bus. Off after one stop. Walk. Bus in the opposite direction (knowing the direction because one way the air was *resistantoily, wetsplinter* the other). Reflection framed in the glass. Blinking when Russell blinked. Mouth open same time as his.

His face about the only original part of him left. Everything else graft.

But it was the face in the glass that felt grafted. A mask.

"What have you done to me?"

Dr Stern jumped as Russell burst out from behind a line of skips. The doctor's car keys clattering across tarmac.

"Russell." Stern pressed against the wing of his car. Overhead, steam rising from a boiler house glowed a rancid yellow in the hospital's floodlights. Making an effort to relax, Stern opened a hand. "I've been worried about you. It's good you're here. Why don't –"

"What the fuck have you done?" Sun becoming hidden by the scowling hulk of A&E, Russell had been hiding in the car park for over an hour. He thought he had been travelling at random. Until he noticed the signs for the hospital repeating, repeating. Russell took another step. "What?"

"You're stressed, emotional, Russell." Dr Stern stooped for his keys, flinching upright as Russell closed a little more space. "I, uh, understand. Listen, Russell, I heard about Mia."

Mia: lingering tactile memories of *softclingingness* becoming *flakedglidesturningwetter*, fleshsight peeling aside the other, poorer senses, driving him until he sank deeper, deeper into –

"What am I?"

Stern did not understand. "The police are looking for you. But I'm sure we can sort it out. Stress of your accident, media attention. If you co-operate, Russell, it's best if you do, I mean, I understand she's likely to recover, so..."

Russell waited until the doctor trailed into silence.

"What." After each word, a step. "Did." Stern pressing against his car. "You." Light making deep furrows in the doctor's face. "Do. To. Me." An arm-length's separation. "What am I?"

"Do? You know. Caused the expression of certain genetic –"

"No. This." Hand flattened against the doctor's chest. Feeling adrenaline surging through the blood vessels below, sweat prickling on skin. *Saw* through direct contact. Each impression mediated by the graft: "A hole. Cavity. Twitching. Sides, sides of angles. Crystals, sliding over tiny barbs –"

Stern jerked away. "Tactile hallucination. The nerves adjusting –"

"It's not." A remnant tingled across the graft's palm. An insight Russell picked up easily. "Something else, this." He gripped Stern's arm, drawing out the same insight again through the graft's palms. "Isn't it?"

"Please stay calm," the doctor stammered, "it's nothing –"

"It is." Flat statement. Russell certain he could trust what he was feeling.

Dr Stern cringed. "In, in a tiny – *tiny* – percentage of cases. It's nothing to worry –"

Russell tightened his grip. "There are others? People who... feelsee what I do?"

Stern tried pulling away. "The technique's successful in the vast majority. It's a few, only. They seem... seem –"

"Dr Stern? Are you okay?" Another doctor. A few cars away. Her mobile held high. "Is this man –?"

Russell was already walking. Conscious of security cameras unblinking. The possibility the second doctor had videoed him.

"Russell, please," Dr Stern called after him. "We must talk."

Russell began to run.

Of course, they knew what he looked like anyway. Hospital records, stories in the media.

Russell crouched in a service road behind a row of crumbling shops. Maisonettes above dark or lit by a scuffed glow that spared nothing for the alley. Two-thirds of the way down, a droop-headed light cast a narrow cone over potholes, broken glass. Russell hunkered further down beside a car with plastic sheeting for windows and stared at the mouth of the alley.

Headlights crawled over the buildings opposite. Traffic noise hollowing the sky.

Russell stroked the car's festering wheel rim. Fleshsight translating the wealth of sensation. Into images. And, increasingly, smells; taste and sound before long, probably. Stern got that much right. Russell's brain was adapting, changing to work with the graft – with *his* skin.

It was getting harder to force things back to the way they had been.

Russell looked at his hands. White shapes in the gloom. Air currents and exhaust particulates silky against his palms. Other sensations coming from across his body. All interlinked, vital.

Only his face was wrong.

It was numb. No, mis-connected.

Russell explored his face.

Wrong. It felt –

But then, it wasn't *his*.

Glass crunched as he walked into the cone of light beneath the single lamp. Water lay in the potholes.

Russell studied his reflection.

Running a thumb down the line from ear to jaw. Again, more firmly. Tried getting purchase across hairline, temple, outer skin stubborn, refusing to budge, peel away. Looked. Until he found a shard that would do. Tried again.

Russell studied his new reflection.

Sirens wailed (*skuttered*) along the expressway, pitch spiralling (*queasing*) before lofting away (*awaywards*), thrumming air beating (*sinelling*) against Russell's ears. He ignored it. The sirens were after somebody else. Probably. Besides – a final glance before dropping the mask-like deadflesh in amongst *jollferant* (mouldering) cardboard boxes, where the rats could find and dispose before it chanced to *leethen* and *tass* (rot and reek) – his newface was enough unlike for anyone looking to not recognise.

As Russell walked towards the opposite end of the service road, he could feel his realface settle, grow more... *nollugous*, more his own. His whole skin felt right at last.

The road dead-ended, leaving only a narrow footpath between two high walls. Following that until it let out into a landscape he did not have words to describe. Yet. There were others who did. Somewhere.

Without looking back, Russell went in search of his own kind.

Making See

Mark Patrick Lynch

My girlfriend turned invisible the first week of April. Just after the flowers bloomed and the skies cleared to blue – *snap*, out she went like a light bulb.

It was a side effect of a rare virus she'd contracted. Unluckily the virus had already given her a severe case of laryngitis and had taken away her voice. She couldn't even cry out to warn me not to walk into her.

We compensated for this by wrapping her in bright clothing. But the invisibility was infectious and soon her favourite jumper and low-cut jeans lost their colours and faded to nothing.

I tried to paint her. But after only a few brushstrokes the black and orange tiger stripes I was applying had disappeared, leaving only an ugly scent in the air. As I'm sure you can imagine, we weren't happy. And when I fell over her discarded, invisible clothes, paint tumbled over the bathroom tiles and onto the dual-flush loo and no amount of scrubbing could clean it off. Right then we didn't think things could sink further south.

The doctor issued me with a jab to protect me from the virus. He assured us that my girlfriend's condition would pass. In the meantime, he advised she should stay in a loose quarantine. Believing him, we settled down to deal with the inconvenience in the short-term.

But things didn't improve as quickly as we'd been led to expect. It seemed the invisibility was a lingering malady.

We did our best to cope and trod around one another warily. We communicated in written notes. Though my girlfriend had no trouble hearing me, I felt that in writing to her I was sharing her world more intimately, demonstrating that I was living my life in sympathy with her own. In this way I was bringing us closer together. Also, on the practical front, I could be sure she received my messages. I wouldn't want to make a fool of myself by talking to an empty room.

Dear sweetheart, she might write, *would you like scented candles over supper tonight?*

In reply, I'd compose something like, *Dearest darling, I would love candles and you over supper this evening.*

We'd dine to the faintest candlelight with comfortable jazz music distracting from the fact that we couldn't make conversation.

Because it was dangerous for her to do so, my girlfriend stopped going outside. Her laryngitis didn't ease up and there was no way of flagging her presence to someone who didn't know she was there. Anything she carried – a cane or a sign with her name on it – would lose its colour and become see-through in a second. For a while she blew on a whistle, but that just caused confusion and frightened people. Crossing roads was hazardous because traffic couldn't see her, and she'd have to walk perfectly in line behind me, and exceptionally close, to avoid anyone marching into her as we strode along the pavements. Even then we couldn't be sure someone wouldn't crash a baby carriage into her from the side, or come running up from behind and leave her rolling on the floor with a broken leg. If such a calamity happened I'd never know where I'd lost her, and she couldn't cry for help. The consequences of an accident were too terrible to consider, so she stuck to the flat and maintained the quarantine.

One day after I came home from work I found a note waiting for me on the mantle-piece.

I'm tired of stomping and clapping around the flat so you can hear me coming. My feet are starting to hurt and my hands are chafing. I'm sure the neighbours below can't enjoy it. Blowing on the whistle hurts my throat. But I've had a thought. Could you go out and find me some bells to wear?

There was a place in the indoor market that sold fabric. Folk dancers used it, and so because there was a demand for them there were strips of cloth with jingly-jangly bells sewn in place already. I bought five strips, thinking it was probably too many, and carried them back in a plastic bag. I got odd looks from people in the street and felt like I was trying to smuggle home a Christmas reindeer.

The bells were a good idea. Now I knew where she was. And if I *didn't* notice the depression she made on the sofa and was about to sit on her all she had to do was shake an arm to let me know she was there. She'd jingle and I'd get the message. Even so, she still wasn't confident enough to leave the building and would even hesitate at the thought of going downstairs to fetch the post up.

We carried on like this for weeks and then months. Eventually my girlfriend found out that she'd lost her job. There was a letter addressed to her, full of "sorries" and "deeply regrets", and ending with an emphatic "given the circumstances, there is no alternative but to let you go."

Because she really loved teaching, she cried for days. She'd missed going into work since her virus got bad and to keep her spirits buoyant she had focused on returning when she got well. After this news was delivered I found damp patches on the carpet, on the cushions of the sofa, on the pillows in the bedroom.

I wrote her a note telling her how sorry I was, and that when she was better we could find her another job.

It was impossible to read what she wrote back. The paper was so wet with tears that the ink had run.

The virus was stubborn and refused to leave. We began to consider that the invisibility might be a permanent condition. It was becoming the norm for us. The doctor came and examined her and shook his head baffled. I got anti-virus booster jabs. We waited for change and feared there wouldn't be any.

From time to time we would look at old photograph albums: my girlfriend and me on top of the tower in which Vita Sackville-West wrote in Sissinghurst; pointing at the wide surf riding into the long curve of St Ouen's bay on the Channel Island of Jersey; damp but not dejected onboard the steam-ferry crossing Lake Windermere. We did it to remind ourselves what she looked like, how the sun touched her hair and made dancing light in the half-moons of her smiling eyes. We cuddled on the sofa and turned pages, looking at what seemed like other people living other lives.

The only time we were together as we had been before the invisibility struck was when we were in bed, with the lights turned out and the curtains hiding the streetlamps. In the perfect dark we knew each other even more fully than we had before the virus.

People have asked me if I was ever tempted to leave my girlfriend when she was at her most ill. My answer is always the same: *I never saw that I could.* Which is not the same as admitting I thought about it, which I did indeed do, I thought about it a lot. But I genuinely couldn't leave her by herself. She wouldn't have been able to cope and had no family to fall back on.

So we stayed together, and in some ways we wound up getting closer than we ever had before. I think she became an ideal for me and the girl in the photographs became a stranger, not the real person with whom I was living. I filled in all the parts of her that I couldn't see with my imagination. There was a strange eroticism in her "there/not there" presence. Sometimes she would leave her bells in another room and sit and watch me as I read a novel or corrected a student's paper. I would feel her breath falling on my neck and then scent her fragrance, blossom talcum powder or Chanel No 5, and I'd be treated to a surprise kiss on the cheek that would tingle like sherbet.

And then one day in the spring, after a year of the illness, I noticed a curious thing. My girlfriend began to cast a shadow. Faintly at first, and not always consistent, but it was there more often than it was not. I didn't say anything at first, in case it gave her false hope.

But in time a surer, stronger shade was visible, in which I could make out a torso, and then arms and legs.

Following on from this came a head and then shoulders.

Shortly after that, I could see something of her actual body, an outline in the air. A haze was visible, like the smoke from a fire passing before the sun. And when she hung onto things there was no seeping of colours or loss of definition to them.

Now, when she took items of clothing off, and as long as she didn't touch them again, they seeped back into grey life. A week without her going near them and they started to find some colour.

When I was sure I was right and something was changing, I wrote an excited note.

I think you're getting better! Maybe you should try and say something?

I saw her lift the note from the mantle-piece. Her bells were silent for a moment, then raced in a flurry of discordant tinkles to the bathroom.

For a moment, I wondered what was wrong. When I knocked on the door to see if she was all right, it took a minute to unlatch and swing open. After stepping back and pausing in case she wanted to leave, I went inside, stepping carefully, calling her name, and with a hand outstretched so that I wouldn't bump into her.

I found the bells discarded on the tiles. If I really concentrated my stare, I could make out their shape, and even catch a glint from them. I lifted them to the light, marvelling at how they had once been clearer than glass.

Then, for the first time in over a year I heard her and my heart all but stopped.

She was sobbing in the living room. At first I didn't recognise the sound and it took me a moment to adjust. I was frightened, though I couldn't say why. Perhaps it's the way someone who thinks he's alone in a house must feel when he hears the tread of a foot in a room that should be empty.

When I entered the living room, there she was, curled up on the sofa. Visible. Her hair hadn't been cut in a year except in big awful clumps from the kitchen scissors – a job she did herself – and she'd put on weight. I could see the strain at the seams of her T-shirt and jeans, the roundness in her cheeks.

She didn't look right and it brought me to a halt. What I remembered – or had imagined in my ideal of her – was different from this person before me. Her skin sagged a little, and where it was once, in my mind, rosy and smooth I saw that it was blotchy and speckled in moles and freckles. Had it always been like that? Her complexion was shot from too much junk food, and her mouth had developed an ugly downturn at the corners. If you're sad for so long, something's going to give, and here it had done so.

I watched her uncross her un-toned arms as she looked up at me – and she saw me see her…

It was too late to hide my expression and impossible to miss the hurt in her eyes.

Sometimes the worst screams are silent.

I tried to make things better, and rushed towards her, forcing a smile to my lips. *I can see you, you're visible,* I told her; *you've come back. Oh darling, my darling, it's so good to see you.*

It was the first time I'd allowed myself to speak to her in months, and I was lying to her and she saw it.

She shrank away from me as I sat beside her. But then, after a while, she edged closer as I put an arm out for her to curl into. I held her, feeling oddly as if someone I didn't know had tucked themselves into my side. She sobbed and her heart beat like a captive bird's.

We sat there a long time, not speaking, trying to adjust to this new change in our lives. Having run its course, as suddenly as it had arrived, the virus had gone.

Hesitantly, almost strangers to each other, we walked around the flat, watching things that had lost their shine return to full colour. The carpet where she'd trodden a path pacing backwards and forwards in frustration regained its pattern. The handles on the wardrobe door were visible. The bedclothes gained in brilliance from a dull buff matt to a blue and white gloss of stripes.

My girlfriend tried to speak, and she said my name, and it was like both of us were listening to someone we'd never met. All the cadences seemed wrong, the timbre in her voice. Her face crumpled, she ran from me, and she didn't say another word for days.

Adjusting to life as a visible person was a slow process for my girlfriend. At first she'd hide away from reflections, start back in fright when she caught sight of herself in the window or distorted by the steam kettle, but eventually she let me put up the mirrors that I'd taken down when she became ill (to shave during this time I'd taken to using an electric razor on the way to work). Now I'd catch her standing in front of her inverted image, pulling at her face as if she didn't know whose it was.

When she realised I was watching she'd shrug and slink into another room, pretending nothing had happened. Now that she no longer relied solely on proprioception to gauge where her arms and legs were, she did everything in a slow ballet of the person, as if the movement of her limbs was the most fascinating thing in the world. I wondered if, like a psychic form of jetlag, her invisible self was pacing ahead of her, dragging this slow dowdy figure behind.

There was a shyness, a hesitation about my girlfriend that had been discarded when she'd been in the deepest anonymity of her invisibility. Now that shyness returned and she was embarrassed to be seen; her cheeks coloured at the sight of me when we undressed together, and she found thick saggy nightclothes to wear, shifting her into shapelessness, another kind of invisibility.

When she finally agreed to step outside the flat, out came a dull brown hat she pulled low on her forehead, unflattering beige and green clothes she would only ever have worn before to decorate the flat in, and a long, heavy jacket into whose pockets she buried her hands. All to hide from the world – and perhaps, I sometimes thought, from me, the one who had seen her so naked when light had so easily passed through her.

She began to apply for jobs, all of them of the kind that would keep her busy at ungodly hours. Overnight cleaners' work, shelf stacking in supermarkets at the witching hour, that kind of thing. Eventually she found employment on the graveyard watch at a local call-centre, talking to strangers who couldn't see her.

Eventually I asked her what was wrong, where had her self-confidence gone, why wasn't she glad to be back as she had been?

She looked directly at me, something she rarely did now, and in her eyes I saw the memory of that first sight I'd taken of her, when she'd left the bathroom and returned to visibility: the expression ever so evident on my face, the honesty of my disappointment at who she was.

It seems that invisible wounds are the ones that scar us the most.

So this is where we are now. We have jobs that keep us apart, so that we're rarely in the flat together, and we leave notes to communicate. We both know that the reason we write these notes is in the hope that the someone we thought the other once was, when the invisibility virus was at its worst, might read them.

The only time we're truly comfortable is when we're in the bedroom, with the lights out and the curtains pulled on. In those moments, I am the man she assumed me to be, and she is the girl I imagined she was when my eyes couldn't settle on her. But this person who shares the flat with me now, visible by sun- and moon- and lamplight, is a stranger. When I stare at her, trying to find the invisible girl I loved, it's as if she's not there.

Sometimes I find myself looking right through her.

The Taste of Turtle Tears
Rhys Hughes

There are certain kinds of butterfly that live exclusively on the tears of other animals. Even butterflies that like to drink nectar will still often alight on the cheeks of a beast that has been weeping.

There is nothing illogical in this action really; for the butterflies crave salt, and tears are one of the richest sources of sodium. Butterflies that dwell near the sea don't need to do this because the wind is already laden with salt and the wind sprinkles it over the flowers.

But butterflies that have their homes far inland will usually find that the salt the wind can carry has been shed long before it reaches them, so they will be desperately short of the vital mineral.

Deep in the Amazon rainforest, far from the ocean, there are flotillas of butterflies that have become specialised tear-drinkers. It may seem a gloomy feast for such a beautiful creature but what choice do they have? Without salt, death is certain and a slow agonising death too.

So they find it essential that larger animals cry; and one way to ensure a regular supply of tears is to encourage these animals to shed them; and the best way of doing that is to make them feel sad.

How on earth do butterflies make other animals sad?

In one small region of that mighty jungle some butterflies have learned a few things that butterflies elsewhere have yet to learn. They know that the tears of the yellow-spotted river turtle are the saltiest and most nourishing of all, and they also know how to speak turtle language.

Actually this last part isn't quite true. They don't *speak* the language but write it instead, in mid-air, with their fluttering bodies. The orange and yellow butterflies form words in the turtle tongue that tell extremely sad stories and the turtles read them and burst into racking sobs.

The butterflies don't need to form individual letters to make the words of a sentence because the written language of these turtles isn't alphabetical but pictographic. Each symbol stands for one word. This fortunately means it takes fewer butterflies to tell a turtle tale than it otherwise might. There is a limit to the number of butterflies that can drink the tears of a single turtle. Having said this, there have been occasions when more than one turtle arrived to experience the sad story that was being related for them.

One memorable afternoon the butterflies had an audience of no less than six turtles, but more than one is a rarity. The stories that make turtles cry aren't especially sophisticated. Simple tragic narratives suffice. Accounts of brave but foolish turtles that ended up as meals for jaguars; doomed loved affairs; stories about ungrateful children being mean to their mother; bitter ironies about what happens to naive turtles in the big bad world.

When the turtles can bear no more, they begin to weep and then it's time for the butterflies to land and take a drink. The turtle tears give the insects the salt they need and they taste great too. The only problem is that the sadness, or at least some of it, comes with the substance.

Yes, it's true. A little of the morose feeling is transferred into every tear, so the butterflies generally feel rather sad themselves afterwards. For the turtle the weeping might be cathartic but not so for the butterflies. They just feel sad without any emotional cleansing of the soul.

One day it occurred to the butterflies that tears are not only produced by sadness. They wondered if they might switch to telling funny stories so that the turtles would cry with laughter. Worth a try!

A comedy that will appeal to a turtle is no more polished than a tragedy that will fill it with melancholy. Turtles like farces best, with lots of characters narrowly avoiding each other in complicated love triangles. The butterflies told these stories and the turtles wept with joy.

These tears tasted sweeter than the juice of sadness.

But they were a little *too* sweet.

The butterflies enjoyed them nonetheless; but one morning while sunning themselves on the river bank among the flowers they held a discussion. Tragic tears were too bitter, comic tears too sweet. Might a way be found to combine and moderate the two flavours into something better? Was there such a thing as *tragicomedy*, a blend of both genres?

They weren't sure but they decided to try anyway.

The next story they told was a masterpiece of plotting and it manipulated the emotions of the turtle who witnessed it in a way that previously would have seemed implausible, swooping from the black depths of despair to the dizzy heights of mirth and back again at a velocity that to a turtle must have seemed horrifying and exhilarating at the same time.

The subsequent tears of tragicomedy were rated very highly. Indeed the butterflies considered them utterly perfect.

They began to tour their performance across the entire region and back to the starting point. It might be supposed they could simply have moved to a new home closer to the sea, where salt would have been plentiful, but the home they already had was far from meddling humans and had its advantages. Why should they emigrate? They liked it here; and now that they had the recipe for the best tears ever tasted, there was no more need to worry.

But giving the same performance day after day meant that they became a little complacent. They put less effort into forming the words correctly. If one of the butterflies was late to get into position the others would go ahead without him or her. Yes, their work became sloppy.

And one awful day the turtle that was the sole audience member started laughing in a different way from usual. The butterflies carried on and when the turtle cried they abandoned the story and took their drink. But the flavour was off this time, very peculiar, and mildly toxic.

It didn't kill the butterflies but it made their souls sick for a few days and in that time they squabbled with each other or drooped their wings pathetically while resting on petals or muttered dark ideas about self destruction or found it impossible to go to sleep. They were depressed.

The problem is that the last performance had been a disaster. So casual had the butterflies become, so cavalier with their theatrical duties, that most of them hadn't bothered to make neat symbols in the air. The pictographs were ragged and badly formed. As a consequence, the *meaning* of the words of the story had changed. It had become gibberish.

And yes, the turtle had laughed and wept, but not because of catharsis or amusement. No, he had guffawed and cried in derision, in contempt, his tears and laughter directed *at* the butterflies rather than *with* them. These tears were pure poison, not strong enough to kill the insects but certainly potent enough to make them feel very bad about themselves.

The solution was to forget about amateur dramatics.

And now the butterflies have a highly organised and superbly disciplined troupe of *professional* actors who give daily shows down by the river. They are even building a special venue there, an open air amphitheatre, though how they are doing this with their little thin legs is beyond my knowing; and the actors in this troupe are never sloppy or slapdash.

It remains to be seen if butterfly theatre ever catches on in that isolated part of the forest. I sincerely hope it does.

Their plan is to make everything as honest as possible, so the old idea of tricking the turtles into weeping is now considered a bit vulgar. A more ethical alternative has been proposed, that the price of admission for a show should be set at two tears, one from each eye, payable after the performance; and only if the show has the desired emotional impact.

Going Dark

E. Lillith McDermott

Marta shut her bedroom door, leaned her head against the wood. Even at the far end of the ranch-style house she couldn't escape their voices. She'd known this wouldn't work. But Angelica wouldn't give up. "Give it a try," she'd insisted. And since they were sisters, Marta had. Social isolation, after all, wasn't good for anyone. Hadn't her military counselor been repeating that for months?

She flung her body onto the bed. A smirk flitted at the corners of her mouth. Easy for him to say. His settings hadn't fused at peak combat. The first step of control: remove at least one of her senses. Unfortunately the scent of cologne lingered in her nose. She closed her eyes, stretched out. She willed her body to focus on the down in the comforter, the memory foam in the pillow. The second step: concentrate on a non-threatening sensation.

Her nerves disobeyed. Adrenaline coursed through twisted arteries, crossed into the tech, reached her fingertips, her toes. Her body hummed with more than just the machinery. She could hear them clearer for being further away. Another *unfortunate side effect.*

Angelica, Roman, their pastor—even with their hushed tones each word hit her like a slap in the face. "So, still no better?" Pastor Franks worried. She'd been one of his flock once too. Before the war.

Her sister spoke in the quietest of whispers. "I think I might be getting somewhere, but then…"

Roman sighed, shifted in his seat. "Mom, it's not like Aunt Marta isn't trying. I don't think you understand —"

"Of course I don't understand! Why do you think I keep asking, begging, her to share? To let me know what I can do? I know full well I *don't understand* but if she'd let me in, even a little… just a few details."

Silence spread through the house. Marta counted the seconds. Nearly a full minute passed before Pastor Franks spoke. "I have some books, about re-assimilation. They might help."

Marta heard the air shift as Angelica shook her head. "Thank you, Pastor, but I've read them all. Everything. Military and civilian… They don't help. Not that Marta will touch them anyway." Angelica's breath went ragged, her pulse throbbed. Behind closed eyelids Marta imagined her sister's face flushing, dark brows furrowed. "We're the flipping US of A! And these are honorable soldiers for Christ's sake! Sorry Pastor. But how can they ask them to go through these…these *mutilations* and then hang them out to dry when they come home damaged?"

Again silence, broken only by her sister's angry sobs, stretched through the house. Marta pressed the pillow to her ears. Her acoustic implants sharpened their resolution in response. The sounds of their breathing filled her room. She took her own deep breath, tried to use the de-escalation techniques from group. Focus on her natural body, not the tech, the real flesh and blood. Her heartbeat disappeared into the thunder of theirs.

Back in the living room Pastor Franks was apologizing for his cologne. Left on his jacket, not fresh, he insisted. Not that it mattered. This battle had been lost at the beginning of the adrenaline cascade. Outmatched by her own body, or, more honestly, by the tech that had replaced so much of her body. She'd have to shut down.

She rolled to the edge of the bed, sat up and yanked her tablet out of a drawer. Retrieving the cord from its autoclave box, she pulled open a surgi-sealed swab. One side to clean the cord, the other for the port under her ear. Blood and nerve were a delicate mix with metal and wires, no need to add dirt and bacteria. As the instruction manual said, "The bionic soldier who takes all sanitary precautions has the longest life expectancy."

With a snap the cord locked into place. When she'd first seen someone jacked in, during orientation, she'd imagined what it would feel like. Would she and the computer be one, like in the movies? She'd envisioned seeing the world as a series of numbers, floating code. Jacking in turned out to be a disappointment. No floating numbers, no disembodied sense of AI eternity. All she got was a vague sense of clicking, like someone typing on the farthest edges of her periphery. At first it had been unsettling, now she barely noticed.

Her program popped up. She slid her diagnostics to the side, opened up her shut down browser. Two taps and the screen flashed numbers. Three hours of silence starting in 90 seconds. She dropped the tablet into its headboard holster and pulled back the comforter. One foot already underneath and she remembered her shoes. She'd gotten too used to *sleeping* with her boots on that even nine months after re-assimilation she still wore them to bed at least twice a week.

With her sneakers arrow-straight under the bed, she lay back, closed her eyes. In the bottom right of her darkened view red numbers counted down the seconds until she'd finally, blissfully, be alone in her body.

Her alert claxon jolted her awake. Not as bad as the danger version, she thought, waiting for her senses to come back online. She'd only experienced the danger *wake-up* once during combat. Once was enough. At least the alert protocols allowed her senses a warm reboot.

Not the terrifying and immediate mechanical response of impending danger. Her tech had her up and running with a fully loaded gun before her eyes and ears were reading anything beyond white noise. Most of the time being a tech jockey meant driving a machine wearing your skin, but that night she'd been nothing more than a disembodied prisoner. She would carry that fear to the grave.

Her eyes focused on the ceiling beams, sent the flashing read *ALERT* to the bottom of her vision. The claxon continued inside her head. With a sigh she squeezed her eyes closed and focused on the *ALERT*, mentally *pressing* the button. After a few seconds of concentration the flashing letters were replaced with a scrolling message:

SGT Duffy, 36ᵗʰ Ambulatory Technical Unit, found dead at 1715 today. All members of 36ᵗʰ ATU to report to mandatory counseling at 0800 tomorrow morning.

Her body turned to lead. SGT Duffy. Dead. Another member of the 36th gone. The ghost of the message still floated behind her eyes, taunting. How many was that now? Close to half the unit was lost during their tour. It wasn't standard practice to replace tech jockeys in the field unless absolutely necessary.

Usually a unit got too small to function and the soldiers were either sent home for re-assimilation or, more rarely, reprogrammed and scattered into other units. Programming and fusing had to match or the unit wouldn't function optimally. The 36th barely completed the tour before their numbers shrank below minimum standards. They'd been home nine months and the causalities continued.

She sat, rubbed her forehead. She needed to know the details. Maybe it was natural, or an accident. She could hope. She started to reach for her phone, remembered she was still jacked. Again she closed her eyes, focused her thoughts. A drop down menu unfolded against her eyelids. A little more focus and the phone rang. Powell picked up on the third ring. "This 's Powell."

"Russ, it's Marta. What'd you know?"

"Hey girl. Not much. Just saw the message same as you. Trying to get in touch with his widow right now. She's not answering. We've been in the same group therapy, he missed this week but I saw him last week. Didn't look too good. I think we can guess…"

Marta sighed. "Damn. And with kids too."

"How many is that now?"

"Six that we can prove. They still haven't found Roberts. But I guess after three months… they probably won't."

"Man, Marta, you'd think they'd be doing more than group therapy and doctor visits. Don't you think someone would have figured out a way to turn these damn things down, or Hell, off?"

"Honestly, I don't think there are enough of us for it to matter. We'll either learn to live with it or wipe ourselves out. I'd say with resources stretched so thin we're a pretty low priority. They've got too many damn wars to fight. They're too busy building more jockeys, not trying to re-assimilate the washed up ones."

"You gonna be okay tonight?"

"Yeah. I was lights-out before the alert. Might try it again."

"Just don't get stuck in your head. If you go dark, go dark. No getting depressed, turn off the lights *and* the thoughts. You and I, we gotta hold on. For each other, okay?"

"Now Russ, when do I spend too much time thinking?" Powell's laughter echoed through her head. "Fine. I promise I won't over think this. At least not until tomorrow. Angelica and Roman are banging around in the kitchen, I'll go get some grub. Calm down a bit, talk it out. Make you feel better?"

The laughter died out. "Yeah. Just promise you'd call me before doing anything…stupid. You watch my back, I watch yours—remember that, girl."

"I'd miss you too, Russ."

"Yeah. Yeah."

Her eye screen told her he'd disconnected. She reached up, unplugged her jack. She'd promised Russ, and a little food didn't seem like a bad idea. She still had two hours before her calorie alerts went off, but she could beat them to the punch.

Of course she'd have to tell her sister eventually, but maybe not tonight. After their disastrous lunch date, Angelica didn't need more worry. It had taken months of struggle to be able to function in a house with her sister and Roman. Not just for her. They'd all done a lot of accommodating. Now they talked in whispers, only watched the television when she'd unplugged – generally lived like monks. For her part, Marta did her best not to scream when they forgot and laughed or answered the phone.

The kitchen exploded with sounds and smells: the refrigerator's hum, stale water in the disposal, food in the refrigerator and power throbbing through outlets and cords. Marta paused in the doorway, eyes closed, allowed her ears and nose to adjust. As much as they could. When she opened her eyes Angelica and Roman stood waiting, muscles tensed.

Taking a deep breath Marta scanned the room. With all three of her hyper-senses running, panic threatened every heartbeat. Even with the lights dimmed the room's color rioted through her nerves. She took it in, focused on her heart rate and the micro-fractures in the countertop. Her sympathetic nervous system came under marginal control.

The flashing read-out in her periphery changed from red to blue. If only she could control it around strangers, or even casual acquaintances. Angelica cleared her throat. "Can I get you something to eat?" Marta nodded. "Anything in particular sound good?"

"You know it doesn't matter. Whatever's easiest."

"I was just going to make some omelets, okay?"

Marta nodded, moved to the table. Roman sat across from her. His eyes darted from her face to his mother's back. He was too young, just 11-years-old, to look so exhausted. Marta relaxed her face. The smile felt foreign. Roman forced a smile of his own. "Are you feeling better after… after today?"

Marta nodded, studied the finish of the table. Beneath the thinning varnish the wood grain ran uneven, a dozen cell layers thicker in patches. Roman sighed. "We'd talked to Pastor Franks, and I really thought he understood. He said he'd done work with other vets."

Marta raised a hand. "No, it wasn't his fault. It isn't any of your faults. You know that, right?" She thought of Duffy's wife, his kids. Roman opened his mouth, closed it again. Behind him Angelica's shoulders heaved. Marta listened to tears trickle down her sister's cheeks.

She didn't have the words. She never did. She wasn't a talker, a thinker. That was Angelica. She was a doer. Like their father. The only difference was he hadn't made it home from the front. She wondered how his first-gen tech would have handled re-assimilation. Returning tech-jockeys were a new enough problem that no one had answers. Maybe her dad had been lucky.

Angelica slipped a plate onto the table. Marta took a deep breath. Smelling her sister's cooking was one of her few joys. It brought back memories of their mother, of times before she'd enlisted. Her nose described the delicate balance of perfectly cooked eggs mixed with peppers and jack cheese. If only her mouth could continue the conversation.

The doctors had explained that her brain couldn't process all five senses; the modifications took up too much computing power. Soldiers didn't need to taste their food. They only needed to remember to eat, and the tech could track that. Years had passed and she still couldn't reconcile smelling the flavors but tasting only cardboard. If it weren't for the memories she'd stick to the packaged MRE's.

Her sister relaxed, heart rate normal, only the smallest capillaries dilated in the whites of her eyes. This was as close to a family moment as she was likely to find. Marta placed her fork on the table. "I have to report to Base tomorrow. They're calling us in for mandatory counseling. Another one of the 36th died."

*

With the group meeting over, Marta sat in a sterile office. Barely big enough to contain the exam table and a worn stool, it was little more than a closet. But at least the walls were thick and the light dim. Marta smoothed the paper gown across her lap, studied the irregularities in the bumps and ridges. With a little focus she could discern the woven fibers. Footsteps crossed the concrete on the other side of the door. She sighed. "I'm ready."

Doctor Henrick opened the door smiling. "You never let me knock. Really throws off my game." Marta didn't apologize. He pulled out the stool, sank down. "So, rough week?" She raised an eyebrow. He shrugged. "Honestly, Marta, I'm not sure what we can do at this point. I'll take a look, but I'm guessing you don't see any changes?"

She shook her head and flopped back onto the table. "Still the same." Doctor Henrick cleaned her port and plugged in a cord. The computer on the wall beeped. Like rain on a window, data poured down the screen. The doctor read a few lines, sighed and pulled back the gown.

He poked at her arm with a monofilament tool. "Does this feel any different?" She shook her head. Her eye message told her where and with what force she was being touched, but the skin over her tech felt nothing. Not like her real skin, or at least her real skin that hadn't been grown in a lab. That at least had some memory of pain versus pleasure.

Doctor Henrick ran the microfilament across her stomach. "I can feel that…or I guess I do." She shrugged. Like her taste buds her brain had given up on most sensations. She was never sure if what she *felt* was more memory than reality. Not that it mattered to anyone but her, why would a soldier need to feel anyway?

Doc Henrick pulled the gown back, sat on his stool "How are the control techniques working?"

Marta sat up. "I'm trying, Doc. I really am. I focus on my weaker senses, touch mostly. And try to eliminate the overloads. It just doesn't work most of the time."

He nodded, pushed up his glasses, squeezed the bridge of his nose. "Same story with all of you. You've got to believe—none of us had any idea. Those first six months after install are so critical, to get those settings locked in. Brass should have known better than to send you kids out so early." He glanced at the closed door. "And the truth is they haven't stopped. Spread too thin. That's the official word. They need you enhanced soldiers about as soon as we can finish the procedures."

"What are they gonna do with all of them…us?" Marta tried not to think how many more Duffys might be headed home.

Henrick shook his head. "Just between you and me, I don't think they're too worried about that. I remember all the way back to your papa, no one even talked about what would happen *after*. That's one of the reasons I tried to talk him out of it, and you too, if you remember." She nodded. She did remember, but just like her father it hadn't made a difference. He smiled, lines deepening across his face. "I'm so sorry for this, Marta. You're good people. All of you."

"So that's it then? They're just going to let us rot here? Or maybe they hope we'll weed ourselves out, like Duffy?"

His shoulders slumped. "Even in my darkest moments I can't think they want that. They're soldiers too, you know. I think they're taking a more *practical* approach. I've seen some funding going toward integrating battle-tested soldiers into new units. Seems pretty promis-"

"Sign me up."

"What?"

"Let me go back, Doc. I'm no good here. I don't have a life, I never will. But I'm good there. That's what I'm designed for, now anyway."

He studied her, took a deep breath. "What about your sister, and Roman? They love you. You have no idea how happy they were when you got scheduled for home."

Marta shook her head. "I know they might miss me, but the truth is I'm no good for them. And deep down they know it. Roman needs a chance to grow up as a normal kid. Sure, they might miss me for a bit, but in the end… They'll realize this is for the best."

He chewed on the end of his pen. Marta waited, listening to the crunch of enamel on plastic. Blood pumped under his skin and the nerves in his forehead tightened slightly. Finally he met her gaze. "Look, I can't promise anything, okay?" She nodded. "This isn't my field, but I know a couple other doctors. And after this many years, I'm owed a few favors. It would have to be you, just you. Any more and questions would start. Questions I don't want to answer, got it?" Again she nodded.

He stood, walked to the door. "I'll see what I can do. It's a long shot, but I promise I'll try." The door closed behind him. For the first time in months Marta didn't have to force a smile.

Marta leaned back in the rocker. Powell's house was one of the few places she visited with any regularity. It was easy to see why he chose it. His small plot of land was about as deep into the mountains as you could get and still be called civilized. Usually sitting outside brought too many sights, sounds and smells, but somehow she'd been able to survive the deck for almost an hour.

Russ kept taking isolation breaks in the basement. He'd been gone for about ten minutes. Marta considered checking on him, but for the moment she was bordering on normal. He opened the sliding door. "Beer?" No need to answer another tech jockey. He could hear her answer shift through her blood and nerves. He dropped into a neighboring rocking chair, set the beers on the deck. "Fine, more for me."

Marta shook her head. "Don't you miss the taste?"

He shrugged. "Maybe. A bit. But I can still feel 'em." She smiled. His tech thrummed, kicked up her own responsive adrenaline. She glanced at him.

"What's up?"

He ran his hand down his leg, smoothed the fabric of his dress uniform, took a swig of beer. "Should know better than to try and bluff another tech jockey. Okay, but I'm really not sure what to think about this. So just keep an open mind, okay?" She nodded. There was no one in the world she trusted more than Russell Powell. "Okay, so today, at the funeral, I ran into Smith."

A headshot flashed into her periphery. She remembered Smith even without the tech's help. "Good soldier."

He nodded. "Yeah, good soldier, and an even better friend of Sergeant Roberts."

Marta leaned back. This was a sore subject for the entire 36th. The disappearance sat like a dark cloud over the unit. Every casualty they'd taken during deployment had resulted in at least some part of a body to send home. With Roberts, they had nothing left to bury.

"Does he have any news? Any fresh places to look?"

"That's just it. I haven't really talked to him much since Roberts… left. But today he was downright chatty. And, are you ready for this, Marta? He doesn't think Roberts is dead."

Marta sat forward. "What? But we all know he was having some serious re-assimilation issues."

"I know, but Smith swears up and down that he didn't off himself. Wasn't the type."

"Okay, fine. Then where the Hell is he?"

"He wouldn't say. Got pretty cryptic. He told me he'd stop by next week. Said he had a lot to talk about. I'll let you know what he says."

Marta closed her eyes, pulled up her diagnostics, scrolled through the lists. She found what she was looking for and opened her eyes. The words faded into sunlight. "It isn't possible. My tracker's fully operational. They'd know where he'd gone before he was even out of town."

Powell nodded. "Exactly! So why can't they find his body? Seriously, what could he have done to himself to damage his tracker? I know the major said Roberts had destroyed his tech to the point they couldn't track it, but does that really seem right to you? Think back to that ambush around Christmas time. You and I were so lost we thought we'd never find Cole's body. But we were able to follow his tracker back a month later. You really think Roberts did worse to himself than Cole?"

Images of Cole's desecrated body flashed up on her retinas. She'd refused to let the tech delete the memories but hadn't meant to call them up so suddenly. Her heart sped, nerves tingled. Powell jumped to his feet. "Need to hit the basement isolation chamber?" She shook her head, opened the door.

"I think I can make it home, go lights out before this cascade gets too bad. Let me know what you find out."

*

"You're really going back then?" Angelica stared at the envelope on the kitchen table. Marta nodded.

Roman shook his head. "But I thought you were done?"

"I was. But they've been putting some tech jock-soldiers into new units. They're really short on upgraded soldiers; they need me. And I'm getting a promotion, I'll be running the ops this time."

"Yeah, but why *you?*" Roman blinked back tears.

"They need more battle-seasoned pros. My country needs my experience out there in the field." Roman kept shaking his head, but fell silent.

Angelica raked her hair. "You are so much like Dad, always were. Neither of you could ever stay out of a fight. No good at home, that's what Mom used to say." The doorbell rang. Angelica jumped. "Roman, would you?"

As he disappeared through the door Angelica leaned forward, drew a cracked breath. "Is this really how you want to… what you want?"

Marta tapped the letter, unable to answer her sister's real question. "Angelica, you know this is for the best. For all of us."

Her sister closed her eyes, squeezed tears down her cheeks. "I'll miss you."

A red alert flashed across Marta's eye.

Powell.

She stood. "Door's for me."

They sat in the cab of his truck. Still too noisy, but better than in her house. Feeding off each other's tension, adrenaline flowed free. Nerves heightened to painful levels. Marta had never missed combat so much. It was only the on the front lines that she could let her tech free. She'd needed to know if birds a quarter mile away suddenly took flight. Here in suburbia that meant a housecat on patrol, not an impending attack. Downtime had required vigilance. Now it required locked doors and going dark.

Powell swallowed. She listened to the cascade of his throat muscles. "So Smith came to see me today." His pulse quickened.

"And?"

"And he told me what happened to Roberts." He turned to face her. "He didn't kill himself."

Her eyebrows shot toward her hairline. "You sure?"

"Smith's sure."

"You trust him?"

"He's 36th, so yeah." She nodded. He took another deep breath. "He said Roberts went off the grid."

"That's not possible. We've all tried to mess around with programming. Doesn't work."

"Not for us. We don't know how. But think about it Marta, someone wrote this stuff, right?" She shrugged. "So someone must know how to re-write it."

"Okay, assuming that's even true. Are you, is *Smith,* saying that Roberts figured out how to hack his own tech?"

"Not exactly. He didn't have the skills, but he knew someone who did. I guess together they wrote a program of sorts. It turns off the tracking systems. Corrupts them, according to Smith, so they can't be turned back on. Roberts used it and took off into the mountains."

Marta sat silent, absorbing the idea. Finally she licked her lips and leaned forward. She lowered her voice, knowing any tech jockey within a half-mile could hear them. "But why not tell us? Why would Brass go to such lengths to make us think he was dead and not just AWOL?"

"I asked Smith that myself. Seemed like Roberts found a solution to the problem of all us aging tech jockeys. But think about it. What do they do when one of us kicks it?"

Understanding tightened Marta's chest. "They salvage our tech."

Powell nodded. "Exactly, each of us is stuffed full of high-priced gadgets. They need us for scrap, to build up the next gen. Add that to the public relations nightmare of a mentally unstable super-soldier running loose... Well, you can see why they wouldn't want this spreading."

Marta knew the answer but asked anyway. "So what does this mean for you?"

"Smith, he has copies of the program. He gave me one." He held up a thumb drive with bio-port adaptor. "We can both use it."

Marta stalled. "Is it safe?"

"Well, they haven't found Roberts yet, have they?"

"Why doesn't Smith use it?"

"His mom. He's all she's got. She's on her last legs, but he said he couldn't leave her, not yet. I think that's his plan, though. After she's gone."

Silence filled the cab. Marta studied the beaten plastic dashboard, unwilling to look into Russ's face. Back in the house she had a letter, her own escape plan. She hadn't even tried to take Powell. Of course Doc Henrick had said it could only be her. But she hadn't even tried.

Maybe Roberts had the right idea. The mountains weren't an easy place to live. And survival played right to their senses. Fight or flight – that's how they were designed. But if Smith and Powell were right, the army wasn't going to let them disappear easily. They'd be hunted, if only for parts.

Her nerves twanged at the thought of a hunt. She couldn't deny it, she craved the rush, the adrenaline cascade. She spent every waking moment fighting off the only feeling that meant she was alive, still human. Running through the woods with Powell, watching each other's backs, it was appealing.

But she was her father's daughter. Like him she'd found a different exit strategy. She sighed. "It's not that I don't want to go with you. It's just that I got deployment orders today."

"What? They can't send you back!"

"I asked to go, actually." His eyes widened. "They have this new program where they're integrating battle hardened tech jockeys into other units. I volunteered and I guess I was a good fit. I deploy in a week."

He licked his lips. "You don't have to report."

"You know I do."

He squeezed his hand into a fist. "How long?"

"Two years."

He closed his eyes. Marta listened to the flutter in his breathing, the swelling of his tear ducts. All his telltale giveaways. He blinked and forced a smile. "I'll come back for you in two years, okay?"

Marta echoed his smile, caught his hand, gave a squeeze. She slipped down from the truck cab, leaned on the door. "I'll be waiting."

He cranked the motor. She stepped back onto the grass. She waved, willfully ignoring the sensory data flooding her tech. She'd had to learn to pretend, they all had, to keep the unit functioning. Mutual unspoken agreements to ignore each other's body fluctuations, their *tells*. Sometimes you have to let yourself be lied to.

Musk
Douglas Thompson

The generally received wisdom is that we cannot detect our own smell. The unique aroma of our own body, that is. The logic to this assumption seems quite sound: that unless we can cancel out this closest and most immediate scent then how can our olfactory system be expected to reach out and analyse all the other scents around us? But what if our scent changes? And it does of course, throughout our lifetimes. Gradually usually: from youth, to middle-age, to old age. Fair enough. At that speed our senses can easily keep up and maintain the cancellation effect. But what if our body's scent changes suddenly? And why would it do that?

I blame Connie. We were just friends at first. At least that's what I went on telling myself for as long as I could keep up the self-deception. Until I realised I was dropping by her flat every second day supposedly to talk about books and writing. But one thing led to another and we ended up kissing and cuddling on her sofa and pulling apart afterwards and shaking our heads in shame as we contemplated my wife and kids and their potential horror at our transgressions. That did it. Musk. My body knew then you see, immoral little bastard that it is, that I was in regular proximity to the body of a new woman whom I had the hots for and I was trying (subconsciously at the very least) to get her into bed. So. I got into the shower one morning shortly afterwards, and before I even turned the dial, standing there naked and sniffing, I noticed my own smell. Musk. Something had changed. I could smell myself, for the first time in my entire life. Of course, I realised this also meant something else: that my senses were extremely heightened. I believe this may be a medically proven fact when people are 'in lurv' or in any kind of state of romantic enchantment. But somehow I had never noticed or experienced it before. There was some life in the old dog yet it seemed.

Very soon however, I began to notice the scent of a lot of other people and things. The breath of every single person I spoke to became clearly detectable to me, as well as the smell of their clothes and their body odour. Sometimes these were acceptable or bland, but quite often (most disturbingly in the case of good friends) I realised for the first time that they were rancid. Walking down the street on my day off to catch a surreptitious train to go and see Connie, I was assailed by all the autumn smells around me: each variety of fallen leaf (freshly fallen, or rotting and fermenting for two weeks into mulch), each bed of earth, every berry, every dust bin, every dog turd. When the first frost came, then ice, I could smell the stagnant water from every cracked puddle that I passed. Bad drains and decaying food and dung on distant fields… the likes of these of course, since such acuity cannot be switched on and off at will, became overwhelming to the point of nausea. I began to lose the appetite for food. But then again that is another symptom of… you know, the 'L' word, being romantically enchanted shall we say, at an age when I ought to have known better.

But it wasn't just smell it seemed; it was some other, spooky stuff along with it. They do say that smell is the sense most linked to intense memories, and maybe there's a clue in there to the connections I began to be able to make. Perhaps the breath and body odour thing should have put me off large social gatherings (fortunately, or unfortunately, I found all Connie's smells enchanting, but as to my wife… well, let's just say it was quite the reverse), but I just tried to drown it out with alcohol. That's when I discovered that the musk was doing other things over and above the obvious. Women would come up and talk to me in a way I had never seen happen before. I think it would be fair to say that I have never been regarded by myself or anyone else as dramatically good-looking. But scarcely would I turn away from the company of one woman in a bar and another one would be engaging me in conversation. But there was something oddly immediate and connected about these conversations. The women would be smiling and laughing almost immediately, talking as if they'd known me all their lives, and one reason for this was a mysterious thing: I found I would say stuff that would astound them, not because I was clever or witty, but because I was unconsciously taking thoughts straight out of their heads and voicing them aloud. I mean I suppose, that I had become telepathic, but unwittingly so. I would simply find an idea in my head and voice it, and people would look stunned: I was reading them as if they were books, wide open with very large clear typeface.

Now I know what you're thinking. I was forty-seven. I was falling in love, probably, with Connie, which was disastrous enough for a married man. I was not going to be asking any of these women for their phone numbers (although many of them freely offered such information and more). My new gift was weird and surprising, but probably of no real use to me whatsoever. If only that had proven to be true.

So the inevitable happened. Connie and I ended up in bed, and I know you don't want details but unfortunately some are necessary for me to tell this story. She smelt great, and felt great when she was naked with me under the sheets, but my bizarrely heightened sense of smell kept drawing me back irrevocably to the epicentre of that smell, and all the words for this are rubbish so we'll just call it her sex, okay? I ended up slowly running my tongue across all the folds and wrinkles of her sex for a ridiculously long time, and although maybe she found that a little odd for a first encounter, after a while she ended up squealing with enjoyment and had to drag me off to perform the more normal anatomical duties of the act of human procreation. So far so good, or bad. The following week and the week after, this sequence was more or less repeated, with some interesting variations you don't need to hear about. What seemed odd the first time, was a delight to her on the second, third and fourth. But by the thirteenth and fourteenth, it was starting to seem extremely weird to her. By the thirtieth and fortieth however, it was beginning to feel to her as if I wasn't interested in copulation, let alone her as a person, but interested only in her sex and her smell. It became in the end to her as if I was trying to devour her, consume her essence, I think. This is a very personal area of the human anatomy remember, statement of the obvious. To admire and taste is delicate, but to gorge and crave is frankly, disgusting. Connie broke it off with me after about three months. She said I was a sex maniac and I was making her feel debased and dirty by helping me cheat on my wife. What she really meant I think was that I was a scent maniac, and my craving for her smell had become threatening and degrading. I was gutted. I had really fallen for that girl, but now I too felt debased, by my own foolishness and moral squalor. But once an adulterer, damned for all time, what have we to lose again?

So I found myself in bars and clubs again, talking to women. Or rather, just letting them all start talking to me, as they became invisibly drawn by my mysterious musk. You'll be thinking by now that this is a dirty story, but you're wrong. I'm just being frank rather than prudish, and actually this is a sad tale. So I slept with a lot of women? It wasn't hard. Sure, I can entertain them by talking and listening and making jokes, but this isn't about my ego. We're talking about a smell. A musk that I just happened to have. God or the devil or whoever the hell is in charge of the universe just woke up one morning and decided to give me this thing, this bizarre gift, which has actually ended up feeling more and more like a curse every day. I try not to sniff too audibly when I first get near a woman, when I first kiss her neck, but they always notice in the end: the way I'm devouring them. They're usually tickled pink at first, then sooner or later it starts to creep them out and suspicion sneaks in that every single greedy sniff is me stealing something from them, a part of their soul maybe.

So I'm not telling you this story to boast and impress you, or even to warn you off from infidelity. This is not a moral tale. I just want to shake the foundations of your safe little suburban life a little and make you aware of some bad news about the human condition that I reckon you don't want to hear. But trust me, I have your best interests at heart, and truth is always its own reward, even if it takes you to some lonely places. You think your life, and more particularly your loves, have been governed by choice and good taste and sanity and quality judgements about the reliability and suitability of your partner or partners. But you're wrong. Your life is governed by smells, pheromones and hormones, unseen invisible forces that just shift our little animal bodies around like so many chess pieces on a big black and white chequerboard. That's not the black and white of moral choices by the way, sane Anglo-Saxon white Christian choices. That's the black and white of Mother Nature's law. Sex and procreation equals more animals equals more survival equals good. Virgin death equals waste of biomass equals bad. Fight to death of two males over one female equals survival of best genetic characteristics equals good. Man has sex with two hundred women equals good. Man joins monastery equals bad. You get the picture?

So here I am on the morning train, clutching my briefcase and my newspaper, disguised as any other anonymous man. But my nostrils are quietly twitching, and in my incredible olfactory receptors I am moving like a dog, back and forward along the aisles, sniffing out the aromas of every fertile woman every time she crosses and uncrosses her legs, and plotting my next project. You might find this distasteful, sordid even. But this is Nature's law, the world which your pet pooch is party to each day and somehow restrains himself from going crazy within. Ever seen the state he gets into when a bitch is on heat even three miles away? Just why do you imagine we humans should be so different? The same mechanisms are at play, weaving their disturbing but necessary work, just at a level below the conscious thought threshold of most human beings with their safely blunted senses. But maybe that's not safer at all, but less so. At least the dog knows he is being driven solely by smell. The human fool in his prime however, believes he is making use of freewill, intellect, choice and good taste, and he is dangerously deluded.

I leave the train at the terminus and walk through the morning streets, assailed by all the smells of aftershave and perfume and hairspray of passing strangers, of the shampoo and soap and detergent and fabric conditioner of all those recently washed clothes, by the stale stink of the unwashed rags of the down-and-outs hobbling out of alleyways. I can smell the rubber, lubricant and semen from a discarded condom two blocks away, the oil leak on the underside of the engine of a double-decker bus around the next corner, the half-eaten fish supper that a seagull is making a breakfast of on a building high above me, the guano dropping from his feathery backside as he takes flight: just quickly enough in fact to enable me to step out of its way as it splashes onto the pavement in front of me.

I'm glad my office is a new one, the carpets still all so clean, the tiled floors and walls all still bright with disinfectant. My day's work gives me a much needed break from all that olfactory cacophony out there. Mostly. But now and again there'll be a distraction, like that new secretary Melanie on Level Two. Seventeen years old. I know she's way too young for me; I'm not that much of a monster, honestly. But her body doesn't know that, it only knows about my mysterious musk, and mine unfortunately, with its oh-so-sensitive snout, knows all about hers. Her mind tells her I am way too old for her, but my mind knows it's only a question of alcoholic mix and quantity as to how to override her mind. But don't worry, I have a daughter her age, who unfortunately I don't get to see much anymore now that my wife has left me. You're safe with me. I'm not an animal, or rather I am, but so are you. Are you safe?

I blame Connie. Beautiful, delicious Connie. I was a safely and happily married man until I met her. She woke something up in me which hasn't gone to sleep since. My musk. Look down on me if you like, dismiss me as a depraved beast. But Connie smelt so good, too good in fact. Maybe a man needs to be protected from an aroma like that, or he goes a little unhinged. Next time you blow your nose, be careful and be grateful that it's so clogged, vestigial and ineffectual. Your sense of smell is pitifully poor compared to mine, your world just shades of insipid grey while mine is a maddening riot of colour. I know every thought in your head before you do, and see all the invisible ropes and pulleys on which you are pulled about in your life like a hapless marionette. I have been awakened, but sometimes I envy you your ignorance, your endless blissful sleep.

Talking of sleep, I must have fainted, collapsed. I think it must have been that garbage truck that drove past me in my lunch break, the last thing I remember before finding myself here. It was like listening like to a deafening orchestra of rats playing an avant-garde twelve-tone symphony at top volume on all their hellish little rat instruments in rat hell. Deafened, yes that's how I feel now, except I mean in the olfactory sense. Is there a word for that? Nasally deadened. Anaesthetised. Perhaps

I have been. Professionally. Looks like I'm in bed in an isolation ward in a hospital, and too weak as yet to even stand and walk over to the window and see where I am exactly. I can hear summer evening birdsong at least. What a relief. And I can see late yellow sunlight landing on the white plaster of the opposite wall, the gently shaking shadows of leaves there also. So my other senses are still receptive at least. I wonder what really happened to me and how long I've been out. What I've been missing in the real world.

Careful, as they say, what you wish for. Did the world wake up after all, while I was asleep? I got too hungry and bored and perplexed at last to wait around any longer, and dragged myself onto the floor in my gown and out of my ward by pulling myself along on hands and elbows. And what a sight met me there. Just as well I can't smell any longer. Dead bodies quickly start to whiff at this time of the year in this warmth. Nurses and patients and even a few doctors here and there, some caked in blood and bruises, some half naked as if raped and abused. It was a relief to get out onto the street on a borrowed set of crutches and hobble over to the supermarket, help myself to the rotten vegetables and tear my way into several packets of refrigerated cold cuts, throw several litres of Pepsi down my throat. And no need to pay anyone any money for it anymore. The guy behind the till lying slumped there with his head staved in with a pickaxe handle.

    The birds are still singing. I like that. It's starting to look like all I'm going to have to cheer me up now. It's as if the little buggers are happy, very happy in fact, that human beings have finally decided to throw the towel in and give them all a bit of peace. I think I read somewhere once that many birds don't have much of a sense of smell, some have none at all in fact, or just two tiny holes in their beak, often vestigial. So like me now, they don't seem much bothered by what must be a mighty cloud of invisible stink rising slowly up to heaven from this huge big abandoned city of ours, full of garbage and dead people. I guess what I had was a virus then, and I should have gone to the doctor. Shucks, I was too embarrassed. Oh boy, was that an expensive bit of shyness. The shame that ended civilisation. The prudishness that prompted an apocalypse. I keep pinching myself. Am I in some weird kind of dream?

I've been walking for two days now. Out of the city and through suburbs and villages towards the sea. Human silence everywhere, and more corpses, signs of struggles and riots, often blood on faces, as if in the death throes it was pouring from nostrils and mouths and ears. Maybe I'm imagining it, but I'd swear my other senses are starting to adapt and compensate and get stronger. Today I feel as if I can see forever, tens of miles, towards tiny specks of sheep and cows pecking happily at grass in distant fields. I swear I can see every blade of grass they're munching on, the gleam of their teeth, and hear, yes, hear every clump and tear of their joyous repast, freed from their tyrannical masters. I feel a strange sympathy for them all now, my only companions. I try to remember to open the gates of every field I pass and let them out to wander along roads and through village squares. I try not to look when I see dogs and even pigs feasting on bits of bodies. Well, how could I bury all of them? – So then why bother with any of them? It's payback time I suppose for the animals. They can handle being animals after all, they're good at it. They know that's what they are and so they just get on with it. No troubling themselves with societal rules and moral hang-ups. Good luck to them.

Electricity will probably run out eventually of course, the major power stations and generators break down. I don't fancy autumn and winter alone in this part of the world, so maybe I'll steal myself a packed lunch and hike it under the channel tunnel and make my way to warmer climes. Better stock up on torches and a whole heap of batteries. Maybe the nasal virus, or whatever the hell it is, hasn't reached there yet and they'll detain me at customs, lock me up like a rabid animal and stick a needle full of sedative up my arse, keep me in a cage for years like a Romanian immigrant, give me a witty nickname like *Nigel Farage*. But I'm no wild animal anymore. I'm the sanest, calmest, most urbane and sophisticated being for miles and miles around, believe me. Benign, serene, king of the castle. Just a little lonely maybe. But definitely sane.

Last night before sunset I found a huge hypermarket with a splendid big butchers department and cold room at the back. Focussing on the thought that the power will run out and all the lovely fresh meat left behind start to go off, I pushed my way in through the clouds of mist past the polypropylene curtains. What a paradise I was met by: of prime joints of mouth-watering meat hanging up all around all ready for the tasting. This carnal emporium seemed to go on forever as I probed deeper and deeper, licking my lips. Whole curtains of red meat with the texture of velvet progressively closed around me, each yielding in tier after tier to my feverish hands. I tried to smell, but could detect nothing. Tried to feel sorrow and regret but felt nothing, only a stone where I thought my heart was, only a terrible all-consuming numbness and a dull ache, the kind of existential loneliness we feel after we have eaten a huge meal and can eat no more. Then I licked. I licked. I bit. I wept, until I saw at last from the corner of my eye that there was blood upon the floor.

The Impression of Craig Shee

David McGroarty

Sight was inevitable. In a world so drenched by the sun, for an organism to draw meaning from patterns of light, from refraction, diffusion, reflection, was always going to be a no-brainer.

Evolution has produced many, many variations on the theme of an eye. Our own camera-lens is not the most sophisticated design in the animal kingdom, and it is riddled with flaws. Of course, you would never know this; as with many of your body's shortcomings, your brain papers over the cracks. But if you knew how little information your eyes actually produce, you might be less inclined to trust them.

As a matter of fact, much of what you think you see is not there at all. (Caron Sinclair, *Perception and Deception*, Barkington, 2009)

The Isle of Porthaven is not an island. This is not the strangest thing about the place, but it can often be the thing that surprises visitors the most: to find that a narrow isthmus connects the Isle to the Mull of Kintyre, making it a part of mainland Scotland in everything but name. On the morning of Caron Sinclair's arrival at that land-bridge, after a two-day cycle ride from Glasgow, a thick fog had fallen across the sea, and Porthaven was invisible. The narrow road to the Isle faded and vanished into the grey with the water, like a bridge between worlds. Caron paused at the side of the road, then walked her bicycle onto the bridge, mounted and pedalled across.

The isthmus was a little over a mile long. Halfway over, she was able to look around and see both the Isle before her and the mainland behind, and the tenuous connection which carried her from one to the other. As she continued, the Mull of Kintyre vanished and Porthaven emerged, layer by dull layer in the fog at first, like a pop-up book, and then filling out in sharp and rich colour. It surprised her that the details – a church spire, the star-shaped outline of a forest on a hillside – though they came together in unexpected ways, felt almost intimately familiar. She had never been to Porthaven, but she felt a sense of returning to a place she had known briefly, forgotten, and then dreamed about many times.

She was inarguably in her mother's land now, more than when her plane had touched down in Scotland. Porthaven was the place that had inspired Mhairi Sinclair's greatest work, the place that had made her famous. It was also the place, many believed, that had destroyed her. On the furthest side of the Isle was Craig Shee, the Fairies' Rock, the impossible thing that had obsessed and consumed Mhairi for much of her life.

The road split into two at the end of the land bridge. A crooked signpost indicated that the town was to the left. It was the only town, and it shared its name with the Isle. She followed the road around a bend until it broadened and became a high street, lined by a squat row of whitewashed shop fronts. Caron dismounted and wheeled her bike along the pavement. It was almost noon, but the town seemed only now to be waking up. There were several shops which displayed faded prints of her mother's famous painting, *The Impression of Craig Shee*, in their windows, some of which remained shuttered. A pub seemed recently to have been named after the painting, as it still carried above the door its old name, that of the Rock itself in Gaelic form, *Creag Sídhe*. Caron chained her bike to a fence by the seafront, sat by the harbour wall, and watched the fog lift and the sun burn through until it reflected on the surface of the sea.

At the front of the pub, a few tourists clustered around a minibus, and a little red-haired woman in a parka told them stories of Fairies' Rock: how the locals had once thought the Rock to be the domain of the fairies; how Saint Columba had arrived at Porthaven from Ireland and castigated them for their fears and superstitions, had declared the Rock a miracle of God and blessed the Isle; how the Rock had later captured the imagination of Italian philosophers during the Renaissance, who tried and failed to rationalise its existence and its effects on the human mind.

Out in the open water, a ferry carried tradesmen and daytrippers around Porthaven to Mull and Bute. The air was still, the sea was flat, and it mirrored the sky.

***Reification:** we build our own worlds, constantly, forever. In every conscious moment, we construct meaning from incomplete and ambiguous data. A smudge of tea becomes a face at the bottom of a cup. A scattering of stars becomes a winged horse in the night sky. Neither awareness of the process nor effort on our parts is needed.*

***Emergence:** when we see the whole, we see it at once. The constituent parts do not queue up for our attention. Complexity emerges spontaneously. That is a tree, not a collection of leaves. That is a house, not a collection of bricks.*

***Invariance**: the worlds that we build are robust. Their structures hold fast, even as their constituents shift around one another. If I turn the table on its side, it remains a table. If I fold my arms, they remain my arms.*

***Multi-stability:** we do not tolerate ambiguity in our worlds. A structure is what it is, until it is something else, and then the change is instantaneous and total. You see* *the rabbit, or you see the duck. You see two faces in profile or you see a vase. You see the old woman in her scarf, or the young woman with her head turned away. You do not ever see some combination of the two.* (Caron Sinclair, *Vision*, Barkington, 2010)

"You look like your mother."

The old publican stared across the bar at Caron with narrowed eyes, head cocked. She wondered if he thought that doing so might transform Caron into her mother, or if it was Mhairi's image he could see, and was trying to dispel.

She shrugged. "So I'm told."

"You don't see it?"

There was a photograph of Caron's mother on the wall behind the bar, between two shelves which were filled with various malt whiskies. In the picture, Mhairi was standing beside the publican as a younger man, smiling, her head tilted to one side, her cheek resting on his shoulder. Her eyes were closed. She looked a lot like Caron.

"Did you know her?"

He nodded. "When she came to Porthaven. When she was painting that," he pointed at the copy of *The Impression* that hung above the fireplace, "she ate and drank here nearly every night."

"I didn't know her then," Caron said.

"She was up on that cliff, making sketches, every day until it was nearly too dark to find her way back, and then she came straight to this pub. We used to be named after the Rock. This was when my old man used to run things. But these days, as much as people come to see the Rock, they're only here because of that painting."

Caron turned on her barstool to look at the picture above the fire. It was at least twice the size of the original *Impression*, which she had seen at the Gallery of Modern Art in Glasgow before coming to Porthaven. But it wasn't a print. It seemed to be a replica, and not a perfect one.

She supposed that it was something in the light. The main elements of her mother's masterpiece were there – the Rock jutting out of the sea, the featureless cliff face, the cave-within-a-cave, the sun-tinged clouds – but the original painting's famously disorienting effect was muted. This copy induced only a mild sensation of vertigo, which passed after a moment's closer inspection.

"It's deliberate," the publican said. "We used to hang a print up there, but punters kept falling off their stools."

"Even when you know it's a trick, you can't stop yourself."

"Are you an artist too?"

She shook her head. "I study perception."

"You mean, like, extra sensory perception?"

"No. Just the normal, everyday sensory perception. I study vision," she said. "I'm a psychologist." The publican nodded slowly, and frowned, as though this were disappointing news. She said, "How we see the world tells us a lot about our minds and how they operate. Especially when we come across images like that, which we find difficult to process."

He glanced towards the door of the pub, like he was planning his escape route. It was a look she had seen in her students.

"Here," she said. She grabbed a beermat, and tore back the printed surface, exposing the plain cardboard underneath, and with a pen she carried in the pocket of her rucksack, she drew onto it two overlapping squares. Then, she drew four lines, one between each of the four pairs of corners, so that the picture on the beermat was the outline of a cube.

"Point to the front face," she said. He placed his fingertip on one face of the cube. "Point to the back," she said, and he did. Then she shaded two sides of the cube, giving it form and depth, and revealing that the front of the cube was where the publican had indicated that the back should be. He frowned, then shook his head. "It's perceptual ambiguity. There wasn't enough information to tell you what you were seeing, so your brain made it up."

"That is something," he said. He glanced towards the door again. "There's a bus about to leave for the Rock if you wanted to go."

She slid the beermat across the bar to him, jumped down from her stool and reached for her rucksack.

"You can leave that here if you like," he said. "Come and get it when you're ready."

As she was leaving the pub she looked back. The old man was leaning on the bar, turning the beermat over in his hand and shaking his head. She left and crossed the main street, and Caron saw that there were only a few empty seats left on the minibus. The driver introduced herself as Shona, handed Caron an information pamphlet, cheaply printed and hand-stapled, and apologised for the two pound fare: "Just keeps this old banger on the road, like."

Caron boarded and squeezed her way down the narrow aisle to the vacant seats at the back of the bus. Most of the passengers seemed to be lone travellers like her. One or two did double-takes as she passed them, and checked against the picture of Mhairi Sinclair on the inside of their pamphlets. A pair of young men in front of her were engaged in an intense discussion in French. They continued in louder voices as the engine started and the bus began to move, only stopping when the driver, yelling to be heard over the clapped out diesel engine, began addressing the passengers.

"Make the most of it, folks," she said. "There's no substitute for seeing it with your own eyes. Take as many photos as you like; but they won't have the same effect. You know, the Italian artist Uccello spent a month dangling from a rope, measuring every curve, and the most his painting ever did was give someone a tickly nose. Mhairi Sinclair is the only person to come close."

The tourists turned their pamphlets over in their hands. Caron looked out of the window. Everything in the landscape – the bent trees, the angled ridges of grey rock that pushed up through the ground – seemed to point towards her destination, to Craig Shee. The last stretch of road was a slow, steep climb, the engine of the bus whining in complaint. There was a car park at the top of the hill but, perhaps knowing the bus would not make it that far, the driver pulled it into the grass verge at the side of the road and stopped the engine.

"This is it, guys."

The journey had taken only five minutes. The passengers shuffled off the bus and onto the side of the road. While they waited in line to disembark, one of the French pair noticed Caron. He held up his pamphlet at the picture of her mother.

"You look like her."

"Yes," she said.

The sightseers started to climb the hill. They crossed the path of a party on its way down the slope to board the bus back to the town. The two groups exchanged polite smiles, and a middle-aged American man coming down the hill grinned and said, "Incredible!"

They followed a gravel footpath from the side of the car park to the summit. Caron could not see the ocean on the other side of the hill, but she could hear it, an urgent roar that seemed to occupy the air and sky. She imagined her mother making the same journey, thirty years before. There would have been no car park or gravel path, but the roar of the sea would have been the same, and perhaps the sense of anticipation, and vague dread, at the prospect of confronting such a marvel on Earth.

Boring's Figure became widely recognised in the 1930's when Edwin Boring used it as an illustration of perceptual ambiguity, but it had been in circulation as a popular cartoon since the late Nineteenth Century. The figure, known popularly as "My Wife and My Mother-in-law" shows a crudely drawn old woman with her head in a scarf, or a much younger woman with her head turned away. The older woman's nose is the younger woman's chin. The younger woman's ear is the older woman's eye. And so on.

What is interesting is that we never see the older woman's nose and the younger woman's ear. We see one figure or the other, entire. And if what we see shifts, it does so totally, and with a jolt that is almost palpable, so intrinsic is this process of perception to our engagement with the world around us. (Caron Sinclair, *Perception and Illusion*, Barkington, 2012)

Caron had walked out of her office at UCL after receiving an invitation to a gala screening of a documentary film of her mother's life to which she had made no contribution. She did not intend to see the film, but the invitation lay on her desk for much of the day, a distraction that became harder and harder to ignore, like the awareness of a trigger being slowly pulled. She had, for much of her adult life, politely dismissed enquiries about her mother, on the basis that she had not really known her. In her early twenties, she found that referring to Mhairi as her *biological* mother could shut down such conversations before they got going, even if she had no *adopted* mother, rather a single aunt who had taken her in during one of Mhairi's more lengthy absences.

At the end of that day, she left her desk, stopped at the faculty office to say that there had been an illness in the family, went home to her flat, packed a rucksack, and booked a flight to Glasgow.

She knew that she had visited Glasgow with her mother as a child. Her dreams had forever been decorated with images she could not place — a cold concrete stair that smelled of urine, an old man having a fit in the gutter of a steep street. She imagined that these images had come from her time in Glasgow. All she remembered for certain was that it was a grey place, wet and noisy.

When she arrived in the city she was surprised by how much colour and light there was, and how much space. She strolled on foot, past grand old counting houses and assembly rooms, in elliptical orbits that always brought her back around by the gallery where her mother's famous picture hung. Eventually, on the third or fourth pass, she went inside, and climbed the stair to the room on the first floor where *The Impression* was on permanent display. The queue began at the top of the flight of stairs, and shuffled slowly into the room, which was dark and lit from the floor, like a nightclub.

The room was unusual because it had only the one painting in it, and because there was a chest-high handrail on each side of the walkway that led visitors past the display, as if it were a bridge over a deadly abyss. People grabbed the rails with both hands. One young man became transfixed on the painting, and could only be moved on when a gallery attendant flashed a pen torch in his eyes.

It angered Caron, for reasons she did not understand, that she was as susceptible as anyone to the painting's influence. The instant she saw it, the image of the impossible rocks seemed to twist and distort not only the canvas, but the fabric of space in which the painting hung, and like everyone else, she felt herself tugged into the image of the cave-within-a-cave, felt her feet lose their connection with the floor beneath her, felt the room expand around her and her own space shrink into the point of a pin. Then, she was being moved on.

There was a photograph of her mother by the exit door, dark-eyed and distant. It was the kind of image she saw often: Mhairi Sinclair, thoughtful soul, troubled genius. Caron had a particular loathing for these pictures because they showed Mhairi as she did not care to remember her. Where the casual viewer saw the haunted eyes of an artist lost in thought, she could only see the vacant stare of intoxication and depression.

Before leaving the gallery, she bought a postcard of *The Impression*, and back in her hotel room she sat on the edge of her bed and stared at it until she felt sick. In the morning, she checked out, hired a bicycle and rode to Dumbarton, where her mother was buried, and then on to Porthaven.

What intrigues me about these so-called impossible figures is that they are patently not impossible. They clearly exist. Interpreted in two dimensions, the works of Escher, the Penrose triangle, are as mundane as any line drawing. And yet, the mind insists on interpreting these images in such a way that they are rendered problematic, paradoxical, brain-boggling. Why do we take this path of greatest resistance? Why not simply see the ink and the paper?

We are creatures of abstraction. We sort. We order. We construct. It's as essential to our nature as is filling our lungs with air, over and over again. (Caron Sinclair, *Perception and Illusion*, Barkington, 2012)

Because of who her mother was, it was not unusual for people to think that Caron wanted to hear their theories about Fairies' Rock. She had heard them all. Her mother, who had shaken off most of the superstitions of her Catholic upbringing, nevertheless believed that the Rock was a wonder of God, placed on Earth so that his children would know the limitations of their own minds. Caron's own theory as a psychologist, though she had tried to avoid the study of the Rock, was that its paradoxical structure would be explained by physics, and that the cognitive dissonance it produced in its beholders was something akin to an optical illusion. It was a fault in the way the brain parsed the eye's impression of the world, rather than a fault in the world itself.

But standing at the top of the cliff, on the edge of the land, finally facing the Rock, Caron was most in mind of another theory. A student, who had later suffered a breakdown, once hijacked a one-to-one tutorial to expound at length his notion that the entire universe was a complex computer program. He produced screenshots from computer simulations that had gone awry. They showed fields of grass spilling up the sides of buildings, mountains that sank into the landscape instead of rising up, cities that melted into the ocean, and canyons that vanished into infinity. Fairies' Rock, he said, was like this: a glitch, a fault in the rendering of the universe.

The roar of the sea had taken on an oppressive quality. It reverberated across the cliff faces and between the rocks, tinny and artificial like a badly tuned radio played too loud, and it limited her capacity to reason. She was again imagining her mother, and the hours and days she must have sat on the edge of that cliff, considering the Rock. Caron could hardly bear to look at it, but she was unable to look away. The Rock, a vertical column of granite, was of one height and aspect with the cliffside, but separated by a stretch of turbulent water, as if the land itself had rejected it and was slowly, over aeons, pushing it out to sea. The cave at its base was a terrible sight, which seemed at once to enter the Rock, to protrude from it, and to open out into infinity. The Rock gave the impression of being in constant motion, and the motion bled out of it into the sea, across the water, and even into the ground beneath her feet. Caron was overwhelmed by a sense that the Rock was not so much a wonder of God as a terrible mistake on his part, and there was no longer any reason to be certain about anything.

One of the young Frenchmen touched her gently on the back of her shoulder. "Are you all right?" He pointed down the clifftop path, where most of the party was making its way over the hill and back to the bus.

She nodded. "I think I'll walk back. It isn't far."

He smiled and turned away. Caron took the pamphlet from her pocket and turned to the image of her mother. She had thought it poorly composed, but now realised that it had been cropped out of the photograph in the pub; Mhairi was wearing the same Arran jumper and Paisley headscarf. She had the same broad smile and her eyes were closed. As Caron looked at the image, it seemed to change instantaneously into the picture of a different woman, someone she did not know, but might have liked well.

At the foot of the Rock, the cave mouth continued to warp and stretch and swallow the fizzing sea. There was the sense of another cave within, and a cave within that, and another, forever, like a hall of mirrors, and somewhere, deep within, a source of light that was not of the Earth. Caron was consumed, fleetingly, by the urge to throw herself from the cliff and drift on the wind through the opening, imagining herself drawn into whatever state lay within.

Then she was walking away and down the hill, but something of the cave stayed with her, an impression, an awareness of a place in her understanding of the world that her consciousness could not reach, like a dream that stays just beyond recollection.

Caron found her way back to the town. The pub was hot and filled for lunch, with tourists and locals, eating chips and toasted sandwiches. The old publican was busy, though apparently not so busy that he felt any need to curb his chatter. He juggled two or three conversations at once while pulling pints, saw Caron and greeted her.

"You're back," he said. "How was it?"

"It was all right," was her reply.

"All right?" he said. "Don't actually think I've heard that one before."

"It was something."

He placed two pint glasses in front of a customer, handed over some change, then came over to her.

"What can I get you?"

"One of those, maybe?" She pointed at the assorted whiskies that surrounded the photograph of her mother.

He laughed. "Which one?" When she shrugged, he laughed again, and said, "Right, then."

She watched him take a bottle from the shelf, but her eyes lingered on the photograph.

"Do you have any more of those photos?"

He poured the whisky into a glass. "If it's too much I can put a little water in for you. This one can be a little intense, but it's a good one." He returned the bottle to the shelf. "No, I don't have any more photos like that one. Sorry. Actually, I don't know where that came from."

As he turned away, she said, "I've never seen another picture of her that I liked."

The whisky tasted of smoke and honey, and faintly medicinal. Caron pulled the little pamphlet from the pocket of her coat. At some point she had folded it back on itself, so that the picture of Mhairi was at the front. It was a poor copy of a copy, dark and fuzzy, and it had crumpled in her pocket. She smoothed it on the surface of the bar, folded it carefully and returned it to her coat. She reached across the bar and picked up a blunt and stubby pencil that lay across a notebook by the cash register and then, with the pencil in one hand and the glass of whisky in the other, started idly to sketch her mother's face onto a beermat: smiling, bright-eyed.

She finished her whisky. The landlord returned and leaned over the bar. "I thought you said you weren't an artist."

"Well, clearly, I'm not."

"How was the whisky?"

She smiled. "It was all right."

"Can I get you another?"

"I think I'm good for now."

She signed the beermat and handed it to him. He smiled and put it on the shelf beside the photograph of Mhari. Then she grabbed another beermat, peeled its surface away, and began again.

Maneater
David Gullen

I should have realised what the Onca male was doing when he destroyed Daron.

We tracked the Onca through difficult terrain, his trail always heading away from the reservation. Late in the afternoon we emerged onto a high bluff looking over a broad river valley. Beyond, primal jungle studded with sandstone mesas – the Onca man's destination.

The sun set behind banks of dusty lavender cloud fringed with liquid gold. On the sunward side the mesas burned red, on the other dense black shadow stretched across a forest dappled dark and bright emerald. Low light emphasised every difference in colour, elevation and texture across the forest.

Despite our mission the three of us were captivated, overwhelmed. Our elevation gave the vista intense grandeur, the sunset palette of burning light and shadow summoned aching emotions I knew were without cause yet still felt deeply personal. It was as if the entire spectacle had been designed for us, that locked inside the colour sense, the geometry and scale were private messages and meanings.

I retained enough sense to keep in cover, not enough to warn Lenzl and Daron as they strolled towards the edge.

"Beautiful," Daron murmured to emself. "Astonishing, wonderful world."

Lenzl hung back from the crumbling edge.

UV laser light twinkled part way up the nearest mesa, half a mile away.

"There! The Onca man!" Lenzl flooded all frequencies and snatched up eir rifle.

Daron laughed at eir panic. "Don't worry, your integument is —"

The laser hit fifty feet away. Vegetation smoked and sputtered; a heavy boulder thumped over the edge of the bluff. Concealed under leaf litter and loose earth a vine noose snatched tight round Daron's right ankle. Pulled by the boulder it jerked em over the edge.

The laser blinked out, a sparse scatter of loose rock rattled down the cliff face after Daron. Four dead brown leaves and three live green ones danced in the updraft.

Lenzl jumped back, overcompensated with eir AG harness, the AG ey explicitly should not have had. Limbs whirling, ey floundered high into the air. A huge jump, an obvious target.

Ey crashed down. I caught em and we tumbled back through the vegetation.

"Do something, Marsk." Lenzl levered emself upright, pushed against me, keeping me on the ground as ey dusted emself down. "Do something."

I checked the ground around the clearing and found nothing, no more traps. The Onca man had achieved what he intended and now he was gone. Of that I was certain. If not, he would have shot at Lenzl.

Crouched low, I ran to the edge. The bluff fell sheer for a hundred metres, the base swallowed in forest. I pushed through the vegetation to where the boulder came from and saw the blackened, laser-cut stumps of the wooden props where it had been set.

A soft explosion came from the base of the mesa, a bright light flared, then faded away. Daron was gone.

I stood up, looked back at Lenzl and shook my head. There was nothing that could be done.

*

Lenzl called me in as soon as the Onca man's escape was discovered.

"I don't want to hunt anymore. I've – retired. I'm going home."

"You don't have enough travel credit, Marsk. Volunteer and get paid, or I'll invoke corvée."

So that's how it was. "Thanks a lot."

"You're welcome."

Lenzl's office was a plain buff box, the furniture functional. No colour, sound-proofed and silent, a place for concentration.

"Lenzl. Greetings. When did he get out?"

"Fifteen minutes ago. This is his third time. I'm out of patience."

"What was the reason?"

"He needs a reason? Animals have reasons?"

"They're biologicals, that doesn't make them animals. Even animals are –"

"A damned nuisance. They won't stay where they're put, they go rogue –"

"Do we know that?"

"He's stolen tech: two AG lifters, an Agency laser –"

"Reservation guards aren't issued with Tech IV –"

"– a MilSpec Tech-V Deuterium Fluorice laser." Lenzl shared data. "We bring him back, or… Or we don't. Really, I don't care."

"We?"

"I'm coming with you. There have been losses – the Agency rep."

"Ey deserved it." First, for being stupid enough to bring Tech V weaponry that close to the reserve, second for being stupid enough to let an Onca take it off them.

"Possibly." Ey looked straight at me. "And so is Daron."

"Three's too many."

"You work alone." Lenzl sighed.

"Yes, I do."

"Not this time. The Agency rep claimed for re-embedding –"

"Self-inflicted wounds. Deduct it from eir personal funds."

"Marsk, listen to me. Insurance are covering it but they don't want any more. Daron is their field rep."

That made me laugh. "I thought Insurance understood risk? I tell you what, you want a man-hunter, you find someone else."

"There isn't anyone else."

"There you go."

"I'll double your fee."

And ey had me. I needed the credit, this was how I earned it. To stop hunting I needed to hunt. One more time. This needed to be certain. "Double for yourself, double again for Daron."

Ey agreed straight away, which told me two things: I should have stuck to my guns and walked, and she had been willing to pay a lot more. Point noted. I stated my terms:

"No tech, no supports, and definitely no weapons above Tech III."

"How will you deal with the laser?"

"I'll have an Override." Breaking my own rules. An Override wasn't technically a weapon.

"That's for close quarters."

"I'm open to suggestions."

I had come to enjoy silences such as the one between us now.

"Agreed." Lenzl confirmed the transaction with a flourish. "And we're done. Anything else?"

"Does he have a name?"

"The Onca man?" Lenzl stared. "Probably. Who cares?"

We met Daron at the perimeter line of the Onca reservation, a two hundred metre wide strip of cleared ground, quad fenced, pair on pair with a deep concrete moat between. The entire perimeter was triple monitored with passives, actives and countermeasures. And the guards.

It was a harsh, ugly place, a scar in a green wilderness. The torn earth and burnt organics jarred and stank, a brutal visual aesthetic crawling with unpleasant tastes and odours.

Daron and Lenzl wore enhanced integuments. Lenzl also carried AG.

"We agreed no tech. Get rid of it." I said. They stared at me. "You're targets."

"The Onca's already stolen AG, he won't need any more," Lenzl said.

"And he's got a DF laser." Daron thumped eir torso armour. "Insurance is paying for this hunt, no way can I go sans integument, it's mandated."

We collected our packs – food, medicine, spare garments – then collected our weapons from the Reservation armoury. The guns were semi-automatic rifles, chemical powered pellet throwers, an old and reliable design. They were lovely things, with antique stocks of oiled wood and mechanisms of blackened metal. I felt the weight, the texture, saw how the metal was worn bright on the corners, round the grip, over the top sight. I ran my hands over the flecked grain of the stock wood, brown on tawny gold, felt the cool curved black of the magazine. Mature technology, an uncompromising design. It was perfect.

Absolutely perfect.

Beautiful.

I broke out of it, looked around and shivered at the contrast between the ruined land flanking the reservation and the pristine forest beyond. A handful of Onca males dressed in their woven breechclouts, gold armbands and feather cloaks watched behind the woven mesh of the innermost fence. Arms splayed, they hung off the wire, muscles bunched under their tawny pelts, claws extended. Their amber eyes looked straight through us, and beyond.

Lenzl and Daron were still absorbed in contemplation of their weapons, lost in the moment, captivated by the intensity of the qualia suffusing their sensoria. Awareness was experience: simple chemical receptors, electrochemical transmission, wavelength, pressure, heat, these physical things arrived in the mind and became – sensation. We detect wavelength: we experience colour. Vibration becomes sound, sometimes music. The same for every sensation, and in us hybrid things, half made half born, most intensely of all. So we told ourselves.

Lenzl emerged first, blinked, and looked at the Onca males. "A million square kilometres to play in and they spend all day looking at this ugly place."

I thought they were looking beyond. They certainly weren't looking at us.

Lenzl stepped gingerly over the burned ground. "Can we go?" Ey looked back at the Onca males behind the wire. "I don't know how they stand it."

"They certainly don't feel it, not like we do." Daron extended eir arm, eir fingertips together. "They don't *experience.*"

"So, fortunate in a way," I said.

"Don't be ridiculous. You may as well say a plant is fortunate not to have a mind because it avoids grief, ignoring the fact it is also excluded from joy. Onca sensoria are evolved, not designed, a remarkable achievement but biology has maxed out. They don't experience the grotesquery of what they made us do here because they don't sense as we do. They don't truly experience." Daron repeated eir aesthetic gesture. "They don't *feel.*"

I led them across the burned strip towards the forest. After a few yards Lenzl hurried past me, followed by a grimacing Daron. The barren zone was a horrid place, we'd debated concreting it so there would be no need to keep suppressing the forest, no need to burn and destroy. One solution felt too permanent, the other too temporary, the conversation stalled.

I reached the forest's edge. The Onca's trail was clear, his pugmarks easy to see in the bare earth, his direction obvious from trampled undergrowth and damaged foliage. He had been moving fast, haste taking priority over concealment. Later in the hunt that would change. Onca had evolved from ambush predators, stealth and patience defined them.

A few smaller figures mingled with the males along the perimeter fence, Onca children. Their mothers carefully watched them from cover in the background as they watched us. Onca children are playful, kittenish, delightful things. They also have needle teeth and claws. Memories came, a sudden pang: tiger cubs of old Earth. Home. I felt it like an ache, it had been too long.

When we went into the forest we were two hours behind the rogue Onca. At first the trail was easy, the forest open, we covered ground fast. The

Onca male was big, the ground soft, the forest air fresh and drying. Within a mile I knew we were gaining.

"Why isn't he using his AG?" Lenzl said. "What's the point of stealing it if you're not going to use it? It doesn't make sense."

Open forest was good terrain for AG. Set it to 40% and he'd bound away from us, the long leaps and soft landing leaving a sparse and difficult trail.

"Why do you expect anything he does to make sense?" Daron said. "He's rogue, he's just running."

"And he's intelligent."

"So why isn't he using it?" Lenzl said.

"I think he's saving it for the jungle and the mesas," I said.

"They're clever, I'll give you that," Daron said. "Clever pattern matchers, like all biologicals. Apart from that there's no logic, it's just instinct."

"Instinct is a form of logic," I said. It was obvious Daron didn't believe me.

The ground rose and dropped, the canopy closed in. We entered a dry, shady glade of ancient trees, forest giants with wide spreading branches. Every branch and trunk was covered in cascades of epiphytic electric blue orchids. Their scent was astonishing, a sweet heady musk, the colour contrast between the blooms and gnarled black bark was superb.

Lenzl clutched my arm. "There."

Up ahead a gossamer white shape descended from the canopy one slow limb at a time. An angel sloth. Two dozen hunts and I'd never seen one, and now, here, a few hours walk from the reservation in a glade I never knew existed.

We watched the angel sloth creep across the length of the glade and enfold flower after flower, sipping and inhaling, the green flecked eyes in its beautiful passive face heavy-lidded with ecstasy.

"Oh," Lenzl and Daron gasped. "Oh, oh."

"Enough." I shook their shoulders, turned their faces so they looked at me, not the angel sloth. "Pay attention. Concentrate. I know why he's not used the AG. He's not running."

Lenzl moaned, a low, frightened sound. "He's here, isn't he?"

"Yes. Watching us."

"Good." Daron unslung eir rifle. I did the same and moved away, alert for any movement, the bright sparkle of the DF laser.

A fleeting tawny shape leapt away through the trees, high and low, left and right. Daron's rifle jerked to and fro as ey frantically tracked the fleeing Onca.

"Gah! I couldn't fix –" Daron put up eir gun then roared with laughter. "I had the safety on."

Above us the angel sloth enfolded another stalk.

"What is he doing?" Lenzl said.

"Watching."

"Why?"

"So he can know us."

And so to the cliff edge, and Daron was gone.

Lenzl could not take eir eyes off the scored earth where Daron had gone over the edge. "What was this, Marsk? Part of the plan?"

"I said three was too many. You insisted."

"I – All right. What do we do now?"

"Go down the cliff."

Lenzl's mouth hung open. "Now?"

The sun was gone, a lone star shone, one of the outer planets. The air cooled, I felt confident, invigorated. Lenzl was out of eir office and I, in a way, was in mine. "We need to get down. We can climb, or do it the fast way."

Ey looked around nervously. "What's that?"

"You have AG so we may as well use it. I hold onto the straps, you jump."

Lenzl gasped. "We'll be destroyed!"

"Perhaps."

Lenzl forced down eir fear. "All right, I'll do it."

It was an insane idea. I had no intention of doing it. "Don't worry. We'll wait, and climb."

"Oh." Lenzl looked pleased. "Was that some sort of test?"

While we talked a small yellow light appeared at the base of the distant mesa, a thin plume of smoke rose into still air. I pointed it out to Lenzl. "He's made camp. We can go down."

"What if it's a trap? A decoy."

"It isn't."

"How –? How do you know that?" Lenzl looked steadily at the distant light. "Where did you learn these things?"

"On old Earth once was a man called Edward James Corbett. He hunted the tigers and leopards that ate men. I read his books. I hunted Onca. I learned from my mistakes."

Lenzl shivered. Corbett had lived and died in ancient times, a mortal human from before the Singularity.

"What did you learn?"

"That the Onca are not tigers."

"What happened to Corbett?"

"In the end he tried to save them."

Lenzl fell silent. That suited me, I wanted to gather my thoughts about the Onca man. What he had done, and what he might do next.

Lenzl stirred, "Why don't you wear integument?"

A good question, and it was nothing to do with Tech. Onca men simply wouldn't wear it. Integument was effective and near silent – but only near silent.

"I used to. Then I realised depending on it makes you careless."

"One of your mistakes?"

"Yes."

"How many hunts have you made?"

"Twenty-four."

"And every time you have –?" Lenzl squeezed an invisible trigger. "Like Corbett and the tigers."

"They're not animals, Lenzl."

Eir brow furrowed. "If Onca were once like old humans, they're not now. They've fallen back, reverted –"

I felt very tired. "We destroyed their technology. Of course they reverted."

For a minute I thought that would be enough to keep em quiet. Then:

"How –? I mean, when you hunt, what does it feel – It's their only life."

"Everything organic dies."

"Not by your own hand."

"No." I turned my back. Down in the valley the lone light flickered, dimmed and grew bright again. "Be quiet, Lenzl."

Lenzl was still for a long time. Then I heard the soft sounds as em removed eir armour.

We moved at first light. When we reached the Onca man's camp the ashes were still warm.

Soon after, Daron came on the earpiece. "What happened?"

"He set a trap. You went over the cliff." I shared data.

"Wait – Yes, I see." The channel went quiet as Daron absorbed the information. "Oh hell. Damn."

Lenzl broke in. "Where are you?"

"Stuck in the recovery facility. Insurance intervened, I've been recovered into a static unit until –" Daron sighed, resigned. "They want to talk."

"Post-mortem?"

"Oh, ha-ha, Marsk. You said –"

"I said three was too many."

Lenzl broke in again. "What was it like, Daron? Can you remember?"

Daron disconnected.

The Onca's trail led us alongside a forest brook, across the water and back again. Superficially it still looked as if he was trying to lose us but I was getting his measure now. He didn't want to escape, he wanted us to follow.

A bend in the stream, a pool, a deep mossy overhang. The trees here were ancient, with massive trunks and vaulting branches. Streamers of feathery epiphytes hung in the still air. Silver light shone down; arching fronds shone acid green, translucent and fragile; the brook babbled and glittered over water-smoothed rocks. Sulphur butterflies, their wings as big as my hand, danced in the dappled light and sank down, danced up and sank down. A rich earthy scent from the soil, a sweeter vanilla aroma rose from trailing orchids and a thousand tiny violet and white-striped moss flowers snug against the tree bases.

Our steps slowed as we absorbed the beauty, the ineffable qualia of sensation: sight, sound, scent and touch. The entire scene was a living poem, a near intolerable distraction.

I struggled to think, to act. "This is… very clever." I unslung my rifle. "Be careful. He has brought us here on purpose."

"Here? Impossible." Lenzl turned on the spot, captivated. "Look, there…. And there. So wonderful, the light – Breathe –"

I pulled the rifle off Lenzl's shoulder and shoved it into eir hands. "It's a trap, he's using our natures against ourselves."

Ey: "No…"

"Take your gun. Hold it."

The stream was the only path, we walked through ankle deep water until we were under the overhang. Half the scene was blocked, dim light, cool air, wet feet. We needed filters, sensory modulators. The idea was repellent, deliberately blinding, deafening ourselves. It had never been needed before.

Lenzl looked around, dazed and gasping. "Why do we experience beauty? This intensity? What is it for?"

"I don't know." My mind was exhausted. For the Onca man it was a weapon. "Take off your AG. Give it to me."

Half dazed, Lenzl obeyed. I hung the harness over my shoulder.

Time passed and it became obvious nothing was going to happen. We'd been obfuscated and delayed, if there was a trap, that was it. All the time the Onca was heading further away. In one way it didn't matter, I knew his trail would be obvious, but I desperately wanted to leave. This place scared me, for the first time on a hunt I was frightened. The Onca understood how we were vulnerable and had shown us that he knew. He had made me terrified of myself. More than anything I wanted the hunt to be over, to end it as it had to end, as it always had.

Lenzl and I left the shelter of the overhang. Trembling with anxiety we walked through a kind of paradise, and nothing happened.

We smelled the angel sloth before we saw it, the rich sweet stink of death. When we saw it, Lenzl wept.

The Onca had crucified it, lashed it to one of the huge trees with thorns, eviscerated it and draped the branches with loops and coils of entrails.

After what we had just seen it was too much. The destruction of such exquisite delicate beauty destroyed the beauty we had seen. I was paralysed, my vision pulsed and flickered, I smelled burning: plastic, organic. Sensory overload. The blood and the meat. And the pain. Dismantled, opened and spread apart, the angel sloth still lived.

My head roared, wild thoughts spun. This was the real trap. The Onca attack.

Now.

"Move." I pushed Lenzl hard, trying to knock em down. I dropped flat, pulled free the AG harness with one hand and groped for the Override in my pocket with the other.

I swear I saw the laser light, saw the DF beam crawl through the air like red rods. I saw them pierce Lenzl's shoulder, eir hip, eir leg. I saw em fall.

I activated the AG and it leaped into the sky, a makeshift decoy. Laser light stabbed at it. My hand found the Override. I flipped the cover, aimed, pressed the button.

The Onca screamed as the laser flashed into overload.

The AG harness thudded down, trailing smoke.

I rolled, came up on one knee, the rifle tight on my shoulder. There, the Onca male, crouched and glaring. I fired, he leaped, and tumbled out of sight.

Rifle ready, I ran towards him through a stink of burnt fur and found a diminishing trail of blood. I walked back; Lenzl was badly damaged, unresponsive. The Onca man was gone, I didn't know what to do, my mind was an empty place. I sat beside em and waited,

"Marsk." Lenzl twitched, flailed and clutched at me. "Help me stand."

I lifted em up. Ey stood unsteadily. "I'm hurt. It's amazing, I don't feel it."

"Those parts have temporarily shut themselves down."

Ey took an experimental step and staggered. "Marsk!" I caught em and ey clung tight. Eir body moved against mine, breathing hard. "Marsk, I thought I was going to be destroyed."

"He's gone."

Eir face pressed against mine. "Show me."

I helped em over to where the mangled DF laser lay, the stock and barrel melted by the overloaded powerpack. I tossed the expended Override onto the ground beside it.

Lenzl prodded it with the toe of eir boot. "What if he had one? What if he stole yours?"

"All it can do is disable higher level tech." I lifted the rifle. "That's why this is Tech III."

The Onca was wounded, I needed to follow. I took Lenzl's spare ammunition and loaded my pack. "What do you want to do?"

Lenzl was excited, confused and uncertain. "I wonder – Part of me wants –"

"You have to decide." I said. "Retrieval is one option."

A very easy option. Just pull out and re-embed. Easy and expensive. Insurance were going to love Daron.

Lenzl hobbled around the clearing, eir damaged leg locked stiff. "I think I can make it back."

"How will you climb the cliff?"

"I'll go round. To the north."

I offered to return the ammunition. "It's not just the rogue Onca. There are some big predators out here."

Lenzl's eyes slid across to the angel sloth. "I couldn't. Not now." Ey laughed weakly, "I'll give them indigestion instead."

I cut em a staff, repacked eir pack. "I'll come back this way, then north round the cliff."

Lenzl touched my arm, my face. "When – If it happens, some big animal, what will it feel like?"

"I don't know."

"I'd rather it didn't. I want – If it happens, if I'm going to be – I want it to be authentic."

That had always been my feeling. "Goodbye, Lenzl."

"Goodbye, Marsk."

*

Wounded, the Onca man could not run so he went to ground. The Mesas were undercut rain-hollowed things. The Onca's trail led to the nearest, up a scramble of jumbled scree and down again, into a vast subterranean space. On the rock of the cave mouth wall, a bloody pugmark.

I paused at the top of the slope before taking that descent into the blackness. He was clever, this one. Buying time, always buying time. Down in the dark his ears would match mine, he had his stealth and I my gun.

The mesa was hollow, a pitch black rock cathedral of slow plink-drips of water and occasional rocks clattering from my mis-steps.

Down a hundred feet to the floor, a motionless lake of black water lay against a silent beach. Water I could smell and touch but could not see. I crossed the beach and found a rock wall. It was wider than my arms could span and higher than my reach, I put my back against it, sat down and laid the gun across my knees.

While I waited, I thought. Why do we experience beauty, and what is it for? And did the Onca really see less than we, do they feel less?

What was it like to have one life?

"Onca man," I said into the dark.

The vast cavern soaked up my voice. A moment later it was as if I had never spoken.

"Onca man. You can't kill us. You know that."

Silence.

Something wet landed on my head. Water? Too viscous, too metal sweet. Onca blood. Fear, sudden actual fear thrilled through me. In total silence he was right above me.

Right above me.

Now he was hunting me.

"What's your name, Onca man?"

Silence.

"I'm called Marsk."

His voice came from the front and side, deep and tired and tight with pain. He had moved again, and again without me knowing. There was nothing to see and he was silence incarnate until he spoke. "Powalgarh, Three and never."

Three battles, three victories, and never defeated. Which meant – the Agency Rep; Daron; Lenzl. Powalgarh was young, he'd never challenged other males and now I was near certain why he had needed two AG units.

"A good run, Powalgarh."

Powalgarh said nothing.

Very carefully, very slowly I stood. The darkness was total, the silence absolute. Far out across the lake a single drop of water fell, splashed, and echoed. I felt a shift in the air, cool and damp, a faint waft of wet stone, organics from bacterial film. Life lives.

Silence.

A low grunt. An unexpected direction. I turned fast and the darkness moved. It *flowed* and I gasped. Out of the black Powalgarh came at me.

He destroyed me. I killed him. It was over.

After re-embedding I went home. Back to old Earth

I decided we are quite stupid in some ways. The Onca Agency only counted males. Only males fought for mates, only males went rogue. When they did the Agency sent for someone like me.

But not me. Not any more.

I pulled a few strings, I made some enquiries. I couldn't be certain because the data just wasn't there but I was sure enough to be satisfied. As well as Powalgarh, two Onca women were missing. He hadn't wanted the AG for himself, he had wanted it for them, so they could get away as far and as fast as they could while we hunted him. Without detection, without leaving tracks. We didn't even know they were gone. Out into a wide, wide world that used to be theirs.

He would only have done that if they were carrying his cubs.

Old Earth. Where the tigers still roam.

Powalgarh, Four and never.

Wide Shining in the Remote
Deborah Walker

"This is where you'll be working."

The room was small, lined with wooden shelves from floor to ceiling. Already Theia felt at home here. There were no windows. It was a dark, book-lined tomb of a room.

It was perfect.

The books were centuries old, leather-bound, inscribed with gold lettering. The bulky scanner and the pc looked out of place in such a place.

"The scanner's very simple to use. I think you know that. Your curriculum vitae tells me that you're familiar with its working," said the Society's librarian and her new boss.

"Yes. I worked with one in the Eldersman Library, Mr Skerrit."

"Call me Vince, my dear."

Mr Skerrit switched on the scanner. It hummed and lit the dark room with a green glow. It was an expensive chrome machine, a bulky piece of anachronology in a room dedicated to the past. Despite Theia's familiarity with the device, Mr Skerrit took some time to demonstrate the scanner's workings.

"It's a little gloomy in here, I'm afraid," said Mr Skerrit. He pushed his spectacles a little further onto his nose. "But you're welcome to take your breaks in the staff tea room. Alas, the Society runs on a skeleton staff. I'm the only member of library staff." He sighed. "It's not like the old days. But if you're looking for company, I usually take my morning tea at 10.30 and my afternoon coffee quite late at 4 p.m. And my door is always open to you if you need anything at all."

"Thank you," said Theia quietly. "And what's through the door?" she asked looking at the north wall and a padlocked oak door.

"Just the de-accessioned stock," said Mr Skerrit. "Don't you concern yourself with those, my dear."

Theia had to choose her positions carefully. She was a chartered archivist, but trends in information science meant that an archivist was sometimes expected to (she shuddered inwardly), talk to people. She needed to be quiet, alone.

Books only spoke silently. When Mr Skerrit had gone, Theia ran her fingers lightly against the spines of the books on the nearest shelf. The old leather flaked to her touch, like peeling skin. She breathed in the smell of old paper.

The Society was an old fashioned institution. Its members came for quiet companionship. Men, and more recently, women came to the club for luncheon and dinner. They'd talk in whispers in the rooms. Sometimes, they'd work under the green lights of the main library. They'd spend their unobtrusive hours in the Society, away from the demands of their careers, their families. The club was a place of uttermost sanctuary.

Theia had been employed to scan The Lord Archibald Collection. Lord Archibald had been an eighteenth century gentleman explorer. His years overseas had led to an interest in the esoteric. When he'd died, he bequeathed his library of theosophy and Asian philosophy to his beloved Society.

"But no one ever comes to visit the Archibald Collection," Mr Skerrit had said. "And it's such a shame. That's why I had the idea of scanning the books and placing them on the internet. The technology's quite astonishing nowadays. Once scanned, a reader can view the books electronically anywhere in the world. It's almost like reading the book itself."

Theia wondered about that. Enhanced access to knowledge was all very well and good. But what was the quality of their experience? Shallow.

She worked in a room, dark, without sunlight. She was content here.

Mr Skerrit was very keen on the project. He kept popping into the office to see how she was getting on. "I haven't seen you in the tearoom," he said a little reproachfully.

"I prefer to work through my breaks."

"The other girls came into the tearoom."

"The other girls?"

"I'm the only permanent member library staff," said Mr Skerrit. "But for special projects, from time to time I employ girls from the library agency. But none have been as dedicated as you, Theia. Can I see the latest book?" he asked. He leant over Theia's shoulder. His breath lingered on her neck.

"Of course." Once scanned the books were reconfigured into an electronic version. The software imaging imitated a real book. When you touched the corner of the screen the image changed, as if you were turning the page. It was clever in its way.

"A very fine job," said Mr Skerrit.

"But it's not like turning the actual page" Theia said. "There's something special about handing a real book, don't you think?"

"It's the knowledge that's important," said Vince. "Not the medium."

Theia asked the question that had been troubling her. "Mr Skerrit, what will happen to the books once I've scanned them?"

Mr Skerrit coughed. "None of them are particularly unique or valuable. They're going to be sold off."

"Oh."

"And this room will be converted to a Skype facility. The members have been clamouring for it."

Theia couldn't imagine the members clamouring for anything. "That's a shame, Mr Skerrit."

"Oh yes, my dear. The relentless march of progress and all that. And do call me Vince."

When he'd gone, Theia sat gazing at the books. It was such a shame. Some of the books would be sold off to collectors. Those that couldn't be sold would be skipped. She imagined the books thrown casually into the skip, forlorn. It didn't seem right. They were crafted items, special books that had once been well loved. In the room the shadows darkened, curling around the north door.

Theia placed the book on the scanner and held it in position while the slow light scanned it. Then she checked the on-screen text to make sure that is had been rendered perfectly. The scan was slow, a few minutes for each page. She occupied the time by reading. She selected a new book: *"A Study of the Remote Pheomena"* by Constance Jemima Alfreton.

Theia flicked through the book. An illustration caught her eye. It showed the upper portion of a man's face. On his forehead was a figure within a circle. Flower petals bloomed from the top of the man's head. She read the text on the opposite page.

Ajna is the sixth primary chakra and is located directly behind the centre of the forehead. Its ksehtram, or superficial activation site, is in the eyebrow region, the third eye location.

Theia ran her fingers through her fringe.

The colour of Ajna is white. Inside the pericarp stands the six-armed Shakti Hakini. She makes the two gestures: dispelling fear and granting boons. She holds a book, a skull, a drum, a rosary.

Above her the downward pointing triangle contains a moon-white lingum.

"You look like you're a hundred miles away."

"I'm sorry," said Theia.

Mr Skerrit had a nasty habit of creeping up on her. And he stared at her so intently. It was disconcerting. Theia repressed a shudder, which would have unconscionably rude. He didn't mean any harm.

Mr Skerrit paced around the small room. He walked awkwardly. Theia glanced at him, looked at his loose skin, his hair that looked feather soft, and she decided that there was something about him that she didn't quite like. Not that she liked any man. But it was an uncomfortable situation. Mr Skerrit had undoubtedly taken a liking to her. Though she'd given him no encouragement.

"There's no need to be sorry, Theia." Mr Skerrit leant against the locked door. "I think that I'd like to be wherever you were."

When he spoke his words rolled with some kind of need, words from a solitary ocean. Theia turned back to the scanner, while the shadows in the room seemed to intensify.

Mr Skerrit was oblivious to her discomfort. "I do thank you, Theia. I've had such a problem keeping girls here. Not everyone likes the quiet like you do." He smiled. "They just disappear."

He kept coming to see her, gently persistent. It was a burden. But she needed the work. And things like this had happened before

In ancient times men and women had a third eye on the brow. Lower animals such as the snake and bullfrog still retain the parietal eye, a sense organ which senses polarised light and which regulates the creature's circadian rhythms. But over the course of history the third eye in humans has atrophied and sunk into the pineal gland.

The bus was crowded. Theia had to stand, clinging to the rail. The bus jerked and propelled Theia into the arms of a man sitting in front of her.

"I'm so sorry," she said, mortified. She grabbed at the rail, trying to disengage herself from the stranger. She pulled herself up, and smiled foolishly at the man.

"Think nothing of it," said the man with a smile.

Charles. Theia saw him. He stood naked in the moonlight on cool white sand, while the tide murmured. Inside the beach hut was the sleeping body of the man he'd met last night. And his wife and his life were so many miles away, and he was perfectly happy. For once, he was so perfectly content.

Theia jumped back, stumbling into another one of the bus's commuters. What had just happened?

Charles. Theia had seen him.

"Are you all right?" asked Charles.

Theia knew him. She knew him.

She had to get off the bus. She pushed her way through the crowd, half stumbled downstairs, and jumped off the bus when it slowed down. And then she was free. Free from that alien vision. Of Charles, the stranger. The too intimate vision of Charles.

And it had been so real. The feeling lingered. The memory made her quiet home seem irreal. As if the delusion has been real, and this quiet night, this blur of televisions, this loneliness was the illusion.

On the bus the next day, Theia held herself rigid, in case it might happen again. It did not.

She came into work and took comfort in the books, scanning them into the computer, adding to their demise. She thought about that flash of insight she'd had on the bus. She'd been too much alone. So, at 4 p.m. the next day she made herself go to the tea room.

Mr Skerrit jumped out of his seat. He bustled around, made Theia a cup of too hot coffee, and sat too close as she sipped it.

"It's so quiet in here, in the Society, I mean" said Theia. "That's what our members pay for," said Mr Skerrit. "I think of the Society as a place of respite. Do you like the quiet, Theia?"

"I do," she said, clutching the warmth of her mug. "Although sometimes I think that it might not be good for me."

Mr Skerrit nodded.

"Sometimes," she said, "I think that working with the Archibald Collection is not good for me. The books are very strange. It's hard not to think about the things they contain."

"We read the books, and they read us? Something like that?"

"Something like that," said Theia, not sure if Mr Skerrit was mocking her.

"You need to be careful, Theia. Especially with esoteric knowledge. Can I tell you something that's not to be repeated?"

"Yes, of course."

"I often work here late at night. I haven't got a family to go home to, you know. And sometimes when it's very late, and so very quiet, I know that I'm the only person in the building, but I hear footsteps. And once…"

"Yes?"

"Once I thought I saw the figure of a girl drifting though the library corridors, holding a stack of books against her chest." Mr Skerrit smiled. "What do you think, Theia? Do you think that there are things that most people don't see?"

"Ghosts, yes," she murmured.

"Yes. Ghosts, unquiet spirits. There have been reports for in all cultures. It's… disquieting to think of such things."

"And other things," she asked. "Can we see other things?"

"That's what the books say," said Mr Skerrit. "I like you, Theia. You're so contained, so assured. I would like to get to know you a little more, yes?"

She finished her coffee as quickly as possible and left.

She talked to the books apologising as she scanned them. If it's not me it will be someone else, she told them. She worked over lunch, forgetting to eat.

Theia stared intently at the screen.

The Ajna chakra can be stimulated by steady gazing, Tratka. And by some forms of breathing exercise, Pranayama.

Her breath was slow and steady. Theia ran fingers through her fringe. She sat in strange postures, unconsciously.

Petals unfolding within the darkness. Pale hands reaching out to her from the shadows. Seeing not the left and right merged together though the mind, but seeing everything. Asking not a child's question: when will we be there, because we are never there, we are always here. And here is everywhere, with the sight of the third eye, opening like a lotus petal.

A few days later, she was buying the paper, when she accidentally brushed against the hands of the newsagent.

Maksymillian. Theia saw him. She saw him at the funeral. She felt his grief, his mind swirling with the memories of his mother. And now he was orphaned. Alone in the world. He smiled as he accepted the good wishes of his family, but he was adrift. And he would never be grounded again.

"My condolences," Theia murmured.

"I beg your pardon?"

"For you mother, I'm sorry."

"My mother? She's not dead. She's in hospital. But the prognosis is good. The doctor told me so."

"Oh, I'm so sorry. I'm confused. I must have heard something… I must have made a mistake… Sorry." Leaving the paper behind, Theia walked quickly out of the shop.

Remote viewing. The books spoke of it. The bridging of minds. Theia read frantically, trying to understand.

But none of the books told her how to stop it. The authors all assumed that it was a desirable thing, this link between minds. It was a gift. Theia didn't want it. And it was getting stranger. She'd seen Maksymillian's future. The customary distinctions past, present and future were dissolving. And she felt the maelstrom of madness within.

Ajna is the eye of intuition and intellect. It is the bridge between two people, allowing the interchange of thought.

"I think that we should go for dinner," said Mr Skerrit. The desperation was hanging off him. Like his ill-fitting suit. He touched Theia lightly on the arm

Vince. Theia saw him. This is what normal people do, isn't it? Those not crippled with shyness, those who can ask a woman out without their heart pounding.

Vince. Theia saw him. Sitting over dinner with Sarah. The silence lengthening like the shadows. She saw the anger building in his eyes. The overwhelming failure.

"No, Mr Skerrit," she said. "I'm sorry but I don't think that we should. It wouldn't be professional."

"Why will you never call me Vince? I've asked you to a million times. What's wrong me, Theia?" He took a step backwards bumped into the shelving trolley. A book clattered onto the floor. They both bent down to retrieve the book "I think... we... should," said Vince. Their fingers touched.

Vince. Theia saw him.

She gasped and scooped the book, cradling it against her chest. She'd seen how the dinner ended with Sarah. Sarah had been the first. And then almost a decade later there had been Rosie. Vince's needs were slow, spread over many years, but they were insistent. Theia saw how Vince's relationships with Sarah and Rosie had ended. She saw him. She saw his need burning within him.

"What's the matter, Theia? You look like you've seen a ghost. You're so pale."

And the words came tumbling out. "I've seen you, Vince. I saw what you did to the others. I saw you choking the life out of them. Oh, you were so strong. I saw it, and I saw what you did afterwards to their poor dead bodies." Theia glanced at the locked door. Behind that door were the bodies of Sarah and Rosie.

Vince smiled. "I've never heard anyone say it aloud. I feel so close to you, Theia. So close. We can be together now that you know my secret?"

"No, Vince."

Cold tears welled in Vince's eyes. "You're like the others, Theia. Aren't you? Why can't I have the things that other people have? Why is that? Why don't you like me?"

"I'm sorry, Vince," she said.

Theia. Theia saw herself. The outcome of this. Her hand moving blindly but surely for the letter opener. Vince advancing towards her with his hands outstretched. Theia stabbing him clean in the eye, with such a force.

Vince falling, pulling a trolley of books to be his marker.

The mind's eye is not limited to the physical ingress of light. The mind's eye can roam through place and through time. It is the new eye, the eye that sees all, goes all. Feeding and growing and growing larger than the whole.

The eye sees Theia. Theia returns its gaze.

Vince is dead.

Theia feels a burning sensation on her forehead. When she touches her brow there is a small raised patch. When she looks into the mirror she sees a small patch of grey like the parietal eye of a bullfrog or a snake. The third eye.

Theia shining brightly in the remote.

Vince's blood soaking into the books.

And on the screen the pages swirl, flicking through the pages. They grow brighter as if feeding, unlimited, illuminated. They had formed a bridge, amongst themselves, no longer discrete. They will be read by others. And then, the secrets will be revealed. Good and bad, all over the world.

The reading will shine with opening of their mind's eye.

Bang, Bang, Thud

Ralph Robert Moore

You're nervous.

It's your first day at your new job. You meet with the woman in Human Resources, sitting in the cramped space of her cubicle, tense and laughing a lot, can't keep the grin off your face, hot cup of coffee you don't even want in one hand, careful not to wave it around while you answer the casual questions, then meet your new boss again, but when he turns around from the other man he was talking to he doesn't recognize you at first. Now here you are in your new office, not a cubicle this time, but a private office, no one in here but you.

The walls of your new office are white.

The ceiling is white.

The carpet is white.

It's very quiet.

You can hear yourself breathing through your mouth. Your breath is more rapid than usual. You sound congested.

There are light gray filing cabinets all around you. You don't know what's in them.

Your new white shirt itches, around the collar and down the back.

The button across your collar is tight.   It moves with your Adam's apple each time you swallow. It hurts.

But everything is going to be all right. This is your first day. It'll get better as you get to meet some of the other people. After a few days, you'll know their names and they'll know your name. You'll greet each other in the halls, joke around, touch each other's shoulders. You're not quite ready yet to push your chair back, get up and walk out into the quiet hallway to look for the coffee machine, but you will do that soon.

A woman walks briskly past your open door, glances in, doesn't acknowledge you.

You feel sweat in your armpits, feel it dampen the newness of your white shirt.

The phone on your big, empty desk rings.

You flinch. Reach out for it.

Your hand is black.

You're looking at your outstretched hand in front of you, veins snaking across the back of it, lateral wrinkles at the knuckles. Your hand is black. In fact, there's even a tinge of dark purple in its sheen. The back of the wrist extending past the starched white cuff is black too, with a plum bruise on one side.

The phone rings for the fifth time.

Answer the phone!

You snatch it up.

– Hello?

It's a white man's voice, deep, casual, as if you and he have spoken often.

– We forgot about the dog. Where are the surgical purses?

Your eyes roll around. What is he talking about?

– Excuse me?

But he's already hung up.

Where are the surgical purses? What does that mean? The company doesn't have anything to do with surgical supplies, or animals. We forgot about the dog. What dog?

You look at the phone. Next to it you've placed the one object in this office which is yours, a black and white portrait of your wife.

She looks happy in the picture, smiling, squinting. You took the picture yourself.

You reach your right index finger out, touch the tip to her forehead, her hair, as if stroking it.

Should you call your wife? Ask her if she knows what the man meant by surgical purses?

Outside the building, you hear a loud bang, bang, thud noise.

What's going on?

You're fourteen stories up. The wide window in your office overlooks the tops of near-distant trees, part of the forest walk the company provides. You need to know the password to get past the gate, to walk under the trees, along the path, along the cool water of the creek. The Human Resources woman whispered it to you, leaning forward. You summon it, to make sure you still remember it. You didn't write it down at the time, thinking she might ask you not to. 1243. Okay. You still remember it.

Bang, bang, thud. Bang, bang, thud.

What is that? Where's it coming from?

Bang, bang, thud.

There it is again! You listen to the uneven rhythm of it.

It's coming from outside. It's coming from above the window in your office.

You swivel your chair away from the window, looking around for something to defend yourself.

Phone, desk calendar, blotter.

A man's voice sounds from above the outside of your window.

He's singing. He's singing in a loud, uninhibited voice. He's singing in a foreign language. It sounds familiar. He's singing in Spanish. Somewhere above your window, on the outside façade, a man is singing a song in a loud, trilling Spanish voice.

Two thick ropes dangle down in front of your window, swinging back and forth violently. You pull your forearms up against your chest, letting out a small noise.

Bang, bang, thud. Bang, bang, thud.

You hear a loud, grating shuffle against the facade.

The two thick ropes jostle even more, lifting, bouncing.

The black heels of two shoes step onto the top of your window.

He's stopped his singing.

As you watch, the soles walk backwards down your window, their owner stretched out horizontal, paying out the two ropes above him, causing the ropes beneath to twitch, until he's standing perpendicular to your window.

His mouth opens, and he starts his flamboyant, almost operatic singing again, soles thumping around as he reaches behind him.

He has a leather harness around his trunk.

From behind his back, he pulls out a squeegee.

You see a white plastic bucket dangling in mid-air from his back.

He dips the wide, skinny blade of the squeegee into the bucket. It comes out dripping a line of soapy water.

You take your hand down from your mouth.

Still singing at the top of his lungs, he starts walking across your window, reaching up to slide the blade of the squeegee down the outside glass.

You hear the squish, crunch of his shoes walking on the glass, the squeaks of the lowering, raising, lowering squeegee.

As he cleans the window, he opens his mouth even wider, his singing getting even louder, pronouncing with even more tortuous enunciation each Spanish syllable.

Is he singing that loud because he's happy, or is he doing it to try to disturb you, to keep you from your work?

While he's shouting out the Spanish song, you notice he's careful not to make direct eye contact with you through the glass. Almost looking directly at you, but not quite. But close enough to where he can watch whatever effect his singing is having on you.

When he walks his soles around on your window, it seems like he's stomping much more roughly than he needs to.

As if it's deliberate.

His soles are right in the center of your window now. You can see a few rough chunks of blue-gray gravel stuck in the soles' tread. Can hear the gravel scratch against your glass.

Behind the soles, his loose, dirty beige pants stretch straight out away from you, so that the seamed crotch of the pants is visible. Stretched way past them is the front of his white and purple shirt, buttons pointing straight up. Beyond the collar of the shirt, rotating up, his singing face suddenly appears.

Still singing, he stares straight down his horizontal body, through the glass, at you.

Holds your eyes, while he continues his exaggerated singing, scrunching his black eyebrows together to help reach a particularly high note.

Stops.

But still stares in at you.

You fidget in your chair.

What's his point?

Silently, he pushes off the glass, looking up at his hands holding the two ropes, his body swinging in against the window, in fact bumping against it.

The frame around the wide window creaks.

Hanging in front of you in a sitting position in his leather harness, arms still over his head, the tips of his shoes kick him away from the window, the return momentum banging his knees against your glass.

And again.

You stand up.

Decide against it. Sit down. Swivel in your chair back over to behind your desk, where you belong. You're going to ignore him.

Bang.

That's all you need, your first day here, getting in a fight with some window-washer, someone who has to dangle outside a tall building for a living. He's blue collar. You're white collar. If worse comes to worse —

Bang.

— You can call the woman in Human Resources, and just explain the situation to her, that one of the window-washers is harassing you. It may not be the first time this has been an issue for the company.

Bang.

This particular window washer may have been warned in the past. He's not going to ruin your day for you. He's not going to jeopardize your job. You keep your back to the window, looking straight ahead, towards the filing cabinets in your office, thinking about your new job, and the duties you have with that new job.

Knock, knock, knock.

Startled, you look up at your door.

There's no one there.

Knock, knock, knock.

You realize the knocking is coming from behind you. From the window.

As far as he knows, you can't hear him. You'll just continue ignoring him. You need to think of the supplies you have to order for your office, and you also have to decide when you should get up and look for the coffee machine.

Knock! Knock! Knock!

You feel exasperated. He has to be confronted. It's difficult to believe he does this at every office worker's window. What you need to do is turn around, stand up, walk over to the window, get his eye, and tell him through the glass that unless he stops bothering you, you're picking up the phone and complaining to building management.

You put both palms on your blotter, push up out of your chair, notice the damp whorls on the green blotter where your palms touched, turn around, squaring your shoulders.

He's hanging straight in front of you, on the other side of the glass. Black, unkempt hair, messy black beard, big nose.

His pants and underpants are down around his ankles.

He's rubbing his cock and balls against your window, squishing them side to side, their brownness lightening against the pressure. Black curly hair all over his balls, cock three-quarters erect, ugly hairy belly-button flattening above.

He opens his mouth, starts belting out his Spanish song again as you stumble back.

Pick up the phone! Hold the phone out, point to the keys, let him know you're calling building management!

His hairy, ugly face breaks out in a grin, but the grin soon fades. He looks in coldly at you. Points, with his right index finger, above him. Holds your eye, cock and balls still swaying against your glass, leans his face slightly away from you, and lets out a loud, piercing whistle.

The smile returns to his lips, but it's grim.

Two more thick ropes dangle down in front of your window, frayed bottoms jumping in mid-air.

From above the top of your window, out of sight, you hear the labored squeaks of pulleys under pressure.

The second set of ropes start twirling, lowering.

You look up.

A pair of small, bare feet appears at the top of your window. As they lower, you see bare calves, then thighs, a woman's thighs, then low-slung buttocks.

The window-washer guides her body down. As the back of her naked body lowers all the way into view, he pushes her spine against the glass, and you realize she's there against her will. She's struggling to get away from him, kicking, her hands clinging to the ropes.

She's not wearing a harness. The only thing keeping her from falling is her grip on those ropes. Although you can only see her back, you know she must be terrified. Fourteen stories up.

The window-washer has her back against the window, laughing at her attempts to kick him. Maneuvering himself in his leather harness around to her front, he takes his hands off his ropes. Although you can't see, it's obvious he's playing with her breasts.

Her knees try to jerk up, to hit at his hands, but she can't lift them that high.

As you watch, stunned, the window-washer slams his cock up inside her.

Starts fucking her against your window.

He laughs at her attempts to get away from his thrusts.

Pulls out a knife.

Looks in at you.

Cuts the first rope above her.

You hear her scream through the glass, cut rope spiraling down.

Puts his knife's blade across the thick weave of the second rope.

Stares at you. Starts sawing.

You bang on the glass, run to the door of your office, run back, slipping on the smooth newness of your shoe's soles, get up, bang on the glass.

Cuts the rope.

She screams.

Doesn't fall.

His cock is holding her up.

She throws her arms around the back of his neck, to keep from dropping.

Wraps her legs around his hips, to cling to him.

Grabbing the front of her face with his right hand, he presses her profile against the glass, for you to see that flat Japanese face.

Her black eye rolls up, looking into yours.

It's your wife.

Your knees buckle.

– What! What?

You grab the back of your swivel chair, lift up the chair. But should you? If you smash the glass, if you can, would that hurt her?

Knock, knock, knock.

The window-washer.

He grins at you, cups your wife's bare ass in his hands, lifts her off his cock, knees her in the stomach to get her to let go of him, and drops her.

Fourteen stories.

You rush out of your office, crying, frantic, run down the carpeted hallway to the bank of elevators, bang the button, bang the button, bang the button.

Get on, press the first floor button, shouting at the doors to slide shut, someone else scoots through as they slide, presses the button for the twelfth floor.

– Why did you do that? Why did you do that?

She backs away from you, frightened, holding her styrofoam coffee cup up to her chest, spilling it on her white blouse, looking up at the progress of the lit buttons above the shut door, looking at you, looking up at the buttons.

The doors slide open.

– Get off! Get off!

People try to get on. You push them back, roughly. Snarl at them.

– Hey!

– What the fuck?

Bang the button, bang the button, bang the button.

First floor.

You run through the sliding doors, barging around people, knocking a woman over. Crying, babbling to yourself, confused which exit leads to the back of the building, guess the wrong one, run outside around the building, people staring at you, your chest hurting.

Back of the building. You look up at the façade, to orient yourself.

Incredibly, the window-washer is still hanging way up there, washing.

Run past the backs of parked cars, looking around the ground, the sidewalk leading to the rear entrance, the foundation plantings, skipping around the few people, who duck their heads, not sure what you're doing.

There.

Lying on her back atop some large palm leaves, naked.

She stirs.

— Are you all right? Are you all right?

She's lifting her head, elbows crinkling the palm leaves beneath her.

Your eyes travel up the trunk of the palm tree. At its top, one side of the dark green circle of palm leaves is missing.

— Are you all right?

Her dazed eyes track. See you. She smiles, still in shock.

— It didn't hurt.

— It didn't…You mean the fall, or…

She dumbly gathers some of the ragged palm leaves around her hips, pulls one up over her breasts, covering them, smacking her lips.

— You mean the fall, or…

— It didn't hurt.

She's clutching something in her left hand. It's the squeegee.

From above, you hear the window-washer singing in Spanish again.

You look up.

He's sitting in his harness, still fourteen stories up, small against the side of the building, but you can hear his singing drift down to you. As you watch, he spreads his little arms apart, hitting a high note.

The outside wall of the building has shallow aluminum ledges, four inches deep, as a design feature, above and below each window.

You put your foot up on the one at ground level, hoist your body up against the glass of the window, reach up for the ledge above the window, hoist yourself up.

Do it the next story, and the next, like a worm inching its way up the façade.

When you're ten stories off the ground, arms stretched up to cling to the four inch aluminum ledge above you, tips of your shoes dug against the four inch ledge below you, the force of the wind this high wobbles you back and forth. You try pulling yourself up to the eleventh floor window, but your arms are too tired, your hands burning, your calves trembling.

Bang, bang, thud. Bang, bang, thud. Bang, bang, thud.

You look across the outside of the building.

The window-washer is paying out rope, gliding easily down the façade, window to window.

Towards your wife.

You look down.

From your angle, hanging onto the facade, the ten stories of the building below you seem concave, bending inwards away from you, all the way down.

You can't hold on.

You look inside the window you're trapped against.

Inside, a woman, sitting at her desk, which holds a small pot of four-leaf clovers, has swiveled around to glare at you. The man standing at the side of her desk, leaning over to hand her a manila file, is also glaring at you.

You pull your mouth open, lips shaking against your teeth. The wind sways you to the right, your left hand sliding off the ledge.

No sound comes out of your throat. You mouth it instead.

Help. Me. Help. Me.

The man inside, still glaring, walks over to the window. Gives you the finger. Shuts the blinds.

Why did he do that? Why won't he help you?

Is it because he thinks you're clowning around?

Or is it because you're black?

A Mimicry of Night

Jon Michael Kelley

At no particularly advantageous point, Dario Frey left the beaten path that cut through the heart of Layton Woods, a sizable run of coniferous acreage that, save for a tiny cemetery and a struggling barbed wire fence, was indistinguishable from the national forest that bordered its fringes. Now in the thick of things, several miles from the nearest town, he trudged along with a watchful eye. In his left hand was a small metal cage; the preferred enclosure for today's quarry.

He was on the hunt, his khaki shorts, climbing boots and safari hat flattering the task.

Ponderosa pine and aspen congregated here, as did juniper, poplar, and any number of deciduous shrubs, all now in full dress. The sun was intervening through a ragged canopy, splashing limbs and boughs in its descent, then soaking finally, patchily, into the dry, needle littered ground.

Butterscotch, the resin scent of the ponderosa, was unusually bold this afternoon, sweetening the tang of yucca and pine. Dario blamed the uncommon heat for that enhancement. It was the dog days of summer, a time that had, decades earlier, prematurely ushered his mother into her own eternal season. She'd raised him in the absence of a derelict father, and it was always her determination to see him achieve his dreams, as menacing as some of them were to her feminine sensibilities. Even when invited, bugs and snakes could make for intimidating house guests. How she would squeal when surprised by one slithering across the kitchen floor, scaling the drapes, or hiding under the toaster. He'd loved her then for her tolerance, and loved her now for not having been the doting, overly affectionate mother, as some were inclined to be when raising alone a peculiar, if not mischievous, boy. Among all other things, she'd taught him to be self-reliant.

Despite his strong independence, he missed her greatly.

She lay nearby in Layton Woods, in that tiny mountain cemetery; put there on an afternoon much like this one, the air hot and redolent with butterscotch. A confectioned aroma that has since become for him a grim reminder of the finality of things. Of death and its callous schedule.

He stopped to dab his brow. At 8,700 feet, the climate was expectedly more temperate this time of year.

The drone of cicadas urged him on: a strident buzz swelling and fading, swelling and fading... The chorus was disorienting yet seductive in its resonance. A siren's song similarly and lastly heard, he mused, as those fabled ship-flung sailors exhausted themselves treading water.

Dario had long fancied himself an amateur entomologist, though would admit when pressed that it was more a love of aesthetics than nomenclature. His young fascination with insects led him in later life to collect and mount them in creative and choreographed ways. Kaleidoscopic and floral-like compositions of the most striking iridescent wings and carapaces deeply framed upon white canvas boards. Some arrangements strictly honored one pigment, one species – corteges of red milkweed beetles or neon blue carousels of vivid damselflies, while others were dedicated to polychromatic tableaus – garlands of pipevine and tiger swallowtails arcing in flight, swirling eddies of dazzlingly white, sulfur and raspberry moths...

His hobby ultimately transitioned into a profitable business, and one to which he owed the taming of his irascible nature. A good many of the brilliantly colored arthropods he chose for his projects were tropical, and therefore had to be acquired through insect farms and butterfly ranches from those regions, with some specimens demanding a hefty price. Customs officials frowned upon attempts to procure those formerly deemed "endangered," but were, most often than not, willing to overlook those offenses if the right amount of cash changed hands. A financial albatross at first, and to a smaller degree still, his artistic vision now had buyers from all over the world more than willing to lessen that burden.

For the prestige, one paid handsomely to own an original "D. Frey."

Less than ten feet away, motionless upon the trunk of a tree, Dario spotted what he'd come to collect. *Okanagana bella*. A Mountain cicada. Perhaps not as exciting as its periodical brethren who emerge every thirteen or seventeen years, this one was of the annual variety and its orange-on-black coloration and purple-tinged wings was just what he wanted, and he would need to collect eleven more to satisfy his next project.

As he carefully approached the insect, the realization came over him that it wasn't any kind of cicada familiar to this region. And the closer he drew, the more he suspected that it wasn't any species of cicada he'd ever seen. Not on this continent, anyway. It was somewhat similar in size to the native species, but its wings were double the normal length and reflected the light with a queerly mirror-like brilliance. Its protruding eyes were a deep magenta, vanguards upon an unusually thin and liquid-black carapace, one supported by six legs that appeared too stout and speckled with orange, as if flecked with a painter's brush.

The color combination was exciting enough, but the potential for having discovered a new species was far more sensational in its implications, both scientific and commercial.

Now within three feet of the creature, he observed an eruption of soil at the base of the tree, and farther up the trunk, just inches from its prior tenant, clung the insect's brown molted exoskeleton. With only one cicada showing, he knew there would soon be more nymphs emerging.

Cicadas were docile insects and not particularly hard to gather up, especially the newly hatched ones sunning in respite, drying on the bark. This part of the year found them in such emerging states, thus his timely efforts.

This one didn't appear as being fresh from the soil, as its wings were straight and dry.

Cage at the ready, he reached out his other hand to gingerly pluck the insect, and the moment his fingers touched that ebony body a momentary blackness enveloped him.

Dario drew away, disoriented, nearly stumbling backward before his vision returned. He barely noticed the buzzing in his fingers before it faded away.

Dazed, he took a moment to gather himself. *Am I having a stroke?* he wondered. Not likely, as the more he considered the lucid quality of the event the more he was inclined to regard it as nothing more egregious than a dizzy spell, one motivated in all likelihood by dehydration – a concerting explanation he was happy to embrace. He normally brought along a canteen when on safari, but this time had, in his haste, absentmindedly left it in the car.

He allowed a few moments for his heart to settle, then refocused his attention back on the insect. But it was no longer there. Searching the trunk, he found that it had skittered to the opposite side. Once again he leaned over and upon touching it experienced a new and more intense bout of darkness. Not any plait of moonlit or even star-filled night, but the blackest of that weave and draping heavily to the ground. This episode lasted a few seconds longer than the first, and this time he wasn't so quick to dismiss it.

Genuinely frightened now, heart racing anew, Dario inspected his fingers. That curious sensation, yet this time more compelling. A litany of medical afflictions again raced through his mind, those of the cerebrovascular variety still front and center. After all, he was well into an age that consorted with those kinds of tragedies, and his family history was a roadmap showing that he was most susceptible to taking that same route. Just ask mother.

Still, he was not experiencing any degree of insentience, disruption of his thought processes, paralysis of limb or facial muscles, all products of ischemia.

It was as if the sun had been switched off. That was ridiculous of course, but it did get him thinking, especially about that tingling in his fingers. What if a mechanism of defense was the stimulus? It was no secret that some animals had the ability to deliver electrical shocks, such as certain eels, rays, and even amphibians – water was a wonderful conductor – but he couldn't recall any arthropods, even the aquatic kind, being known to possess those talents.

However, his knowledge of such things had atrophied over the years, an unfortunate consequence of advancing age, and those right-brained principles that the creative community fostered as a way of life.

Regardless, it was a plausible theory, especially if this cicada were truly undocumented. After all, hundreds if not thousands of new arthropod species were discovered every year, more so than any other phylum – and one of whose maligned characters were notorious for their adeptness, charlatanry, and resilience.

Did he dare try to capture it again? What if those first volts had been just a forewarning, he wondered, followed up secondly with a harsher caveat? Would a third provocation guarantee something more painful? More enduring?

Yes, a less personal approach might be the way.

When his attention went back to the insect, his heart found a new reason to surge. It had again disappeared, hopefully only having dashed out of sight of its molester to another reachable section of tree. It had, and Dario sighed with relief. His next attempt was the safer one, coaxing the bug to crawl onto the end of a loose stick, then gently easing it down into the metal cage. It worked splendidly, that successive and potentially more aggressive zinger avoided. He slapped shut the lid, then left the mountain upon a profound sense of wonder; one not even the pitiless smell of butterscotch could spoil.

And, once down, he would immediately call his good friend and entomologist, Doctor Casper Seventes.

From atop one of the city's more impressive foothills, Dario's town home peered out over its southern edge and down upon its busiest district, a contortion of railways, interstates and lesser roads, all slipping in and out and through one another in holiday-bow fashion, if one was of the inclination to see it so festively.

Dario never found his good friend Casper Seventes to be of that persuasion, the incurably happy sort, but neither did he ever find him courting the other extreme: the profile of the rigid, white-coated academician manifestly addicted to pie charts and boundless contemplation. Older than him by a handful of years, and as many inches taller, Casper Seventes was a layman's scholar, well-grounded in manner and appearance, domesticated to established theory, and most approachable. His only eccentricity, besides being able to lull a casual audience into tedium with his crowded intellect, was collecting prosthetic glass eyes. It was a side of the man Dario found uncharacteristically macabre.

A bachelor, Dario's two-level residence denied him that stereotype, showcasing a modest array of Persian rugs and fine porcelains, with just enough frill to suggest that a woman had sneaked in at some point. Dario had never been married; a prospect rich in claustrophobia, and one he intended to keep maintained at a safe distance. His hallways were shrines to his most intrepid works, his mentor's unseen influence in many of them. And Casper would always tour them first when over, his appreciation never seeming to wane.

Today's visit was the exception to that rule.

Staring down at the cage's unique resident, Dario couldn't help but smile along with his friend, who was beaming ear-to-ear and nodding with unrestrained joy, the same way a small child does when a trip to the carnival has been proposed.

Dario had made it clear that he didn't want Casper handling the insect. This request had visibly struck his friend as mightily odd, but he continued to be the well-mannered guest, keeping his hands down at his sides. Clearly, it was killing him.

"Those wings!"

"Yes, remarkably brilliant," Dario agreed.

"A proud find, Dario," Casper said. "Let's not break out the champagne just yet, but I am rather confident that our little friend here is unclassified." He finally tore his eyes away and turned them on the bug's incarcerator. "Have you thought of a binomial name yet?"

Smiling even wider, Dario nodded that he had indeed.

"Well?"

"Monsmontis noctis."

Casper winced at the sophomoric attempt. "Yes, mountain for its origins, but night? Why so? Is it the color...?"

"I was waiting to hear your verdict on its identity, or lack thereof, before presenting you with this next bit of excitement," Dario said, brimming delightedly. "You see, I believe that this cicada has a unique defense. When touched, it administers something of an electrical shock! Or, at least that's what I think it's administering, as electricity is the only thing I can imagine that would cause a... a momentary lapse of vision."

Casper's radiant smile darkened. "Say again?"

"I've so far only touched it twice, but on each occasion felt tingly, and was rendered sightless. Only a few seconds the first offense, mind you, but lasting quite a few more the next. Funny, it didn't feel exactly like traditional current, but then I've never been so similarly assaulted by an animal and therefore have no comparative frame of reference." He shrugged. "There were obviously enough volts, though, to make its wishes known."

"It's amperes that kill," Casper said, attempting some levity. "Besides, Dario, there's no insect, at least on record, that uses electricity as a defense. Chemicals, yes; venom, yes; pheromones, yes. Even bioluminescence. But electricity? No."

Dario held up a finger. "Yes – *on record.*"

Casper was shaking his head. "I fear your little episodes are unrelated to anything this insect could manufacture – and certainly something you should address with your doctor should they continue." He chuckled. "Remember, there is the cost-versus-benefit rule in insect defense. Simply, if the expenditure of a defensive mechanism exceeds the benefit, then it won't be passed down to the next generation. And the requirements necessary for any insect to maintain such a thing would be acutely burdening. Of course, there are other reasons factoring against such a theory, but, suffice it to say, that's why nature has given us no examples of it in the arthropoda phylum."

Then, as if to punctuate this very point, Casper reached into the cage.

Just as he did, Dario grabbed his arm. "Wait–"

Then impenetrable darkness.

Outside, in what was just moments earlier a bright and busy afternoon, pitch dark night pressed against the front window glass, and as Dario continued to stare in that direction his mind's eye retained the ghost image of that rectangular frame, recalling the curtains as being parted and tied back midway, lending the memory the allusion of some kind of knowing, sinister smile. And in the close distance beyond those panes was an interstate in the throes of rush-hour traffic, absent the blaring horns and sirens and collisions that would surely be the resulting cacophony of a sudden and most premature incursion of night.

No car or adjacent streetlight shone in; no light of any kind sparkled or twinkled or flickered, inside or out, all suffused in a midnight consommé.

Either the whole world had gone dark, or just his own eyes. His instinct was holding tenaciously to the former, a persistent notion that, despite it being frighteningly unfathomable in its own right, was helping to slow what should have otherwise been a rapid descent into panic.

Casper had gasped tellingly, but was yet to utter a word. That was all Dario needed to hear to know that his friend had been blinded, as well. He could hear him breathing steadily; could almost hear him thinking.

"So then, where are your damned eyes now?" Dario finally asked. He was of course referring to Casper's creepy collection. That both of them had simultaneously been rendered blind was daunting enough in its insinuations, but as the phenomenon's duration continued to maturate so did his anxiety. It wasn't time to panic; not yet. But it was fast approaching.

Dario guessed that they'd now been in complete darkness for well into half a minute, and counting.

In his surprise, Casper had dropped the insect. It landed on the tabletop, and Dario heard it scrabbling away, its chitinous legs swimming against the glass surface. It reached the edge and fell to the floor with a quiet thump, where it continued its escape until it could no longer be heard.

Both men stood motionless, grasping the backs of dining chairs, still caught in the immediate stasis of a blackout. Outside, the ambient sounds of an unmolested city continued to betray their situation, strongly indicating that they were the only percipients of this bizarre event.

"Lights," Casper finally whispered, as if the bug was listening. "Find a switch."

Dario fumbled for the nearest one, found it, flipped it up once, twice, a third time, but no radiance ensued.

"That's... interesting," Casper offered, dourer now.

Dario was already feeling his way to the adjoining kitchen, a search that grew more desperate by the moment. "Found it!" he said, then began cursing when the flashlight failed to produce even a dim glow.

Casper sighed. "Might you have some matches, and a wick?"

"Candles, yes," Dario said, not liking the creeping resignation in his friend's voice.

As Dario began another frantic search of his kitchen cabinetry, Casper verified that he was indeed acquiescing to their unfortunate situation. "I'm afraid power outages and full solar eclipses and biblical plagues of darkness offer little explanation for our predicament. We're going to have to accept a far grimmer possibility."

This last comment confirmed that Casper had, too, in those first moments, felt the darkness to be an external demonstration, but had since come to surrender that notion.

Just then, Dario found the stove matches; fumbled with the box. There was nothing peculiar about the first match and the flaring sound it made when struck, nor was there anything different about its acrid sulfur fumes. He could even feel upon his fingers the heat from its flame. He just couldn't see it.

Dario shook it out, then lit another. This time he let it burn all the way to his fingers, and even then endured the flame until he could absolutely no longer hold it, as if the pain might keep him fastened to a sane world quickly giving way to far worse alternatives.

He turned to Casper's lingering statement, and said, "What did you have in mind?"

"Blindness – and of the short-lived variety, let's pray." Casper said. "You were right about a defense mechanism, but electricity is certainly not the culprit here. Rather, think Phasmids."

"Of course, The American Walking Stick." Dario felt a bit embarrassed at not having already thought of that ideal example; an insect that was well-known for spraying its aggressors with a potent chemical – one toxic enough to cause temporary blindness. But he quickly realized why such a potentiality had been evading him: Pain, specifically. Or rather its absence. Such an attack would cause severe irritation to the eyes, but he'd not experienced upon this or either of the two prior episodes even mild discomfort, just that strange buzzing in his fingers. And he wasn't hearing Casper cursing any distress either. Besides, the onset of his total blindness was too immediate. Where was that deteriorating interim between assault and complete loss of vision?

And if the poison was a fast-acting enzyme or protein absorbed through the skin, that made some sense – up until this last attack, where he'd not touched the insect at all. He had been stricken just as he'd grabbed Casper's arm, the very same moment the man picked up the insect – and that implied a transference, a conductivity; one that looped back to his initial theory of electricity. But now he wasn't even buying that as plausible. And because he'd had prior physical contact with the cicada, it would be the most amazing coincidence that he would suffer a relapse from that alleged contamination at the very same instant his friend was afflicted.

He posited these concerns to Casper, then proposed another eccentric theory: "What about camouflage?"

"How so?" Casper said. His tone was more receptive than Dario had anticipated.

"Your first impulse was to turn on the lights. Mine, too. It just strikes me that if this is a blindness brought upon by the secretions of an insect, then its onset should not have been so effortlessly abrupt. So... thoroughly engulfing."

"The lack of any sequence is rather curious," Casper calmly acknowledged.

But Dario feared that his friend was only paying him a courtesy, and that there would be no pulling up Casper's pragmatic roots, as they were firmly entrenched.

"There's just this persuasive feeling," Dario continued, "this... nuance, that what we're experiencing is being perceived on a different, less physically-induced level." He sighed. "Therefore, given this stubborn intuition, I'm growing more inclined to believe that this insect has the ability to inflict darkness – the transient kind, if I may take my recent experiences into account, those intervals having been directly proportional to the perceived level of threat, lasting just long enough for the cicada to dash out of sight. With your more aggressive handling of it, well... You pissed it off, is what I mean to suggest."

Still with that tolerant tone, Casper said, "Escape is exactly what it has accomplished – but only by conventional means. Your creative if not fanciful sensibilities are masquerading as logic, and are providing your own wishful escape. Not at all surprising given our grim prospects. Naturally, you'd want to ascribe this experience a brief and painless lifespan, and certainly one with a happier ending.

"No, Dario, I'm afraid common sense and clearer heads must prevail here. Trust me, we have become – and yes, frighteningly so – the recipients of an arthropod's wrath. Nothing paranormal about that."

"Still–"

"No. It's time we leave conjecture and start searching for that insect. If we've been poisoned with a neurological toxin, and given our symptoms I believe that may very well be the case, then we need to capture that bug and make quick and proper arrangements to get it studied, and for us to get to hospital. I'm beginning to fear that our only hope is for an antivenin. I don't want to discourage you even more, Dario, but if we are fortunate to have one made, it's not likely to reverse the damage already done, but will only prevent further harm. Our loss of vision may only be the first of many ailments yet to come. Just so you're prepared."

Dario drew in a sharp breath. "Alright, you take the living room. I'll start in the kitchen."

Upon Casper's request, Dario painstakingly navigated to a nearby hall closet and retrieved a box of surgical gloves, then dispensed each of them a pair. The gloves were used when handling some of his more exotic specimens chosen for display. Not for his protection but theirs, as his fingers' natural oils proved detrimental by dulling iridescences, lifting wing scales, and tarnishing luster.

Now on hands and knees, the two blinded men proceeded quietly and systematically about the wood floors, alerted for specific sounds that would direct them to the insect's location; a quiver of membranous wing, a scratch of chitinous claw.

After Dario finished with the kitchen, he progressed to the adjoining hallway, his intention to sidle the baseboards and continue a methodical sweep of the floor with his hands.

It was stop and listen, stop and listen...

As he searched, Dario began noticing that the darkness was subsiding, but only feebly; a peripheral adjustment so minor that he wasn't sure if his vision was actually returning or was just the glow of wishful thinking. It was so meager that he didn't feel it worth mentioning to Casper. Not yet. But it did give him renewed hope. And unsettling confidence that perhaps his exotic theory was worth reconsidering; that the longer the insect remained unmolested, the safer it began to feel, and thus...

Casper called out from the living room; a loud whisper. "I think I hear it."

Now at the opposite end of the hallway, Dario turned and braced his shoulder against the wall. Remaining on hands and knees, he moved determinedly toward his friend's voice.

"Yes!" Casper said, soft but assured. "I think it's on the curtains."

Just as he reached the threshold of the living room, Dario sensed a measurable displacement of air, adding a dimensional quality to the darkness that seemed to take it to a new, more evolved stratum.

From just a few feet away a sound leeched up from the basement stairway; heavy, stealthy, the sound of something large.

Then those promising boundaries of his emergent vision once again yielded to inkier realms.

"Dario?" Casper whispered.

Dario did not answer, and in that breathless silence he heard the cicada rub its wings. A slow, deliberate chafing, as if in some kind of contemplation.

Dario noticed then a drifting aroma of butterscotch.

"It's right above me," Casper said. Then: "Got it!"

Upon Casper's exclamation the stairway erupted with more determined sounds. Intentioned sounds. Dario was certain now that whatever was there had reached the top steps. Then, from what was surely that very entry, came a low, predacious growl, as deep and paralyzing as the night that encapsulated them.

"No," Dario warned, confident now with his assumptions. "Let go of it."

As if waiting for that very decision to be made, the unseen thing hesitated, its throaty respirations thrumming against the blackness. Dario was sure that Casper was hearing it too, for he'd gone stone-still, and just as quiet.

The smell of butterscotch was overwhelming, as was what it implied. His heart pounding now, panic in full bloom, Dario said, "Just open the window and press out the screen."

Within the mercurial acoustics of a dream, the thing released an eerie caterwaul as it leapt from the stairway entrance, then set upon a predatory course toward the bug's present captor.

Almost instantly, Dario perceived its impressive size as being utterly out of sync with its speed, as the distance between it and his friend should have been achieved in a single leap, yet the enduring clamor of pad and claw across the wood floor suggested that it was advancing by means of a hamster's wheel. Dario was reminded of the classic nightmare chase across a fogbound moor, where the pursuer seems always to be in imminent, grasping reach of the dreamer's trudging heels, until finally—

"Casper!"

"I…I can't seem to move," Casper whispered.

"For God's sake, *set the damned thing loose!*"

As if to offer one last chance, the thing halted its determination, then remained absolutely still in the fluid blackness. Only its slavering, cadenced breath gave away its position, one that Dario now imagined to be right at Casper's very own feet.

If not encouraged by Dario's verve, then certainly by the looming consequences of remaining idle, Casper found the handle, cranked open the window, then pressed the screen from its mooring. In moments the cicada was heard to take to the wing, its noises receding swiftly away upon what Dario was confident to be illumed escape.

There was not a gradual return of light, but an onslaught. Dario was blinking madly, and accompanying this brightness was an almost palpable warmth, one slowly thawing the nightmare gloom around him. Instinct was urging him to define this reemergence as that from a dream, but such a seething hallucination wasn't going to surrender its nocturnal temper so willingly, he feared, and certainly not to any fading memory.

He found Casper leaning against the picture window, squinting. A mild summer breeze fluttered the lace curtains, their nonchalance recaptured in the daylight, now seemingly oblivious to the previous extempore of night; one that, outside of its duration, differed only in depth from the kind seen countless times before, just beyond their balcony seats.

Whatever had been nearly upon his friend was gone; had perhaps slunk back down into the murk that had been giving it asylum.

For a very long moment, in a rescue of thoughts, both men stared at one another.

"It appears that I may have to concede to your imaginative side," Casper finally said, his tone authenticating a reluctance to do so.

"In what way?" Dario said, returning shakily to his feet.

"Think Phylliidae."

"Leaf mimics?

"Indeed, the grandest of morphological strategies. Those insects mimic their foliage down to the minutest detail: shape, color, texture, veining – some to the extraordinary efforts of appearing gnawed upon by caterpillars. They even parody the wind as they move about, rocking and swaying as if in a breeze."

Nodding in his attuned and now reverent regard for the light, Dario was staring past his friend and out the window. "Remarkable camouflage."

"Yes," Casper said, curiously grim. "Camouflage." Then, reflecting upon a more esoteric demeanor: "When long immersed in the night we are left no other option but to prepare for its denizens, especially those birthed from the basement of our perpetual anxiety. Our escapist battle with them is, in a way, I suppose, our species' own mimicry defense. We become the impersonations of our deepest fears and hope that, like the leafhopper, they don't recognize us as we sit trembling on the branch."

"Did you…smell anything…peculiar?" Dario asked.

Casper stared at him quizzically; an expression that struck Dario as being oddly incompatible with the lingering bizarreness.

"No," Casper said. "Nothing at all." He pulled the gloves from his hands. Then, as if reason were a scheduled train, he glanced at his wristwatch, and said, "Shall we call it a day, then?"

From the approaching distance it appeared as if the trees had anticipated his intentions and, to deny him the pleasure, set themselves afire until thoroughly scorched. But it was only the thick infestations of a black and undocumented cicada that covered their trunks.

Inflicting darkness was only part of their defense; was only cover for things far more cruel, more remorseless, more dangerous. Our most indomitable fears, always on the prowl.

The forest's sepulchral aroma of butterscotch was again strong today, as if in defiance; perhaps to remind him that his inevitable end would arrive just as spontaneously.

He sat aside the gas can, then looked in the direction of the cemetery, his mother's final resting place, just over the ridge and out of sight. Nothing that he was about to do would destroy her memory.

He recalled his friend's tragic inference; that when crouched upon the night we are the interlopers of our own infected minds.

Then he commenced setting the mountain in enduring light.

Space
Terry Grimwood

1

There was too much space, too much nothing, between Nyk and the hatch. The hatch promised dark and tunnels and walls to give him boundaries, walls to give him back the borders of his world.

Walls to touch.

He lay on his belly, palms pressed against the open, wide, floor. His eyes were tightly closed. A moment ago he had looked up and seen that the room he was in was vast. There was no sign of its walls. Its distant blue roof was stained by what looked like distant puffs of grey-white steam.

The room was lit by a dazzling, hot illuminator, so bright he could not so much as glance in its direction. Its heat burned into the back of Nyk's head. Yet it seemed so far away.

Far.

A terrible word.

Why was he here, in this immense room, this titanic module of nothing, this place full of farness? Was this a punishment? If so, he was sorry. He wanted to shout it out to them, but he could barely draw breath, let alone force words from his throat.

So he lay flat and touched the floor with as much of his body as he could and wondered how long he would be here and tried not to believe that they may never want him back in the complex.

*

2

The alarm shattered Nyk's sleep with its announcement of a new workday. The light in his womb-module snapped on; bright, stark and cold. Nyk's eyes stung, as always, as he blinked against the sudden wash of light. He twisted his head and latched onto the nutritube. There would be wholefood later, but for now it was a sweet, puree that assuaged his wake-up hunger and energised him for his shift.

The womb's hatch swung open and Nyk slid out, feet first, into the main dormitory tunnel. Along the narrow passageway, other workers were emerging from their modules. All, like Nyk, were naked and bleary-eyed. Each head was shaved, each face aglow with a healthy pallor.

Nyk joined the flow, his back and shoulders moulded into his habitual slouch. The iron ceiling was low, the iron walls close. The illuminators were set for morning level. Not too bright, high in the orange scale. The workers moved quickly shoulder to shoulder, shoulders against the walls.

And there was Shen, glimpsed ahead of him, visible-gone-visible between the workers that separated her from Nyk. She looked back. Nyk gave her a shy smile, which she returned.

Nyk stayed close to the cold, rough wall and relished its textures and the orange crumbs that scraped and stained his skin. He needed wall. Some workers were content with the brush of shoulders and arms, but arms and shoulders were inconstant, and moved in and out of touch too quickly.

The stream stopped, started again, stopped. People were passing through the shower, always a bottleneck.

When it was his turn, Nyk huddled himself against the smooth shower wall and luxuriated in the power of the spray. He glanced up and saw Shen. He stared at her, breathing hard. His face felt as if it was on fire. Shen looked at him and smiled again then threw back her head. Water ran over her face, spilled down the sides of her bare scalp, traced the curves and lines of her body. Nyk could not stop watching the water, and could not stop wanting to run his fingers over her in the same way. He wanted to feel her.

Then he realised that he was hard, as if he was watching pleasurevids. He turned away, faced the wall, pressed himself against its whiteness and closed his eyes for shame.

Wet bodies slid passed, battered, pushed and pulled at him. He waited, trying to gauge the amount of time it would take for Shen to finish her shower, then opened his eyes and turned back. She was there, in front of him. She stared at him, as if puzzled, or amused. Then she touched his lips with her fingertips, laughed and was gone.

Touched his lips.

Which tingled now. He reached up, placed his own fingers on the spot and felt a huge wave of joy surge through him and burst out as laughter. The other workers passing through the shower stared at him. Some grinned, others shook their heads. Some even hurried through as if frightened by his mirth.

3

He had to move. There was nothing here, no food or real heat or real light. Nyk opened his eyes, lifted his head and looked towards the hatch. He took a deep breath, a hard, dry-mouthed swallow and began to crawl. His belly scraped over the rough floor, which tore at his skin and made it raw. It wasn't iron but smooth and grey. Something like green hair grew through its cracked surface

After a while he could stand it no longer. He closed his eyes again and realised that to get to the hatch quickly he was going to have to stand up.

Which was impossible.

No, not impossible.

He pushed himself onto his hands and knees then waited until he stopped panting. He struggled into a crouch. Then he stood. He wavered, dizzy and weak. He reached out for support, an instinctive action, rocked, and almost fell. There was nothing to touch. Nothing. The vast room spun about him.

*

4

The workers streamed down the tunnel towards their duty positions. Dressed now in overalls, Nyk slid along the wall, confused, euphoric, desolate, more than ever in need of touch. There was nothing in his mind except Shen. She was no longer in sight, already at her machine no doubt. He was unable to work out what to do about these unfamiliar and disturbing feelings. There would be opportunities to meet, in the refectory, in the communal cell, when they watched instructional films, but what did he say? How did you do this?

He tried to press himself into the shadows, tried to disappear. But there was little room, too many others in need of the wall.

Nyk was a Components Quality Inspector. He had no idea what the components were for, or how they worked, but he had an instinct, highly prized in the complex. He could tell, simply by looking and touching if the component was sound or faulty. There was no magic, the item either felt *right*, or *wrong*.

Today, however, it was he, Nyk, who was *wrong*.

Thoughts of Shen were constantly in his head. He dreamed of touching her and feeling her touch. He wanted to kiss her, wanted to crush her to himself. The day wore on with dragging slowness. He grew tired more quickly than usual and, unthinkably, dropped behind the quota. More and more devices and components piled up. The other workers on the conveyor system grumbled.

Panic was on him as well, stirred up by the bleak truth that he didn't know how to make this happen. Here in the iron dark, crushed and surrounded by the other workers, unable to be alone with anyone.

(First time he had ever thought of the complex that way, as a dark place, a place where he was crushed. Crushed? Surely no one could live without being crushed, without crowded tunnels and closed-in walls. The idea puzzled and unsettled him.)

Not that he could imagine what *alone* was like. He had never been alone, with himself or anyone else, except in his womb cell. The thought of it was too terrifying to imagine –

"Nyk, please report to the Supervisor's office module."

*

Nyk clanged up the iron stairway to the Supervisor's office. He kept his right arm against the wall. Trying to find comfort in the contact, wanting his womb-unit, wanting the routine of the conveyor.

He reached the door, its metal solidity broken only by a single glass porthole and a huge lever, which Nyk pressed down. The door swung open and he stepped through.

The office was too big.

Nyk stood by the door, crouched against the curved wall, finding what comfort he could from the cold iron surface. The Supervisor was a long way away, sitting behind her desk.

"Nyk? Come along, come along. Sit down." The chair indicated, was opposite her distant desk.

Nyk moved slowly round the edge of the spherical room, pressed against the wall. His mouth was dry now, his breathing shallow.

"Hurry up, please. I am very busy, I need to talk to you urgently."

Urgently? Why would the Supervisor want to talk to *him* so urgently?

He pushed himself away from the wall, lunged at the chair and sat down. The chair was big, and seemed to fold itself about him.

The Supervisor templed her fingers, elbows on the desk, which was made of some heavy, shiny brown material. There was little on its surface, some papers, a computation terminal. She was tall, slim and sharply beautiful. She wore a suit, which was spotless and razor creased. She seemed kind enough. Her smiles were warm and comforting.

So this was what it was like to be alone with someone. Strange. Nyk glanced round, continually expecting to see other people here, disturbed by the empty spaces.

The wall behind her consisted of a huge porthole. Nyk could see the endless conveyer belts and the distant machineries beyond them, vast structures that dwarfed their operators to tiny specks. The grey, smoke-misted air was punctuated by the flare of furnaces. The office thrummed to the rhythm of giant hammers and presses.

"It has come to our attention –"

Ours?

"– that you would like to touch Shen."

"I'm sorry. I…" Nyk had no idea what to say, but was sure he was supposed to say something.

"It's all right, Nyk. Touching Shen would be a good thing."

"Good?"

"We noticed your reaction to her in the shower."

Nyk opened his mouth again, horrified that his hardness had been seen by the Supervisor and whoever else *our* might mean.

"So we want you to have the chance to touch her." The Supervisor's smile hardened somehow; a smile, but not a smile. "Would you like that chance?"

Yes, oh yes, he wanted nothing more than that –

"Nyk?"

"Yes, I want to touch her."

"In that case," the Supervisor stood and waved towards a second hatch set into the office wall, off to her right, "she's through there."

Nyk stared at her. "You mean…"

"What else could I mean?" The Supervisor sounded irritated now.

Carefully, slowly, Nyk stood then stumbled across the intervening space to the hatch. It opened as his palm hit its surface. On the other side there was a tunnel. Nyk crawled in and scuttled towards a light that glowed at the end. The tunnel was small, tight. It touched him on all sides. The security and comfort of that contact released a hunger in him. She would be waiting for him, down there, in that light.

5

He didn't fall. Dizzy, sick, but standing, he tried to take a step towards the hatch. He lifted his left foot. Now only the sole of the other foot touched the uneven, dirty floor. He concentrated on that part of his body, on that tiny contact and brought his left foot back down. He panicked, grabbed for something to hold on to, but there was nothing.

Breathing hard, Nyk managed to lift his right foot.

He walked, tottered, but walked, keeping his eyes fixed on his destination, feeling that faraway roof bear down on him. He tried not to look up or to look left or right. Nyk was quickly exhausted and wet with sweat, which was chilled by the air. He wondered where the air was blown in from because there were no fans or vents visible. Nothing was visible, no doors, no walls —

The hatch.

There at his feet.

Nyk dropped to his knees, shaking, panting but so happy he laughed. He had walked without touching a wall, without support and now he could go home. He saw the pad, covered it with his palm and felt the familiar electric tingle.

Nothing happened.

But hatches always opened. He touched it again and again then hammered at it until his hand ached, numbed, then bled. He shouted. His shouts became more and more anguished until he was screaming.

The hatch remained shut.

6

Shen, naked, stood in the centre of a huge, softly lit chamber. She looked up as Nyk stepped inside and her gaze locked with his. Then she turned to look over to her left. Nyk followed her stare and saw another hatch through which another male worker entered.

A third hatch opened. A third man.

The distance between the hatch and Shen was impossible to traverse. The floor was a flat metal grid through which red-lit machineries could be glimpsed. Their roar and thrum hammered at Nyk's skull and added to his mounting panic. He stared at Shen then at the space. It was as if his whole body had jammed the way the conveyor sometimes locked up and came to a juddering halt.

The second man to his right took a faltering step. His arms were out, as if trying to touch the distant walls of the chamber. The third man dropped to his hands and knees and began to crawl. Good idea. Nyk did the same. He dropped to the floor slowly, carefully and almost cried with relief to feel the floor beneath his knees and palms. It was better, but there was still too much *nothing* around him, a suffocating wall of it.

He looked up and saw the walker was already moving slowly and clumsily towards Shen, who was watching him, *him* and not Nyk.

Nyk dropped to his belly and began to slither towards Shen, the woman he wanted to touch. But it hurt and it was slow, so he raised himself up onto his hands and knees and crawled. The third man stopped and began to whimper then curled himself into a ball and sobbed and was done. Only the walker to beat. But he was already halfway across the space, his steps clumsy and slow, but ahead of Nyk and catching too much of Shen's attention.

Then she looked at Nyk and even at this seemingly enormous distance he felt her plea for him to hurry. It gave him strength. He began to crawl, exposed, alone, with nothing but the grid against his hands, knees and shins. He filled his mind with the touch; the feel of Shen's skin under his fingertips, the taste of her. It was beyond imagining, but something in him, some collection of awakened inner senses seemed to know already how it would be.

The walker was almost there.

Nyk scuttled like the cockroaches and beetles that infested the tunnels. Not quick enough. He was going to lose her. And suddenly he felt a new emotion, anger, not the irritation, occasional shouted arguments and brief flurries of blows and shoves that were part of a normal day. This anger was as strong as his need for Shen. It shuddered through him and splintered the bright glow of imagined touch with images of blood and fists.

Crawling was too slow.

He needed to walk.

The realisation was too immense to grasp. He needed to walk, here, now, across the remaining vastness of the chamber.

Slowly, Nyk hauled himself first into a crouch, then up onto his feet. He wavered, reached out for walls that were too far away to offer anything more than a taunt of unattainable security. He held his breath, dizzy, paralysed, then collapsed back onto his knees.

A moment later the walker lurched the few remaining steps into Shen's arms.

She held him tight, but gazed at Nyk over his shoulder with eyes that held longing and a disappointment so intense it might have been scorn.

The hatches burst open and four bulky-suited Keepers rushed in. Two of them prised the weeper roughly from the floor. The other two bore down on Nyk who managed to get to his feet, but too late. They grabbed his arms and hauled him towards the hatch. He screamed Shen's name until something metallic and sharp was pressed against his neck. There was a hiss, a stab of pain and darkness.

When he woke he was in the great nothing.

7

When Nyk finally stopped howling at the hatch to open and was curled on the floor, nestling his bruised and bloodied hands to himself, he understood that he must be *outside*.

The thought was too awful to accept. It had slipped into his mind and no matter how much he tried to push it away, the reality of it had already seeped into every nerve of his body. It rang in his ears; it painted the dark of his tight-shut eyes with barely-understood images of endless space and loneliness, starvation and death.

And they, *they*, the Supervisor and the Directorate, that amorphous, featureless smudge of authority imprinted in his view of the world, they had done this to him. What crime had he committed? The Supervisor told him that wanting to touch Shen was a good thing. He had done as he was told. He had tried to get to her.

But failed.

So he was outside.

His fear slowly fractured to reveal anger again.

He did not have to die.

He must not die, because *they* wanted him to die.

His mouth was so dry it was difficult to swallow. It had never been difficult to swallow before. He had never even noticed swallowing. But now, his throat worked against an almost impenetrable thickness that made him gag. Water, he needed water.

Perhaps there were other hatches. To find them, however, he would need to walk around the room. Well, so be it. He sat up and tried to look away from the floor and at the space around him. Above him, the steam clouds were thickening. Some had turned grey. The ventilation had been turned down as well, the air now cold enough to make him shiver. Nyk struggled up onto his knees then onto his feet again. He swayed, dizzy. He closed his eyes for a moment then opened them and looked down at the floor, which seemed too far away. He started to walk, slowly, carefully. He concentrated on each step, which was good because it meant that he stopped thinking about the space around him.

Where did this place end? He had always known where things ended. He had always known what was around the corner of every tunnel he traversed through the complex.

There was a structure ahead, formed into a tunnel although its sides were ragged, made up of columns. The roof was a web of what looked like green fabric or netting that waved and hissed in the moving air. As he entered the tunnel the light faded and the air cooled further still. A tunnel must lead somewhere. The thought eased his hunger and thirst a little and gave him hope.

The columns were strange, their surfaces roughly textured. Other columns could be seen stretching away into the dark green space behind the tunnel walls. Devices flitted around between the columns and in the roof, fast and agile. They twittered and whistled, but appeared to have no purpose that Nyk could see.

He came to the end of the tunnel and the room opened up again. Its floor sloped away into a distance that drove Nyk back against one of the columns where he wept and whimpered and covered his face with his hands.

He forced himself to open his eyes again. The floor sloped down, rough, brown, grey and green, then rose up again a terrible distance away. The far floor was hidden within another of the sprawling green structures.

Water flowed along the bottom of the slope, silver-grey, wide and fast moving. Objects protruded from its surface and broke the flow into swirls of foam.

Water.

Nyk tore himself away from the shelter and security of the structure and stumbled down the slope. There was water down there and he had to drink.

When he reached it, however, the fear came back and drove him onto his belly.

The water was wide, the floor running along its edges, empty and broken. Nyk clutched at the floor, pressed his cheek to the coarse green fabric that protruded between the cracks and stared at the raging, deafening torrent. He relished the feel of the floor against the entire length of his body. The space around him pressed in, the light, dulled now, but all-pervading seemed to burn into his eyes.

Slowly, he slithered towards the edge of the water. He had to drink. He would stay here. Someone would come looking for him. Wouldn't they? He reached the edge of the water, where the swirl and rush was gentler. The floor here was cold, smooth and dark grey. The floor was wet and unpleasant. Nyk splashed water at his face, then, without thinking, he formed his hands into a cup shape and scooped water up and into his mouth. The cold was shocking on his tongue but it slaked his thirst.

Exhausted, he crawled back towards a group of columns that stood a little way from the edge of the water. The rocf had darkened, now completely covered by the grey steam which seemed frozen into bulging, heavy shapes. The air had changed, had become heavy, cold and somehow damp. Then the water came. Great drops of it thudded onto the floor and onto Nyk's head and back. The drops quickly became more frequent, heavier, faster until the world was turned into an icy, grey blur and Nyk was beaten onto his belly by its relentless hammering.

Desperation drove him to his feet again, hunched double, barely able to see where he was going in the water-drenched mist, he launched himself at the structure, careered over the rough floor and grabbed at the nearest of the columns. Then he collapsed again. The structure leaked badly, but gave some shelter. He clutched at the nearest column, unheeding of its roughness and the grazes it made on his already damaged hands and face. He held it tight, curled up and escaped into darkness.

He woke, suddenly, breathless, confused. The light had changed to night-dark, broken into an uneven patchwork of absolute shadow and silvery grey.

There was a noise, something moving, nearby.

8

Wet, shivering and disorientated, Nyk pushed himself away from the column and peered into the dark. Nothing -

No, movement again, the sound of feet rustling through the fabric on the uneven floor. The sound of breathing. Not good breathing, but human breathing nonetheless.

"Hello?" Nyk called out. He was frightened but he needed these people. "I'm Nyk, I'm a Quality Inspector. Who are you?"

He was answered by a brutal fit of coughing, and voices that sounded rough and angry.

Nyk tried again. "I'm over here. I need to get back to the complex."

Something deep inside him, some unease, a voice almost, clamoured for him to keep quiet, to run away. But he was alone, he shouldn't be alone, and these were people.

Then they came.

Three, four, rushing at him from the shadows, their movement shambolic, but fast. The closest burst into a pool of silver light and Nyk saw long hair, ragged clothes.

The man grabbed Nyk's throat and they crashed to the floor. The man stank: his body, his breath. The smell was ripe and overwhelming: sweat, rotten food, and something else Nyk could not name. He grabbed at his attacker's wrists. The man's grip loosened and he seemed to simply give up. Nyk shoved him away and he rolled off and onto the floor, into a pool of light.

The man's face was a ruin, his skin distorted by huge swellings, some of which had burst to bleed thick, foul-smelling fluid. Nyk stood over him, breathing hard, fists clenched, but the man made no move to get up. He began to shake, curled himself into a ball and trembled and whimpered, then coughed.

A moment later, Nyk was shoved aside by another of the figures who knelt beside the man and began to cry. This second person was a woman. Her sobs were chesty, wet, wheezing noises, punctuated by fits of coughing.

"Help us, please." It was the third of the group. A man. He sounded young.

Nyk backed away, sensing more of them, closing in through the shadows. These people were ill. Illness meant infection, contagion, terrible words he understood only by their use in the complex. Anyone who became ill was taken away. Nyk had seen it, weak, coughing, shivering men and women hauled off their conveyor belt stations, out of the showers or the communal hall, by the Keepers. They were never seen again.

If someone became ill, you had to get as far away from them as possible, which was not far in the complex, but was very far out here in this vast and awful room. Suddenly the nothing out here was no longer a bad or frightening thing. Nyk ran, as best he could out of the structure and across the rough, broken floor, following the water, for no reason other than it was a marker, a *way*.

His chest was tight, it was hard to breathe and now he was afraid that *he* might be ill. It had never happened to him, he didn't know what it felt like. He slowed to a walk. He was tired but too frightened to rest. There might be more ill nearby.

He looked up. The roof had changed.

The sight of what it had become, stopped him dead.

The action was impulsive. He *had* to stop and feel this…this vast strangeness. He reached out to it and opened his hands and grasped at the emptiness, He was looking up at a roof now lit by a huge silver illuminator, and scattered with countless, sparkling white lights. And for the first time the empty vastness of this place filled him with wonder. For the first time, *nothing* felt good in his hands.

Someone shouted his name.

He turned and saw bulky figures detach themselves from the shadows; shapeless suits, the burred, artificial voices; Keepers.

Now his fear was edged with anger. They had torn him away from the complex, thrown him outside. He didn't want to run away from them anymore, he wanted to fight, to strike back at them, to hurt them. For a moment, crazed with desires and thoughts of punching, beating and kicking, he almost ran *at* them. But there were too many, and they wore those suits and would be armed with tranquiliser sprays and electrosticks, or worse. So, face burning, rage boiling through him, he broke into a run.

He stumbled over the rough floor, crashed through the structures, dodging and darting, the way he had learned to run in the complex; see a gap in the never-ending flow of people, take it, weave, dodge. On and on until he was too weak to go any further. Clawing for breath, he staggered to a halt, one palm against a column. Beyond, the room opened out again, and this time to expose ruin.

It stretched away as far as he could see, structures, some squat and ugly, others vast and thrust high towards the light-speckled roof, but all crumbling, broken. He staggered to the nearest wall and found it rough and caked with dirt. He huddled against it, drinking in the comfort of touch. In the silver-black dappling he saw a debris-choked passage, roofless and wide, walled by the ruined structures. There were broken vehicles, many much bigger than the runners that dashed through the tunnels of the complex. Somewhere at the heart of the ruin there was a dazzling, stark glow that filled the roof and washed out the other, more beautiful lights.

If he stayed here he would be caught. He had to move. He pushed himself away and ran. The darkness helped.

The water was channelled between two crumbling walls, the far wall many metres away. There was a walkway beside it, cracked and pierced by that odd fabric that seemed to grow from every floor. As he picked his way along the path, he saw other vehicles in the channel, dark hulks, rotting where they floated. The fast-running water slapped at their flanks.

Voices, up ahead this time, his name, orders to stop and wait. He looked and saw more Keepers moving towards him. He glanced behind and saw his original pursuers, closing in. There was no other choice. He pushed himself away from the wall and out into the water.

The cold stabbed him with a million knives, seared into his flesh and paralysed his muscles. He couldn't breathe, couldn't move. It was as if his life was swirling away from him, bleeding into the wild writhing of the water. He thrashed and struggled but was thrown and shoved by the torrent. It sucked him down where the roar became muffled and overridden by the pound of his own heart, then up again and away. He stopped fighting, let it take him.

No.

He began to beat and thrash at the water again, weakly, ineffectually, but he could not let it take him.

Solidity smashed into him and knocked the breath from his lungs as he careered into the side of one of the hulks. He saw a rope connecting the vehicle to the water and grabbed at it, found it cold and slimy but held on. He closed his eyes. Why not let go? Why not just let the water take him down into the comforting dark?

He held on.

Until the Keepers came.

9

"Tough is an understatement, we were supposed to find you curled up and whimpering by the complex's exit hatch like all the others. You led us a merry dance, Nyk." The speaker, a woman, was sitting in the entrance to the womb module in which Nyk had awoken hours (days) ago. "And better still, you're immune."

"Immune?" Nyk was bruised, aching, but warm in clean overalls and safe in the module's padded closeness.

"To the plague. You were in close proximity to victims over twenty-four hours ago but your bloods are clear and you're showing no symptoms."

The victims, those weak, frightened sobbing wretches who had tried to attack him. "Why are they outside? Why aren't they in a womb like this one?"

The woman had long hair, light brown and fine. Hair he wanted to touch. She wore an overall which was white and clean. "There's nothing we can do for them." She sounded sad and wouldn't look at him as she spoke. "The plague was almost the end of everything. Ironic though, what started as a weapon of war brought humanity together in time to build the complexes, and the arks."

Arks?

The woman smiled. "Come and eat. I want to show you something." She held out her hand. "I'm Sara by the way, from Recruitment and Psychology."

Nyk held her hand and found it to be soft and warm. He was reluctant to release it.

They seemed to be in a complex, one that was much less crowded and more spacious than Nyk's own. Its tunnels were too wide and high, though comfortingly metallic and utilitarian. Nyk found that now he was able to walk the tunnels without his natural terror of space overwhelming him completely.

There was a communal eating hall, large and disturbingly open. One wall of the hall was formed out of a huge window through which the outside could be seen. It was daytime, the sky once more hidden by grey steam. Water ran down the other side of glass.

The view was of the ruin, and something else: an unthinkably huge cylinder, held in place by a web of girders and towers and bathed in stark, white light. Its flanks were decorated with an endless mosaic of tubes and pipes which issued clouds of white steam or smoke. The cylinder tapered to a point at its summit, which was so high that at moments it was obscured by the water and grey steam. Even from here, it bore down on Nyk, filled him with both awe, and the need to hide from its immensity. The thing seemed alive with some barely restrained violence.

"Impressed? You helped build that, Nyk, you and the other workers in complexes all over what's left of the world."

"What is it?" Nyk asked.

"Hope," Sara said. "An ark. One of five. There's nothing left here, we have to find another home for our children. The ark is a giant womb, mother to a billion embryos, all tended by a handful of crew."

"Why was I sent outside?" Nyk asked.

Sara was obviously taken aback by the sudden question. "It was cruel," she said. "Certain people are watched, people with potential. Shen was offered to you as a test -"

"I failed."

"No, the man who got to her first was bold and reckless, good breeding stock. The weak ones who were too afraid were sent straight back to work. You though, you were cautious, but brave enough to try. Once outside you became a walker, an explorer, one of the few who have enough fight in them to leave the teat and survive." Sara tapped the glass with her fingertip. "The type we need as crew. The people we'll send to the stars."

"Stars?"

"You saw them, that night you were outside. You saw the stars, Nyk."

"Yes," Nyk said quietly. "I saw them, I wanted to touch them."

"It's not all romance," Sara said. "The arks' living quarters are a little cramped; economy of space and mass. It would be premature burial for someone like me, your Heaven, my Hell." She held both his hands, gazed straight into his eyes. "The choice is yours. You're free to go home, back to the complex. We owe you that."

Nyk felt a rush of relief: home, the tunnels and press of his fellow workers.

But then there were the stars.

Nyk pressed his forehead against the cold glass, only millimetres from the grey water that streamed from the distant roof, and experienced an odd panic he had never felt before.

He could not decide because both paths frightened him.

10

The alarm shattered Nyk's sleep with its announcement of a new workday. The lights in his womb-module snapped on; white, bright, stark and cold. Nyk forced his eyes open. They stung, as always, as he blinked against the sudden wash of light. He twisted his head and latched onto the nutritube. There would be wholefood later, but for now it was a sweet puree that assuaged his wake-up hunger and energised him for his shift.

The womb module door swung open and, naked, Nyk joined the other workers as they travelled the narrow, curve-walled metal tunnel. Once in the shower he saw Ynna, who glanced shyly at him. She showered quickly, but as she hurried away, looked back and offered Nyk a smile before disappearing to her workplace.

Pulling on his clean overalls, Nyk scuttled the remaining distance to his own post. He climbed through the hatch into the control module. The module was small and enfolded him on all sides. Its walls were made entirely of glass. Outside was night-black vastness beyond comprehension, and all splintered by the sharp-bright glitter of uncountable stars.

The Sound Cyclones
David Turnbull

A fevered dream that recalled the trauma of searing pain – a memory of near death on the muddy bank of a river at the tail end of a nasty little war. Tash Owen could feel the anxious thrum of her pulse as the bed sheets twisted around her ankles. In the dream her scream was silent.

She became aware of someone shaking vigorously at her shoulder. For a moment she couldn't decide whether this was the ashen-faced medic who was hovering over her in the dream or whether it was reality. Gasping for air she opened her eyes.

Slowly became aware of the familiar slate grey tunic of a Warden's uniform. Tash blinked several times before she was able to make out the short black hair and olive hued complexion of Maria Hernandez.

Tash propped herself up on her left elbow and signed with her right hand.

"What?"

Hernandez signed back, mixing expressive facial gestures with rapid hand movements. "Signalman on the pylon."

Still a tad unsettled by the aftermath of the dream, Tash clambered out of her bunk and pulled back the heavy netting on the dorm window.

The bright Catalan sun stabbed at her sleepy eyes and again she had to blink several times before she was able to focus properly on the foam-insulated pylon that rose from the rooftop of the opposite building.

A code red alert was being raised by semaphore signal.

She watched the Signalman's rapid hand movements expertly positioning and repositioning the short poles of his red and blue flags. The message that he was spelling out to his counterpart on the next pylon two blocks further on was clear and unequivocal – *'C-Y-C-L-O-N-E / A-P-P-R-O-A-C-H-I-N-G'*

Tash knew that as the signal passed from pylon to pylon across the city a complete silence would descend upon the hearing populace. She could already see people on the street below walking swiftly toward the entrance of the soundproofed neighbourhood bunker, padded slippers deadening footfall on rubberised pavement as they hurriedly donned insulated facemasks to muffle the risk of renegade coughs and sneezes.

Hernandez tapped her on the shoulder.

"Get dressed," she signed. "What are you waiting for?"

Tash splashed water onto her face from the dorm faucet and pulled on her own grey tunic and trousers before slipping into her wide soled sound-suppressing boots. Having fixed her blue beret in the mirror and set it at the regulation angle she signed to Hernandez.

"Ready?"

Hernandez creased her brow in mock annoyance and signed back.

"More ready than you'll ever be."

Tash gave her the middle finger and slid swiftly down the station pole from the first to the ground floor. Once Hernandez had joined her she opened the door to the equipment locker and began handing out items of hardware. They signed back and forth as they checked off two sets of inventory.

"Decibel monitors and wristbands," signed Tash.

"Check," signed Hernandez.

"High powered rifles and silencer attachments."

"Check."

"Bandoleers."

"Check."

"Two times six sets of tranquilliser darts."

"Check."

Hernandez began slipping the darts into the loops on the bandoleers.

"Ear protectors," signed Tash.

"Check."

This time Hernandez signed back with a cynical wink.

It was a huge joke amongst Wardens that the authorities still stubbornly insisted on deaf veterans like Tash and Hernandez somewhat pointlessly wearing ear protectors. There was no further damage a *cyclone* could inflict on them. The tiny hairs and fragile bones inside their eardrums were already destroyed beyond repair.

Tash recalled seeing the diagnosis scribbled down on the medical records clipped to her bed frame in the field hospital where she had first been treated – *irreversible neural hearing loss caused irreparable damage to the vistibulochlear nerve*s. She remembered feeling somewhat morbidly glad that she would never have to attempt to pronounce those particular words out loud.

Tash selected the next pair of items.

"Toughened goggles."

"Check," signed Hernandez.

Tash pulled on her goggles and rested them on her forehead while she strapped on her bandoleer and attached the decibel monitor to her left wrist. The goggles were designed to protect their eyes from the flying debris often churned up by the energy tossed around when a *cyclone* came in.

"Ready?" she signed to Hernandez.

"Love you," Hernandez signed back and leaned forward to kiss her.

Tash turned her head and dodged to one side.

"Not when we're working," she signed.

Hernandez scowled and then shrugged her shoulders. There was a brief moment of discomfort as their eyes met and locked before the two of them shouldered their rifles and walked out into the baking mid-morning heat.

*

Tash could feel the tensing of every nerving ending in her body. Having been amongst the first casualties of the use of a *sound cyclone* against combatants she knew exactly what it was like to be caught in the juggernaut path of one of these roaring monstrosities.

Electromagnetic warfare could be traced back to high-frequency aural research programmes and atmospheric geo-engineering experiments that had commenced as far back as the 1960's and *sound cyclones* were the pinnacle of this experimentation.

In simple terms, they consisted of a rapidly rotating core of oxide particles through which an electrical current was driven. This created a magnetic field that drew to it all audible sound within a half-mile radius.

Cyclones had been deployed with cold and incautious recklessness by rogue states during the secession wars that had flared up within the European Union during the second quarter of the 21st century.

The day they were hit her unit, mainly Brits and Belgians, was skirting the shoreline of the Moselle River, shell-pitted vineyards rising steeply on the opposite bank, studded with claws of vines that had been blast-blackened to charcoal. Here and there they could make out ghostly remnants of farmhouses and wineries, reduced to piles of rubble by weeks of intense blanket bombing.

They had all felt it at once – a sudden electrical charge in the air, a tingling that raised goose bumps on flesh – then the low rumbling noise of something approaching. Thinking that they had strayed into the path of an advancing armoured division their commanding officer had given the order to take cover.

Tash and two others had stationed themselves behind an outcropping of charred rock on the lip of a shell crater. The sight of hundreds of swallows momentarily filling the sky in a flight of terror had sent a shiver through her to match the feel of the cold mud seeping through the knees of her combat trousers.

The shiver gave way to an almost convulsive trembling when she witnessed the *cyclone's* approach, a semi-visible swirling cone, twenty foot tall, descending down through the slope of the blighted vineyard, churning up devils of dust and ash.

"What the fuck?" yelled one of her companions.

Tash winced.

The din that the *cyclone* was making was becoming increasingly uncomfortable.

The whirling cone crossed the river, slicing a white water trail like a frosted scar.

Then in an instant it was upon them and they were suddenly hearing a wild cacophony of random and arbitrary sounds –the chinking of cutlery and coffee cups, the tribal chanting of a crowd at a football match, screaming heavy metal guitars interlaced with snatches of classical music and operatic arias, the pounding of a pile hammer, the roar of a jet engine, the banshee wail of a siren, the dull thud of distant artillery, the clamour of church bells.

These sounds and dozens more like them merged and melded into one terrible blaring uproar. From the communication device pinned to the lapel of her flak jacket she could also she could hear snatches of confusion ensuing within her unit's chain of command – garbled orders issued, rescinded, countermanded – the sound of bewildered sobbing, rapidly drowned out by screams of terror and agony.

The *cyclone* was right over her by then and she felt the searing hot poker of high frequency white noise drilling into her head. It was like every sound she had ever encountered in her life compressed and concentrated into an unremitting mass. Her nose began to bleed. Her ears began to bleed. She could see members of the patrol thrashing on the ground in agony, some of them fleeing into the river and diving beneath the surface to try and escape the remorseless noise.

Her vision became increasingly hazy as blood vessels ruptured in her eyes. She felt as if someone had wedged the narrow end of a crowbar beneath her cranial plate and was cruelly levering an open gap into her skull. She became vaguely aware of herself rolling in the wet mud as the pain drove her to the brink of insanity.

Then, all of a sudden, there came an instant moment of relief as something popped audibly inside her head. She was still conscious of the *cyclone* swirling around her but, other than a sharp and incessant whistling that was clearly internal rather than external, there was no longer any discernible noise. And she realised with a cold and unsettling certainty that her hearing had been destroyed, torn from her in the most cruel and violent manner imaginable.

Several members of her unit had died that day – some from heart failure, others rendered unconscious and washed downriver to drown. Tash and the remaining survivors had initially been airlifted to a field hospital in Dusseldorf before being transferred to a hastily established rehabilitation centre in Barcelona.

Here she had undergone counselling to help her cope with the effects of post-traumatic stress. Here too she was tutored in the basics of sign language and semaphore. And it was in Barcelona that she had remained, enlisting as a Warden when the proliferation of *cyclones* became a real and ever present threat to the civilian populace.

The zone that she and Hernandez were assigned to patrol consisted of a number of narrow streets that ran off from the famous market area of the Ramblas. Their job was to ensure that the populace was secure and safe within the bunker and that any residual noise remained as far as possible suppressed till the all clear.

Even outside of code red alerts all sorts of precautions had to be taken.

Subtitles in cinemas and for television broadcasts had become standard. The use of heavy machinery was subject to prohibition. Live music was a thing from the golden heyday of a nostalgic past. Dogs had been systematically culled to eliminate the risks posed by their barking. But babies still cried – waves still crashed against the shore – and *cyclones* came with distressing regularity.

Not only did they come; they multiplied, too. In certain prevailing crosswind conditions a *cyclone* could collapse in on itself only to rise again, giving birth to a second or a third smaller but nonetheless equally potent whirling dervish of compressed noise.

Tash had witnessed this for herself from a Signal Pylon while learning the basics of semaphore. An incoming *cyclone* racing towards the area around the famous Barcelona football stadium had suddenly lost integrity and blinked out of view. A moment later two separate spirals had ascended – with a third, considerably smaller funnel, trailing in their wake like a child chasing its parents.

The first duty assigned to Wardens during a code red was to ensure the door to the neighbourhood bunker was closed and sealed. Tash and Hernandez reached the entrance of their allocated bunker in time to see a somewhat harried looking police officer assisting a primary school teacher to herd her pupils into the main passage.

As soon as he set eyes on Tash the policeman began gesturing wildly, sweat pouring down his forehead beneath the peak of his cap, his mouth moving rapidly as if he was shouting something at her. Tash shrugged her shoulders helplessly. She hadn't yet mastered the basics of lip reading let alone lip reading in Spanish or Catalan.

She tried to tell him this by speaking out loud. But although she could feel the vibrations in her larynx she had no idea whether she was yelling at him or whispering. She turned to Hernandez. Hernandez studied the man's lips and translated with her hands. "He says there are looters in the area, avoiding the curfew."

Tash gave him a quick thumbs up to show she understood the message.

The last of the pupils were in the hallway now, ready to descend the stairwell into the main bunker area – their teacher clucking around them like a fussy mother hen. As soon as Tash bustled the policeman inside to join them Hernandez began pushing the heavily insulated doors shut.

When the rubberised seals kissed together, Tash yanked the lock into place and punched in the numerical sequence of the security code into the raised keypad. The bunker would remain sealed until the *cyclone* had passed and the signalman had spelled out the all clear from the pylon.

Now the focus for Tash and Hernandez would be to track down and apprehend the looters. Tash despised the stupidity and selfishness of looters. While she and Hernandez were expending all of their efforts into trying to apprehend them some poor elderly citizen might be struggling towards a bunker door that was already sealed. Biting angrily down on her lip she loaded her rifle with one of the tranquilliser darts and watched from the corner of her eye as Hernandez did likewise.

There were a couple of pharmacy stores in one of the nearby streets. *Cyclones* had brought Europe's economy to its knees. The price of over the counter medicines had skyrocketed and looters usually made a beeline for the type of high end and easily portable medication that could be sold quickly on the black market. Tash signed her hunch to Hernandez.

Nodding her agreement Hernandez shouldered her rifle as the two of them turned left out of the main thoroughfare.

Although she could not actually hear it Tash knew that the *cyclone* could not be far away. There were little telltale signs all around – a noticeable drop in temperature, gooseflesh on her arms, underfoot vibrations rising up from the rubberised surface of pavement, a visible trembling of the toughened plastic glass in shop windows.

She checked her wrist monitor.

The needle was creeping past 100 decibels.

Not enough to cause permanent damage – but enough to cause severe discomfort.

Like hungry monsters *cyclones* honed in on noise and seized it for their own. It was important, therefore, for the two of them to proceed with caution. The slightest sound could draw the *cyclone* in their direction, placing both the looters and any stray citizens at risk. Increasingly Tash couldn't help thinking of *cyclones* as living, coldly calculating predators – like wolves prowling down from mountain lairs intent on slaughtering the lambs in the valleys.

She hurried in the direction of the first pharmacy, Hernandez jogging silently at her rear. The pavements in the streets off the main drag of the Ramblas were not rubberised so both of them had to run in the awkward, sound-muffling, soles of the feet gait they'd been taught at the Wardens' Training Academy.

They were ten or so yards away from the pharmacy when a figure dashed out of the doorway, struggling to slip his arms through the straps of a backpack that was no doubt overloaded with painkillers and asthma inhalers. The stylised depiction of an Argentinean bolas embroidered onto the back of his denim jacket signified him as a member of *El Gaucho*, a street gang who had recently been engaging in increasingly reckless looting activities during code red emergencies.

When he saw them he turned to run, losing his grip on the backpack in the process. It fell heavily to the pavement. The chances of the *cyclone* picking up on the sound of it falling were high. Tash raised her rifle and curled her fingers around the trigger.

Suddenly something came at her in a rapid blur from a side alley and before she had time to react a second gang member knocked her from her feet. Pain shot through her shoulder as she landed awkwardly. He leapt over her and sprinted after his friend.

Hernandez fell onto one knee and fired the dart from her rifle at the first gang member. Her aim was as perfect as ever. The dart pierced his shoulder. He stumbled, control over his legs immediately giving out to the instantaneous effect of the powerful sedative.

Knowing Hernandez didn't have sufficient time to reload Tash sat up and fixed the second looter in her sights. Just as she pulled the trigger he dodged into another alleyway. The dart sliced against the wall leaving a jagged trail of blue sparks.

Hernandez hauled Tash to her feet.

"Do we give chase?" she signed.

Tash checked her monitor. The decibel reading was past 110 and climbing.

"No time," she signed back. "We need to bin this one before the *cyclone* hits. His friend is going to have to take his chances. He knew the risks."

From a rack attached to a wall a short way along the street Tash retrieved a flat, four-wheeled trolley and pushed it to where Hernandez was crouching down to remove the spent dart from the unconscious youth.

He couldn't have been more than fourteen years old. Tash shook her head when she saw that he was wearing a pair of stereo headphones padded out with bubble wrap and duct tape – as if that would offer any real protection in the raging eye of a *cyclone*.

Taking his limp arms and legs they laid him out on the trolley. Hernandez grabbed the fallen backpack and dumped it on his belly. Its illicit contents would be used as evidence later when the police retrieved him from the bin. Tash looked at her wrist monitor – 115 decibels. They'd have to move quickly now if they were going to avoid their ward suffering permanent ear damage.

Crouching low, they pushed the trolley into the Ramblas. The ground was shaking more violently underfoot, the air sharp and spiked with static. They headed for bin number 4 – a long coffin-shaped object situated between two of the street vendor kiosks. Tash started punching the security code into the bin's lid while Hernandez slipped her arms around the youth's chest and hefted him up.

The lid hissed open.

They laid him inside the sound insulated interior.

Again Hernandez dumped the backpack onto his belly.

Tash pushed the lid shut and watched the seals kiss.

She punched in the code to activate the lock and set the red *occupied* light flashing. This would alert the police once the all clear was given. When the boy finally came round he'd find himself in a cell, waiting to be charged for theft and violation of the city *cyclone* ordinance.

Tash looked up at the pylon. The signalman had strapped himself into position. He was spelling out another semaphore message with his flags. This one was meant for Tash and Hernandez.

"C-Y-C-L-O-N-E / H-E-A-D-I-N-G / Y-O-U-R / W-A-Y"

They saw it sweeping slowly across from Plaza Espania into the mouth of the Ramblas – its semi-visible vortex swirling wildly as shafts of sunlight sparked back from it. Ahead of it came a frantic airborne dash of gulls and starlings and emerald coloured parakeets. Tash tried to remember if she had ever actually heard the call of a parakeet. Whatever it sounded like the panic of the birds was almost certainly dragging the noise hungry *cyclone* behind it.

In her mind Tash could see rapid and random flashbacks as she was once again forced to relive the nightmare of her riverbank encounter. She looked at Hernandez and knew from the wide stare of her dark eyes that she too was being drawn back to the day another *cyclone* had ripped away her own hearing faculties.

For a moment the two of them stood perfectly still as all around them the pavements, the shop windows and the vendor stands were shuddered and shaken by the intensity of the noise generated by the *cyclone's* approach. Tash stole a glance at her wrist monitor – 145 decibels and still rising.

The *cyclone's* advance was slow and ponderous as it diligently harvested the minutest of noises within its vicinity. The rustle of a newspaper blown along the pavement, the barely audible clicking of an insect in a crack in a wall, the buzzing of an errant fly – all were fodder for its voracious appetites.

Ahead of the *cyclone*, bits of grit and detritus were already being tossed up, stinging Tash's cheeks and bouncing away from her goggles. Hernandez tapped her on the shoulder. "We should move," she signed.

The two of them turned and began walking swiftly in the direction of the Warden's booth that was situated near the Columbus monument.

By and large *cyclones* tended to follow established routes, influenced to a great extent by prevailing atmospheric conditions. The likelihood was that this one would follow the previous trajectory set by its predecessors, skirting the coast northward for several miles before turning back inland.

It would then have a free run till it hit Andorra. There was unlikely to be a living soul in its path. Like most of the European countryside vast swathes of rural Spain had become largely depopulated.

The wealthy had fled to North America, Brazil and India – anywhere that money could oil their questionable immigration status. The poor had congregated in cities where they were assured of the protection afforded by soundproofed bunkers. The desperate had crossed the Straits of Gibraltar on precariously flimsy rafts, clinging to the hope of a new life beyond the squalor of the North African refugee camps.

It was a bizarre reversal of fortunes – but in comparison to the grinding daily poverty of self-imposed and largely self-inflicted silence endured by Europeans, Africa's population remained rich and affluent in unfettered and unlimited sound.

Tash turned and looked back.

The *cyclone* was now half way down the Ramblas, hovering and spinning almost level with bin number 4. She hoped the looter wouldn't come round early and start thumping on the lid, giving the monster more noise to fatten itself up on.

They were about to hurry across the road to where the booth was located when Hernandez grabbed her by the elbow and swung her to the left, pointing frantically at a convoy of four armoured electrical vehicles that was speeding towards them.

Panic shot trough Tash.

What was this?

Who'd be crazy enough to drive into the path of an approaching *cyclone?*

Her first thought was that it was members of *Los Gauchos,* out for revenge for the arrest of the pharmacy looter, recklessly ignoring the imminent risk. Cursing the fact that she was only armed with tranquilliser darts, she hurriedly loaded her rifle. Hernandez followed suit.

Instinctively, the two of them stood back to back, moving in a slowly paced defensive circle, rifle barrels facing out. The first vehicle sped past and swung around before coming to a halt. Within moments they were surrounded. Sweat beading on her brow and heart pounding, Tash decided that she wouldn't fire unless Hernandez fired first.

The door to one of the vehicles swung open and someone in a more stylised version of their own grey uniform stepped out. Despites his goggles and ear protectors Tash recognised him straight away. The broad shoulders and shrapnel-pitted face were those of Günter Saddler, former EU Special Forces commando and now unit commander of the Barcelona Brigade of Wardens.

"Stand down!" he signed.

Somewhat reluctantly, the two of them lowered their weapons.

Now more people came streaming out of the other vehicles, dragging assorted sections of strange looking equipment with them. They were dressed like astronauts: padded one-piece boiler suits, heavy boots, wide goldfish bowl helmets with glass visors. The writing on the back of these helmets appeared to be in Mandarin.

Could have put money on it being the Chinese, thought Tash.

It was common knowledge that the Americans were developing a process (optimistically called the *Giant Killer)* that involved a thermal lance of intensely hot air shot through the disambiguation of *cyclone* and into the oxide core in order to bring it down.

However, American foreign policy had become increasingly insular and it was also common knowledge that the Pentagon was far more interested in the potential for imposing *cyclone* diplomacy on certain inconvenient Central American states in their own back yard than it was in extending offers of assistance to its former European allies.

The Chinese were far more pragmatic. They had clear and unashamedly global economic ambitions. Tash felt sure that whatever deal had finally been thrashed out between Brussels and Beijing it was going the involve Chinese tiger reaping huge fiscal benefits in exchange for bringing back the luxury of noise equality to a cowed and grateful Europe.

Tash watched as the pieces of equipment were rapidly assembled into a mass of wires and grilles and coils. A folding table was set up and a laptop placed on it. An operative began booting it up. The *cyclone* was only a few hundred metres away now, swirling up dust and litter, thrumming vibrations deep into the ground and sending the dial on her decibel monitor into crazy spasms.

"Into the booth now!" Saddler signed.

Tash and Hernandez exchanged glances.

"Now!" signed Saddler more insistently.

Giving a cursory salute they hurried over to the booth, a construct made of toughened glass, fashioned on an old style phone box, but wide enough to accommodate a team of two Wardens. From behind the glass partition they watched as the Chinese version of the *"Giant Killer"* was put into action.

The person operating the laptop started tapping his glove-encased fingers against the keys on the keyboard. A shimmering haze began to pulse out from the assembled equipment. As it rippled through the air into the path of the *cyclone* the *cyclone* itself seemed to pick up pace, as if rushing to meet it.

All at once the hazy miasma engulfed the *cyclone,* spinning around it like a serpentine predator, easily matching the velocity of its revolutions. With each circuit it seemed to push inwards, cogently compressing the cone, forcing it to meld into the oxidised core. Smaller and smaller the cone was condensed, till it looked like a narrow length of string stretching skywards.

Then – a blinding light and shuddering of the ground that almost dislodged the booth from its concrete base. When Tash looked, the *cyclone* was gone. She held her breath and waited for it to multiply and rise again as an unholy trinity.

Nothing.

She looked at her decibel monitor – eighty-five and falling rapidly.

Outside the Chinese were giving high fives and bumping helmets in celebration.

Hernandez grinned like the Cheshire cat

"Fucking hell!" she signed.

*

When their shift finished at sunset, Tash and Hernandez linked arms and made their way back through the narrow streets towards the small apartment they shared on Calle de Luna. They could see that the hearing populace had become cautiously optimistic – whispering animatedly to each other as news of the miraculous event on the Ramblas became common knowledge.

"We're about to become redundant," signed Hernandez as they passed the endlessly unfinished gothic spires of the Familia Sagrada.

Her mood seemed deflated.

"Not yet," signed Tash.

No one knew how many *cyclones* were endlessly crisscrossing the continent. It would take months; years even, to drive them to extinction. They'd have work to do till then at least.

"We'll be the forgotten heroes of a forgotten war," insisted Hernandez. "They'll have no use whatsoever for us any more."

"We'll have each other," signed Tash.

Hernandez unravelled her arm and stepped to one side.

"Are you sure?" she signed. "*Cyclones* are the only reason we're together. Without them there would never have been any Wardens and we would never have met. Once the *cyclones* are destroyed the Wardens will be disbanded. There will be no reason left for you to stay with me."

Tash felt her face flush red.

"How could you even think that?" she signed.

"I've absolutely no idea how serious you are about me," Hernandez signed back, face becoming even more solemn.

"Of course I'm serious about you," signed Tash. "I love you."

She was surprised at how instantaneously the words formed on her hands. It was the first time she'd said this without Hernandez first initiating a response. Hernandez pulled her close and kissed her. This time she didn't pull away.

As they turned into Calle de Luna, the signalman on the neighbourhood pylon saw them. He began to spell out a message with the luminous flags that the Signal Corps utilised on night duty.

"B-L-A-C-K-O-U-T / P-O-W-E-R -L-I-N-E-S   / D-O-W-N / D-A-M-A-G-E / F-R-O-M / C-Y-C-L-ON-E "

Tash noticed that the streetlights were out and the windows in all the buildings were dark. She linked arms with Hernandez again as they passed cautiously into the dingy hallway.

Their apartment, gloomy at the best of times, was pitch black. The darkness unsettled her. Her hands were struck dumb by their sudden invisibility. The worries that Hernandez had expressed on their walk home seemed to close in on her all at once. An anxious little knot twisted itself into her belly.

What challenges might a future without *cyclones* present?

With the Chinese pulling the purse strings would there even be a severance package once Wardens were surplus to requirement? Would the authorities come up with a plan to reintegrate afflicted veterans back into civilian society? Would there be any place for them at all when everything clicked back into place? Or would they be condemned to begging on street corners like the limbless veterans of previous conflicts?

Hernandez took her by the hand and led her to the bedroom.

She pulled her down onto the bed, smothering her in kisses, tenderly removing her clothing – fingertips on naked flesh, following through with the warm wetness of lips pressed against intimate places. The musky scent of arousal filled the room. She felt the sleek glisten of sweat on Hernandez' back.

Hernandez hugged her closer and her anxiousness began to dissolve against the feel of dozens of passionate kisses smacking against her neck. She responded in kind and lost herself in the moment. For a little while the future and whatever it may hold for them could wait. Taste, smell and touch were the only senses that mattered.

And no words, signed or spoken, were needed.

A View from a Crowded Street Corner

David Buchan

The man jumped about on the roof, flailing his arms wildly as the flames danced around him, and I was suddenly reminded of a scene from an old silent movie.

I couldn't remember which movie it was, or who had starred in it, whether it was Charlie Chaplin or Buster Keaton. But I knew I had seen it somewhere.

There was something comical about the way he moved. Obviously, the firemen knew that he was stuck up there, but the man still waved frantically, like a bad actor giving an over-the-top performance. The only thing that was missing was a damsel in distress.

A part of me felt bad for being here, for standing on the street corner, along with all of the other people, people who were complete strangers to me. This really wasn't my place.

But I knew that if I just walked away and carried on going home that it would later affect my sleep. Not knowing if the man was going to live or die would bother me.

I didn't know how long the building had been on fire, but considering that all eight storeys were now ablaze, it must have been quite a while. Even from where I stood, I could feel the intensity of the heat, despite the cool November evening. Something tickled my upper lip. I wiped it with a forefinger, and the digit came away smeared with sweat.

Many of the firemen were training thick streams of water onto the burning structure, but they seemed to be fighting a losing battle. I wondered if anyone had yet entered the building. When I looked toward the main entrance, all I could see was a gushing wall of flame. The man trapped on the roof still had some hope, though: a massive Simon Snorkel cherry picker suddenly pulled up in front of us, its siren blaring.

Some people in the crowd started clapping and whooping – whether out of support for the man on the roof or for the added drama that the cherry picker would provide, I couldn't tell.

Above, the man still danced with the flames. Now they completely surrounded him, and the ones that lingered behind him revealed his tiny, moving form in silhouette.

"Poor guy," said a woman standing next to me, her right arm raised in front of her as she filmed the scene on a mobile phone. I glanced around the crowd and saw that a few other people were doing the same thing. Somewhere behind me a man with a loud voice was giving a blow-by-blow account of the whole event to somebody else.

Before us, a fireman stepped into the cherry picker's caged platform and began to fiddle with its controls. It was taking far too long. He'd never get to the man in time.

Somebody shouted out that the man on the roof was naked. I squinted at the figure above, but there was too much smoke in the way. I supposed he must have been asleep when the fire began. The old department store had been empty for years, and it was rumoured that illegal immigrants had been using it as a squat. Perhaps the fire had been started deliberately. Certainly, there were enough right-wing nuts out there who would have loved nothing more than to rid the city of unwanted foreigners.

Finally, the fireman began to ascend through the smoke, rising past entire storeys engulfed in flames. A fat man at the front of the crowd punched a meaty fist into the air and shouted, "Go on, my son!"

I swore that once the man was safely in the caged platform that I would turn around and go home. But I knew even then that there was no guarantee that the man would still make it. He must have breathed in a ton of smoke, if he hadn't already sustained serious burns to his body. Those flames were awfully close. Anybody else would probably have jumped by now.

The fireman was almost there. The man teetered on the edge of the roof, arms stretching out toward the approaching cage.

With only a few feet to go, the cage suddenly stopped. The crowd issued a collective groan. Something was wrong with the crane, I realised, trying to see through the eddying smoke. Above, the fireman was now level with the man on the roof, and his figure appeared just as diminutive. He seemed to be just standing in the cage, doing nothing at all, while the man on the roof reached out to him with both arms.

The cage started to move again, but away from the building.

Either the crane's mechanism had gone completely haywire, I thought, or the fireman was seriously neglecting his duty.

And then the man on the roof jumped.

Remarkably, he reached the cage, even from a standing jump. He clung onto its railing with both hands as his legs dangled beneath him. He appeared to be pulling his body up into the cage itself.

The woman next to me screamed. I turned to see her covering her mouth with one hand and somehow still filming the scene with the other. When I looked back up I saw what had made her scream, saw what I hadn't noticed before: the fireman had raised one of his heavy boots and was stamping on the other man's hands.

"He's murdering him!" cried the woman. I couldn't disagree. There was simply no other way to describe what was happening. I pushed my way to the front of the crowd. Somebody shouted at me, but I ignored the protest.

The fireman had succeeded in dislodging one of the man's hands, and was now pounding the remaining hand with his fists.

After a few seconds, the man fell. He plummeted to the ground, arms and legs thrashing as though he were trying to swim through the air, and the nearer to the ground he got the better we could see his plastic-looking limbs and featureless mannequin face, until the whole thing hit the concrete and shattered into a dozen separate pieces.

Watching the Ashbless Bloom
T.J. Berg

I was about to walk through a solid wall of concrete. My back was turned to the audience so I could see the gaudy sign advertising my show: *Theodore's Music, Madness, and Magic.* We were almost to the last act and there was an appreciative silence as the audience awaited the moment of magic. I played a tune on my slide whistle. I stumbled. The tell-tale jerk, like all my skin was yanked left while my body continued to travel forward. Laughter flitted through the crowd. A tingling itch rushed along my side. *A worm* my body screamed. Why now? I tried to cover the awkward moment by vanishing the whistle and pulling it from the tuba. Then I walked through the wall, turned my head to give a cocky wink, and disappeared in a twirl and swish of my cape. Standing still beneath the stage, I paused for a breath. The applause thundered down through the floor, but there would be no more show tonight. Hunched slightly beneath the low ceiling, I jogged to the stairs, back stage, then to the green room. I snatched up the telephone and made the call.

"I'll need to stop at my flat," I told the Commissioner. She was pissed, but it had been over three months since the last worm and I'd left my kit at home. Did she think I would carry all that gear and weaponry everywhere I went? Just because I had the misfortune to carry some rare, inexplicable sensitivity to the worms? It wreaked enough havoc on my relationship and my career.

I dashed into the drizzling night and hailed a taxi. It jerked down on gangly legs with a hiss, flopping open a door that clanged against the cobbled street. The racket of metal against stone startled an ashbless tree into releasing several unripe bladders. They floated up a few feet and burst into flame, raining ash into my hair as I climbed the steps of the taxi's door. A pair of tourists snapped pictures of the sprinkle of ash. One wore a stupid shirt with "Ashbless You!" embroidered across the front. I shook my head and gave the cabbie my address, tried not to breath in the vomit smell that mixed unpleasantly with the St. Valmore's air freshener bouncing near my cheek.

"I'll double your fare if you get me there in less than ten."

"You betcha." The cabbie grinned into the teloptic trans. The taxi extended its legs. My ears popped as we skated down the street, skimming over low-riding carriages with graceful lifts of legs and only the occasional spark of wheels skidding too fast over cobbles. One leg shot up, braced the cab against my building, and swung us to a halt. Less than eight minutes. I forked over the double fare, asked for a receipt, told him I'd double it again if he waited, then stumbled down the door platform.

Feet on solid ground again, I felt the tug, the whole right side of my body itching and tight with it. It was getting strong fast. I dashed up the stairs. At the door to the flat, I paused, tried to muffle the noise of my keys in the lock, not wanting to wake Matthew. When I opened the door, however, light streamed down the short entrance hall from the kitchen.

Damn. I hurried into the brightness of the kitchen. Matthew sat at the table with coffee and a book. A tuna can filled with cigarette butts rested on the windowsill. The torn green curtain fluttered. The faint smell of smoke still lingered under the smell of coffee. *Damn again.*

"I left a message with the venue," Matthew said. He marked his page by sticking a finger in the book, closing it and opening it gently. "Your mother called."

"Oh?" I worked on untying my cape, my hands clumsy on the knot. I whipped it over my head in frustration.

"She's been arrested again. Another protest."

I bundled up my cape and threw it at our bedroom door. "Dammit I can't deal with it tonight. She's just going to have to sleep it off in jail."

Matthew closed his book and pushed it across the table. His gaze trapped me in the doorway like a sudden, heavy rain, furious and indomitable. "Another worm?"

I itched all along my right side. "I have to get changed."

"You shouldn't have to do this."

"It's not like there's a choice."

"They have a task force for this."

"They'll never –" be as good as me, as quick as me, as accurate as me? Matthew knew that. I didn't know why he was arguing now but I had to go. Every second counted. "You know I can't have this argument now."

He stood, shoved the window open, lit a cigarette. "I'll deal with your mother." He blew the smoke out the window.

"Let her sleep there. You have to work early tomorrow." There was a visiting urban ecologist at the university. Matthew met with him every Monday morning.

"I'll deal with your mother." He waved a hand, dismissive fingers flicking me on my way. "Someone has to put family first." That again. He wanted a family, thought I could manage being a dad even with the worms and my magic show. Did he know how much work a baby would be?

I cursed inwardly. This was no time to argue. The worms could sporulate at any time. I crossed the kitchen, sparing him a quick squeeze to his shoulder, trying to crush down my annoyance. Did he not remember the photographs out of Wrentown? The worms couldn't be allowed to get out of control. "I do this because I care about my family, about you, keeping you safe," I said. "Maybe you could figure out where the worms come from and I could quit. Until then…" I just let it trail off. At our bedroom door, I kicked my bundled cloak aside. I kept my worm clothes on a hook on the wall. I stood in the doorway as I changed.

Matthew sat back at the table, pushed his book in little circles. "She's right you know, to protest." He chewed at one dirty fingernail, pulled it away again to clutch his book.

"I know, but some of us have jobs." I struggled into the leather trousers, blotchy and stained from past expeditions.

"Things won't get better if the government doesn't change its policies on trade with countries with shitty labor conditions. People will just keep buying cheap crap and watching their jobs go overseas."

I tied the flaps of my leather jerkin tight around my waist. Did he really think now was the time to talk about this? My skin crept and itched and tightened. I pulled the knee-high boots on and picked up my case with the mask and helmet.

"We can talk about it when I get home. Have fun with my mom." I kissed him on the cheek. He scowled.

"It's a shit world we live in."

I felt terrible just then, leaving him. It was unlike him to be so negative. He was clearly down about something, but I really had to go. Didn't he realize I was protecting him?

"I know. But hey, I think the ashbless trees will bloom tomorrow night."

His scowl deepened. "You know the puff addicts are spreading the ruby ash borer on purpose now? Pretty soon they'll have killed off the source of their own drug. And this city's tourist money."

Poor Matthew. He'd spent so much of his life studying the ashbless trees. He loved them, the glory and mystery of their fiery blooms, their delicate ecology. Now they were dying, and all he wanted was to protect them, but he kept getting pulled away, switching gears to study the worms, to stop me going out and risking my life finding them. Even with everything pulling me toward the door, I couldn't leave him dwelling on those thoughts. I put my hands in his hair and turned his face toward mine and kissed his forehead gently, then pulled him in for a hug. "I love you," I said. "Fetch my mom if you can. Tomorrow we'll work on saving the world. Tonight –"

"Yeah, I know, tonight you've got to go be Theodore Thomas Stone, Worm Hunter, Hero." I gave him a bow and he gave a barely-smile and then I had to go.

Rebecca Mason, the Commissioner of the Worm Crew, was waiting outside the station, arms crossed over her chest, smoking a cigarette. When the taxi door dropped to the ground and she saw me, she crushed the cigarette out against a wall and tossed the butt to a waiting swallower. So many of the little rubbish beasts had become addicted to nicotine. It snuffed and chewed, purred after it swallowed. The thick tendrils that covered its body waved, seeking more. The Commissioner hit a bell on the wall and a large door scrolled up the front of the building, clattering.

"We're ready," she said. And obviously had been for too long in her book. She stalked toward the door.

"I had to get changed, Rebecca."

She snorted. The reek of cinnamon off of her was strong now that we were out of the cloud of her smoke. Her crew slouched on their velocipedes, low voices silenced when I walked in. There were six of them, all strapped into their leathers and reeking of cinnamon. The crawlers were somewhat repelled by cinnamon – it burned their skin. But the spores, and the adult worms, couldn't care less. My leathers were cinnamon-free. It gave me a rash and interfered with my detection.

Visors snapped down and engines whirred to life. I clipped my bag onto the back of the commissioner's velocipede and climbed up behind her. I wrapped my arms around her waist. "Left out of the building," I said.

We roared out of the bay, and I shouted directions until the ache and twitch of my skin, the simmer heating closer and closer to a boil, erupted at once all across my body, and I clutched tight around the Commissioner's waist and we stopped.

You never knew what you were going to find.

We found ourselves in Paul's End, built up, destitute, built up again, and destitute again. First home to immigrants. Several came to windows and doors as our engines settled, curious at this rare arrival of authority. A group of women, faces hidden by scarves, stood in front of the building that shivered across my skin. It was four stories. Used to be a factory. Half the windows were boarded up and the others contained broken glass, jagged glaring in the street lamps. Some had been tacked over with parchment paper or decorated with colorful curtains. One was sealed with a beautiful religious scroll. Squatters in the upper floors. But we'd be going below.

The scarved women glared at us, only their eyes visible. The Commissioner bristled. She balanced her velocipede on its kickstand, threw down a line of phosphorshield and told the women to clear out. The crew unloaded equipment. The women shuffled, reluctant.

"Nothing in there," one said.

"Go home," the Commissioner growled. She didn't mean where they lived. She meant out of the city, to wherever they'd come from. She was convinced they'd brought the worms somehow. If it wasn't the worms, she'd blame them for something else. But the worm thing annoyed me. Matthew was trying to find a pattern, a source, a biology that made sense, but her team wouldn't follow any of his leads. It was brought here, they believed, and that was all they'd investigate.

I snagged a sleeve of a passing woman. "There *is* something in there." I nodded up where the squatters surely lived. "If you know anyone up there, you might tell them to get out."

The woman tugged her arm away, glanced up and down my body, said something to the other women in another language, then strolled across the street into a market. A man had come to the door, feet bare, one foot hideously twisted and swollen. He closed the door with a sad shake of his head. Two floors above him, lights flashed in a window, flash flash flash pause flash flash flash. It went on.

I grabbed my bag, walked to the head of the Worm Crew. I hated this part. Whether stepping into a shining new bazaar, a defunct church, or an old factory like this, the dread was complete. The worm was in there, throwing out its spores. There could be berserkers. And crawlers. But still, I had to go first. I was the worm hunter. The Commissioner, her pistols loaded with exploding acid bullets, was a presence at my shoulder. Each of my hairs vibrated in the tension of my sense.

I wrapped my hands around the metal bar, still warm from the day's heat, felt the ridges where the brass had tarnished and decayed, pushed. It was so loud. *Bang clank* in the vast echoing hall in front of us, filled with machinery that should have been defunct but was not. Recently abandoned, but clearly operational: red fibers of wool or cotton like shreds of blood caught stretched on looms. A half-eaten apple, not yet brown, had rolled under a chair.

The worm was not up here. It was down. It was always down. My feet might have been dipped in the acid the Commissioner's crew filled their bullets with. I dragged my stinging feet across the room, opening doors along the way. One led to a room of tattered pallets with a few worn children's toys: a yo-yo, a balding doll. I came to a heavy door, solid metal. I tugged. It wouldn't open. Not locked – the knob turned. I pulled harder, thinking it was stuck. A tap on my shoulder and the Commissioner pointed up. There was a padlock above my head. One of the team carried over bolt cutters.

A piercing thunk and clatter and the door was unlocked. I swung it open. The Commissioner slammed into me, sending me sprawling as a spore whirred through the air. We both leapt up to meet four berserkers as they burst through the door. The Commissioner shoved me aside. My hand convulsed by my pistol. The berserkers were children. One had taken a spore in the neck. Her left arm twitched and waved in the air like some silly child's dance as she dashed out the door, wild to spread what she carried. Her arm burst and crawlers poured out, sausage-sized, pale and squirming, heads up and wavering, scenting for us, for food. Their circular mouths, filled with grinding teeth, all turned toward me.

I pulled a balloon from my bag and flung it hard, sending acid over the crawlers as it burst. They sizzled and hissed and melted. The Commissioner and her team dispatched the berserkers, unfazed by their being children. Nona, the team's newest member, spread the desiccant powder over them before she headed through the door and down the stairs. I looked back over my shoulder, at the looms. So this was child labor, hidden in our city, maybe making cheap shirts for tourists. And down the stairs? The bosses had been warned of our arrival and thinking that we had come to raid the factory, had locked the children in. With the worm. How many children were down there? Could I go down?

I drew my machete. It would be close work again. The broad flat blade was perfect for batting away or slicing the head-sized spores or the soft-boned berserkers.

Dead children littered the stairs, bodies shriveling beneath desiccant powder, the occasional crawler writhing from the skin. At the bottom of the stairs, blocking a narrow hallway, two men lay dead. One had taken a spore in the face. It had swollen, stretching the skin and sucking one eye in, popping the other out, bloodshot and seeping. The crew had thrown phosphor lights all over the walls, illuminating the scene in ghoulish pale yellow-green. I could hear the panting screams of dozens of berserkers coming from down the hallway. I raised my machete, jumped the dead bodies, and ran.

Just as I neared the end, a spore shot into the hallway. I slashed with my machete, splitting it in two. I ducked as another soared past. The worm was still alive then, not that I needed spores singing through the air to tell me that. I rounded the corner, thanking my magician-quick hands as I sliced through two more spores. The crew had formed a semi-circle ahead of me, wielding machetes and acid balloons and desiccant powder with zeal in the closed space. The bullets would be saved for when they found the worm. I could feel it off to my right, but the crew was moving straight ahead, unable to turn their backs on the panting, screaming berserkers, their heads swinging and arms twitching, violent spasms throwing crawlers out to hunt and tear. Even our tough leathers were only a few seconds work to a crawler, but the team met the onslaught with a barrier of acid and desiccant.

I whistled. The Commissioner looked up at the piercing sound to see me wave them in the direction of the worm. My machete whispering through the air in front of me, I cut my way through the spores toward my target.

I tossed my own phosphor lights as I went, sent them flying through a door that led to another room. I crossed the threshold, felt the heat and searing pain of the worm sense erupt all along my left side, turned and ducked. The worm towered, the biggest I'd ever seen, its head bent down beneath the ceiling. Its pale ring of eyes, white embedded in the gray flesh, seeped sticky liquid that splattered the floor as it swung its body about, spitting spores from erupting pustules.

Trapped on the other side of the room was a woman with six children. She stood in front of them, their backs pressed against a door. She must have hoped to take them through that to escape. The children hunkered behind her, no screams or crying, some with fists tucked into their mouths. The woman wielded a cricket bat, swatting spores away from the children with rapid, hard hits. Her headscarf had fallen free, revealing sweat drenched hair. She was tiring, arms shaking.

I opened fire on the worm. The blasts from my pistol distracted the woman. A spore careened into her chest. She dropped the bat, clutched at the spore, trying to fling it away, but it was already dissolving, its pale pink darkening to rust as it melted around her hands, ate through her clothing as she screamed. I slammed another clip into my pistol, emptied it into the worm as it seethed, hissing boiling sounds erupting inside it, wounds gurgling out thick gray ichor, rank smelling as decay. Boots stomped down the hallways. The team was coming. The woman's screams shifted in pitch, from human pain to the berserker hissing pant. I couldn't shoot her or throw an acid balloon, not with the children still behind her.

I raised my machete. One of the boys behind her darted out and grabbed my leg, wailing words I didn't understand. I flung him away as the crew stormed into the room, the ring of pistols firing, the bitter sour stench of acid. I cut off the woman's head. It squished almost flat when it hit the floor, her bones already softened to feed the crawler larvae. Plump, immature crawlers squirmed and fled as I dowsed the head and body with desiccant. The boy pounded my side, as if angry. Maybe she'd been kind to them.

"Cover your eyes," I shouted, but they just stared. I tossed two acid balloons on the woman, realized how light my bag was. I'd used a lot of ammunition. The boy tried to grab the bag, hit me again. "She was already dead." I bent, grabbed his face in my hands. "She was already dead." His tears streaked across red cheeks. "Come on." I took his hand but he pulled it away. "Come with me," I said to the children. I waved my hand. The worm was dead. The crew had already started clean up. The children didn't need to see that. "Come with me," I said again, gesturing emphatically. They cowered.

Sighing, I pulled a coin from my pocket. It was my lucky coin, from Matthew, the tip he'd tossed in my hat when I was performing on the streets. I flipped it into the air, caught it and revealed it was now a whistle. I put the whistle to my mouth and played a tune, made the tune go sour, made faces, spit out the coin. It was grotesque, this silly act in front of these children, as if it could make them forget. Then there was a giggle – a single giggle pitched high as if slightly panicked. I put the whistle back in my mouth, started to play again, found again the tune gone sour, and spit the coin out again. I gave the whistle a perplexed look, then tried one more time, this time spitting out a mouthful of coins when the tune started to twist and warble. I handed out the coins. There were no more giggles, no smiles, just blank stares, but they didn't run from me.

"Come with me," I said. "We'll go somewhere safe." I mimed eating and putting a blanket over shoulders.

Perhaps they understood, because the boy didn't pull his hand away when I took it. I led them out past the carnage of dead, dissolving children and up the stairs and out of the basement, past the looms and finally outside, to stand in the ring of phosphorshield. The day's spring warmth was fading. The children shivered. I brought blankets from the saddlebags. Manuel was the medic on the crew, and his saddlebags had energy bars and water. I passed them around. The children watched me as they ate, still not entirely trusting. They also watched the windows of the stores and homes around them, glanced down the street which dead ended at St. Paul's Green. The Fallow River twisted a branch through there. Litter shared its steep bank with puff dealers, but in the settling coolness, all that could be seen was street lamp-dazzled fog obscuring flower-laden trees. The white blossoms shone, shy in their beauty, not unlike the city.

One of the girls, thick black hair standing up off her head to reveal an ear that looked chewed, put out her hand. I went to fetch her another energy bar but she shook her head and pointed at the whistle that poked out of my pocket. She dropped her eyes when I touched it, but she nodded. I handed her the whistle. She examined it, flipping it over in her hands several times, then put it to her lips and played a tune, haunting and soft, working the slide with expert hands.

She played until the crew came up, sticky with worm offal, rancid sour smell too thick to breathe. She extended her hand to return my whistle. "What will you do with them?" I asked.

"Unless we find they have families, they'll go into the foster care system," the Commissioner said. Her lips were tight. She seemed somewhat disgusted by the children.

"What about the people running this?" I waved toward the factory.

The Commissioner shrugged. "I hunt worms," she said. She started speaking again before I could protest. "I'll write it up in my report. Someone will deal with it."

By tomorrow, all the evidence would be gone. Anyone in the community here would be too scared to speak up. This would just be another worm hole, another bit in the news to show how the Worm Crew saved the city from yet another worm, and desolate pictures of the creeping horror that was Wrentown would send shivers through the viewers. Who had time for abused immigrant children when there were worms to be afraid of?

"Get them lined up for me," she said. "Need to scan for latent spore infection."

It was a procedure required of all survivors when we responded to a worm. Most people hit by a spore showed rapid signs of infection, transitioning to berserker within minutes as the micro-spores moved through the blood stream to the brain. Within an hour they were usually making mature crawlers, which in turn could chew into a new human and form a full-fledged worm. The problem was: some people were immune to the berserker stage. They continued as normal, sometimes with almost a day of dormancy before the crawlers chewed their way out. A thing like that in a densely populated area was a serious threat. We knew all this from Wrentown. What we didn't know was where the isolated worms were coming from in our own city. One thing the Worm Crew intended to be sure of was that there would never be a latent spore infection.

But this time it really made me squirm. We'd only ever found a handful of survivors, and they'd all been adults. I was hesitant about stripping down a bunch of children. "Listen, if you don't want to line them up, fine, I'll get one of the crew to do it."

"I'll do it," I said. "But we should at least put up some kind of screen."

The Commissioner shook her head, lips pinched in disgust at my weakness. "Just hurry up," she said, then stalked away for a post-worm smoke.

I made a makeshift screen using the blankets and my belt, a streetlamp, and a velocipede. Above me, a woman leaned out her window and beat a broom against the wall. I lined the children up and told them what would happen, hoping they understood. They'd be behind the blanket and take off their clothes and Manuel would dust them down with a special powder that would make sure no nasty worm bits got on them. I expected crying, objection, fear. It was disheartening how meekly they went along. They'd been through worse.

As they got their examination, I comforted myself that things would be better for them. They'd be going to foster homes, be cared for, educated, or even reunited with families. When the girl with the short black hair stepped out, she smiled at me, brushing dust from her gaunt cheek. I handed her my whistle and wrapped her fingers around it, pushing it toward her chest. Her smile faltered, then resumed. I thought about fostering. Matthew had brought up adoption before, and I'd always hesitated. But what of these kids? Maybe we could foster this little girl, maybe more of them. A sense of lightness, like the blooms from the ashbless trees, buoyed up from my stomach.

"I've called a van to pick up the kids." The Commissioner, arms crossed over her chest. "I'll take you home."

I didn't really want to ride with her again, but I was floaty with excitement to tell Matthew about my evening, ask him what he thought of fostering one or two of the children. Even the Commissioner's sour rants about immigrants bringing in the worms couldn't dampen my mood. She thought we were fools, looking for something in the worm ecology to explain them. But I knew Matthew would find something. The worms would be stopped one day.

The Commissioner paused just long enough to say to come by the station tomorrow. "I'll have full ammo bags for you, since you still insist on storing your stuff at home."

She zoomed off, engine roaring. I bounded up our stairs and into our kitchen, not caring if Matthew was home and sleeping or not. I startled my mother in the kitchen. Her arm jerked, sending a mug flying across the counter. She turned from the kitchen window. The sink was filled with sudsy water, the foamy top still smooth and undisturbed.

"Mom?"

She'd been crying. Eyes red, tears still wet on her cheeks.

"Mom?"

I ran past her, flung open the bedroom.

"Where's Matthew? Mom?"

Thick, warm arms and softness wrapped around me. "There was a protest," she said. Her voice was surprisingly in control. "I'm so sorry. There was a protest in front of the police station, about us getting arrested. It turned violent." Then her voice hitched. "Matthew." Caught again. "Matthew was shot in the confusion." She was bawling now. "They had live ammo. Oh lord I don't know why they had live ammo." She was bawling and holding me close but I couldn't cry, just felt my eyes burning. Through the window the ashbless trees bloomed, throwing beautiful fiery globes into the air, raining soft white ash onto the streets below.

The Crystal Gazer
Stanley B. Webb

A human colony thrives on the planet Scry, in orbit around the star Alpha Centauri. Scry is unique in the known galaxy, being composed entirely of transparent crystal, excepting a large inclusion of meteoric iron. Science is mystified by Scry's strange ecology, and astonished by Scry's ability to support human life.

Because the colonists' private business is perforce in public view, a psychological reflex known as 'social blinders' has developed. This reflex has resulted in a society remarkably free from vice. Under certain circumstances, however, the 'social blinders' fail. Professor Spektar Glazier, once the colony's preeminent Scryologist, provides a case study.

The new endoscope stood three hundred meters above the campus of Bravais Lattice University, its diamond girders shining in Centauri light, its magnetically stacked lenses almost perfectly transparent. Spektar was in the objective chamber at the endoscope's summit. A flock of ruby birds swept by, their wings flashing as they swerved around the tower. Spektar had just put his eye to the objective lens when his assistant, Nascent, called to him.

"Professor, Mrs. Glazier is on the resonator."

Spektar sighed. "Take a message, will you?"

After a period of discreet mumbles, Nascent's voice intruded again.

"Professor, she asks if you'd like to go out with her for lunch."

"Of course," he said absently.

There was a bit more mumbling, and then silence.

Spektar adjusted the focus knobs. His perspective tunneled through the transparent crust plate below, penetrating shimmery fault lines, and bubble-caverns. One huge cave held a sea of liquid crystal, which supported an ecosystem of quartz alga, glass fish, and salt crustaceans.

A fault line reflected the light of Alpha Centauri, and he flinched away from the glare.

"Nascent, activate the anti-lumens."

"Right, Professor."

Attached to the endoscope's lenses were crystals which could absorb light in their internal facets. These crystals began to glow as they bled the excess lumens away from Spektar's objective.

"That's better."

His view blurred as he descended through varying crystal strata. Spektar constantly adjusted the focus knobs. He passed through the core, and traveled out to Scry's opposite surface. He found himself below a major city.

"What are my coordinates, Nascent?"

"Um, you're looking at Carbondale, Professor."

Spektar watched the crystal traffic flow along the crystal streets; he saw men and women at work in crystal mills; he got dizzy when crystal lift cars approached and receded in his view.

He paused when he came upon a young couple trysting in a bedroom. Spektar was trained to observe through the endoscope, and his social blinders were down. He was shocked by what he saw.

"Naughty," he muttered.

"What was that, Professor?"

"Nothing!"

Spektar quickly shifted his focus. His view jumped, and he suddenly found himself looking at the Inclusion. Millions of Earth-years before Man had conquered interstellar space, a huge iron meteorite had impacted with Scry. The meteorite had fractured a crater deep into the crust, the heat of impact melting the crystal. The molten crystal had flowed back in over the Inclusion, but fault lines distorted his view for kilometers around. The Inclusion had also melted, and quantities of iron had flowed from the main mass, into the fracture lines. As a result, the Inclusion resembled a monstrous tumor, metastasizing in the body of Scry.

The Inclusion was a popular tourist destination. Spektar watched as crowds descended the crystal galleries, which had eroded along some of the old fault lines, and disappeared into the mass of iron.

"Bloody opaque thing," he muttered. "Nascent, I need refraction."

"Refraction on, Professor."

Spektar's view wiggled, and then side-slipped around the Inclusion. He was viewing with light that had refracted through the fault lines. The full extent of Scry's faults was unknown. Some colonists feared that the planet might crack apart. The government had provided funds for several universities to construct endoscopes. In return, the universities were expected to map the faults system.

Spektar's view returned to the surface behind the Inclusion. He found himself beneath a forest of branching crystal structures, locally known as trees.

"What am I looking at, Nascent?"

"That would be the Emerald Forest."

Spektar followed a narrow track, which meandered among the trees. At the end of the track, parked in a secluded location, was a crystal car. A young couple was engaged in the back seat, her buttocks pressed into the garnet-flax cushion. Spektar adjusted the focus until her quivering rump filled his eye.

He felt omniscient.

Then, he heard the lift rising.

"That must be Mrs. Glazier," said Nascent.

Spektar shifted his view.

"Why would she be here?"

"You're going to lunch together."

"We are?"

Spektar looked down through the tower, and saw Clarice smiling up at him. Shiny and pink in her mica silk robes, she was fifteen years younger than him, a trophy for his aging ego.

A moment later, she stepped out of the lift, onto the transparent floor.

"How is your day going, Spek?" Clarice asked.

"Very well."

"I've gotten us reservations at Pane's Window. Afterward, I thought you might come home early."

He glanced at the objective.

"I'm sorry, Clarice, but I'd forgotten completely about lunch," he said. "I've accepted a heavy workload today, and I'm afraid I must cancel."

Clarice's smile faded. "We've not had an hour alone in two weeks."

"We sleep together every night."

"Sleeping is all we do."

Spektar wanted to return to the forest before the young couple had finished. He called out to his assistant, who was discreetly occupied in his own duties.

"Nascent!"

"Yes, Professor?"

"Do me a favor, and have lunch with Clarice."

Nascent blushed. "Oh, Professor, I couldn't do that."

"Of course you could. Darling, this is Nascent, my assistant. You wouldn't mind if he substituted for me, would you?"

Clarice gave her husband a dry-eyed glare, and then smiled at Nascent.

"Of course not. Let's go."

She offered her arm. Nascent hesitantly accepted. She steered him into the lift, and they floated down to the surface.

Spektar felt relief. Even Nascent's presence was a distraction. He waited for them to hail a taxi, then returned to the endoscope.

His breath caught at what he saw.

Spektar was so engrossed in his research, that at first he failed to hear the woman calling on the resonator.

"Professor Glazier? Professor Glazier! I see that you're there, would you please answer?"

He startled upright, his face burning, and looked out toward the administration center.

"I'm sorry, Coordinator Salta, I didn't hear you."

"We had a meeting scheduled fifteen minutes ago."

"Oh, I am sorry! I'll be right there."

He took the lift down, and crossed the campus to Salta's office. He bowed before her desk.

"What were you viewing with such avidity?"

"The Inclusion," he blurted. "It's a fascinating object."

"It must be," said Salta. "You have been neglecting your fault mapping for some time. We have an obligation to the Colony, Professor. You need to put yourself back on task. If you can't do the work, I'll assign it to a professor who can."

"*If I can't do the work?* I'm the best Scryologist you have."

"Not to judge by your recent efforts. Also, your students have been failing their requirements. You seem very distracted, Spektar. Is there a personal problem on your mind; a problem at home, perhaps?"

"That's ridiculous! Clarice adores me. If you want maps, Salta, then you'll get maps; the best maps that you've ever seen."

"I hope so, but you should consider this as a performance warning."

Spektar's mood was vindictive as he returned to the observation chamber. He looked down the objective, which was still set to the forest. The young couple was gone. He felt a surge of fury, and he yanked on the refraction control. The view spun. Spektar leaned back, suddenly dizzy.

When the nausea passed, he twirled the controls more cautiously, until his view was refracted one hundred eighty degrees. He was visually beneath the University. He focused on the administration center, and Salta's office suite.

She was seated in the Ladies'.

He snickered.

By the time he arrived at home, he could hardly keep his eyelids up. His shoulders and spine were sore from the hunched posture of endoscope viewing.

His mind was whirling with the things he had seen.

He found the supper table empty.

"Clarice?" Spektar called.

"I'm in the bedroom."

He looked through the house. His view was distorted by the intervening diamond joists and walls. Clarice appeared to be naked.

"Where's supper?"

"In here."

He went to the bedroom.

She *was* naked, stretched out on the glass-fiber comforter.

"You look tired," she said. "Undress, and I'll give you a massage."

Spektar felt tingles.

"That would be just the thing, Clarice."

Clarice poured a handful of warm quartz oil across his back. She straddled his hips, and kneaded the oil into his muscles.

"Ooh," he said.

"Does it feel good?" Clarice asked.

"Yes, ooh."

Her hands went up and down his back, and his tingling concentrated. Clarice leaned down, pressed her breasts onto his back, and put her tongue in his ear. His day at the endoscope had left him excited, and his sensations peaked quickly.

"Oh, Clarice! Oh, my God!"

Clarice giggled.

Spektar's peak ebbed, letting him down into a warm, comfortable place.

Clarice's tongue probed his ear again.

He snored.

At work the next morning, Spektar found a young actress cavorting like a shapely spider in her okenite-webbed bedroom. He had watched the girl's recordings many times, but he had never before seen her perform like this. He remained unaware of the lift until its door opened, and Clarice stepped into the objective chamber. He spun the refraction dials, and turned to face her, staggering with transient vertigo.

"Clarice," he said. "I'm busy."

"I've not come to bother you," she replied. "Nascent, will you join me again for lunch?"

Nascent's face turned crimson, and he stuttered. "Mrs. Glazier, I, I don't think that's proper."

Spektar experienced a rush of joyous relief.

"Of course it's proper!"

Nascent looked at his boss with surprise. "Is it?"

"Certainly! Off with the two of you."

Spektar watched them float away. He was pleased to have found such a simple solution for Clarice's interruptions during his time at the endoscope. His inner tensions relaxed.

He returned to his viewing, and restored the previous coordinates.

The young actress was still at it.

Sometime later, Salta interrupted him by calling on the resonator.

"How is today's mapping coming along?"

"Very well," said Spektar, trying to mask his annoyance.

"Are you certain?"

"Yes!"

"Because, I can see you from here, of course; you've been at the endoscope steadily, but…why are you wiggling in that manner?"

"Salta, you've been *watching* me?"

Her voice became discomfited. "Not from any prurient interest, I assure you."

"If you must know, I have an ache in my back; due, no doubt, to the poor ergonomics of this viewing station."

"All right, I'm sorry; you simply looked so… never mind. Bring your preliminary maps to my office after you're done."

He froze for a moment, but he didn't let it show.

"Of course, Salta."

Spektar was too distracted to return to the endoscope. He had to show Salta *something,* but he had not enough time to produce any maps. He dithered a moment about the ethics, then took up his piezoelectric etcher, found a scroll of isinglass, and created a map out of whole cloth.

His life was good for some days afterward. Clarice and Nascent occupied each other, and Salta accepted his fake maps. His time at the endoscope was his own.

Then, a day came when Nascent offered rebellion. Spektar was viewing the locker room at a women's talc skiing competition, when Nascent cleared his throat. Spektar tried to ignore the noise, but Nascent then spoke.

"Professor Glazier, don't you think that you should take your wife to lunch today?"

He looked up from his work. "What for? Is she bothering *you* now?"

Nascent reddened. "Clarice is a wonderful woman, and she still loves you very much; you should give her some attention."

"Do I look like I have time? You're aware of my work-load."

"I'm not sure that I am, Professor."

Spektar scowled. "Whatever do you mean?"

Nascent turned even more crimson. "It's just, the coordinates that you've been viewing; I'm not sure what the, the research value is."

"What the Devil do you know about research value, young man? How dare you to question me. Perhaps you would like to find another mentor?"

"Perhaps I would, Professor. I'll speak to Coordinator Salta."

Nascent departed.

Spektar grumbled for a few more minutes, and then he shrugged.

"It's for the better, really," he said, as he returned to the locker room.

*

Salta called him shortly thereafter.

"Professor Glazier, Nascent has just requested that I assign him a new mentor. He won't tell me why, but he's alluded to some failure in your technique of research."

Spektar blushed.

"That's ridiculous!"

He glanced at Salta's office, and was reassured to note that she was too distant to see the color in his cheeks.

"As a result of this," she continued. "I've reviewed the data which you have submitted, and I find that it does not correlate with any data collected by other endoscopes."

"They must be incompetents," he snorted.

"I want to see your viewing coordinates for the past few weeks."

Spektar was flustered, but he could think quickly.

"I'll admit it, Salta; it's true that I've been supplying you with doctored maps, but only to protect my data from dishonest researchers. Scry was once a perfect crystal globe. The impact of the Inclusion created the fault systems below us."

"I want to see your records."

Spektar took a deep breath to spout his next objection, but then he realized that there was no objection to make. He had backed himself into a corner.

"Of course, Salta. I will need a day or two to collate my data."

He shuddered after the call, but he could not show any overt sign of his distress. The world was filled with voyeurs, as he well knew. He glanced at the endoscope, and he hated it. He had not known how his recreational voyeurism would become a compulsion. There was nothing to do now but cover his rear end, figuratively, and forge several weeks' worth of data to support his claims.

He knew that his efforts were futile.

His shame would be exposed.

*

He went home preoccupied with such forebodings. The light had the watery quality which came of evening, when Alpha Centauri's rays passed through the mass of Scry. He was squinting and muttering, and he did not notice Clarice's absence until he found her laser-etched note on the otherwise empty supper table.

Dear Spektar, the note said. *My sister has taken ill, and I've run off to be with her.*

Regards, your wife Clarice.

Which sister, Spektar wondered, but his worries soon banished her from his thoughts.

The miracle occurred on the following day. He was mapping fault lines to the Inclusion, in the hopes of finding a few which he could use to corroborate his claims. To his amazement, he found that *all* of Scry's fault lines converged to the Inclusion.

Obviously, he was cleverer than even he himself knew. In his research on the private activities of Scry's colonists, his subconscious must have recorded data of which his conscious mind was unaware. With facts to support him, he quickly assembled the data which Salta had requested, and hastened to her office.

She was duly impressed.

"Spektar, I will never criticize your methods again. I've always heard that the true genius was an eccentric, but I've never encountered one before."

"That's quite all right," he replied. "It's a pity that Nascent didn't stick around to share in the glory. Who have you assigned him to, by the way?"

"The boy's on leave," said Salta. "He had to run off due to an illness in his family."

Spektar returned to the endoscope with the strange sensation that he had overlooked something. The feeling did little to dampen his good mood. He wanted to boast of his triumph for Clarice. Since he did not know which sister had taken ill, he might have to call all of them to find her.

He considered a better method. He looked up his in-laws' addresses, and focused the endoscope on each. He found one sister in her fluid saline bath, another between gossamer silica sheets with her husband, and the third trimming gypsum shrubs in her garden, but he did not find Clarice.

The sensation of missing data returned. Spektar broadened his search to the multifaceted shops and parks around her sisters' homes. He did not find Clarice.

He was suddenly aware of how long a time had passed since he had boasted to her, or walked arm-in-arm with her. Ever since the endoscope was constructed, and he had discovered the diversion of voyeurism, he had not even taken her to lunch; instead, he had sent Nascent in his place.

With fear suddenly piercing his heart, Spektar returned to the objective. He stayed at the endoscope all night, through the precession of the Inclusion's shadow, and searched the world for Clarice. By the time that Centauri's light came clearly over the rim of Scry, he was exhausted, but too enervated to rest. Although he had not searched every location on Scry, he had searched enough to conclude that Clarice must be someplace where he could not look.

There was only one such place.

Spektar bought a ticket on the next diamondwing, and arrived at the Inclusion nearly a full day later. He looked incredibly disheveled, but he had the funds to pay his way into the iron mass. He was amazed by the throngs of tourists who surrounded him, even though he had seen it all remotely. He wondered what it was that made the Inclusion so popular.

He entered the first iron cave. Scry's liquid daylight vanished. Strange tubes on the cave's roof emitted flickering pink light. There was a motion close beside him. Spektar jumped back, and looked down. He saw his shadow. He had never had a shadow before, and he was unnerved by how it followed him.

A woman in a clinging mica dress approached, stalked by her own shadow.

"Do you need a date?"

"I'm married."

"Of course you are. Do you need a date?"

He walked away from her.

She approached the next man. "Do you need a date?"

The new couple linked arms, and wandered off with their shadows.

The Inclusion was a den of vice, filled with saloons, gambling halls, and brothels. Many couples engaged in open nooks, where crowds gathered to watch. Drunken fistfights were common, and also attracted voyeurs.

Spektar became increasingly uncomfortable. He lowered his eyes, only to see his shadow.

"Stop following me!"

One sleazy woman asked another, "What's wrong with him?"

"He must be a greenhorn."

"Maybe we can loosen him up."

Spektar hunched over himself, and hurried on.

He came to the end of the inhabited caverns, and entered the first darkness that he had ever seen. At first, he was relieved by the absence of his shadow, but he soon began to fear the dark. Anything might be hiding there.

Then, he noticed a dim, pink glow in the distance. He hurried toward the light.

He was quite near when he heard two voices, a man and a woman. They did not speak, but grunted in unison. Their voices were familiar. He identified Clarice first, because he had heard her make such sounds before. The man's voice was more difficult. Spektar had just reached the edge of the light when he realized that the man was Nascent.

In his weeks at the endoscope, Spektar had watched many couples do what Clarice and Nascent were doing, but this was different. He could smell Nascent's sweat, and Clarice's arousal; he could hear the rapid pressing of their flesh. Clarice was astraddle Nascent, and her expression was rapturous. Spektar thought that months might have passed since he himself had caused her to look that way.

"I'm sorry," he whispered. "I didn't see what I was doing to you."

Spektar turned away. He put his hand to the iron wall, and groped his way back into the darkness.

The War Artist
Tim Nickels

1

On the day before the war ended, Monksilver walked across the Sandalwood Bridge and offered himself up for surrender. He was still in uniform but had removed his decorations, progressing with a pronounced limp and appearing a good ten years older than published photographs had previously suggested. Nevertheless Monksilver's course was steady as he nonchalantly drifted through the tracer fire as if it were a light rain, deviating only to avoid the corpses of men and pack mules. He was immediately arrested by astonished commandos who transported him to divisional headquarters eight kilometres behind the front line. There he was subjected to DNA swabs to confirm his identity and was deemed fit to stand trial. Presented with a pen and an induction form, he unhesitatingly scrawled his current occupation as *War Artist*.

The prime minister wired the area commander with a firm instruction: Monksilver should be treated with dignity but was to speak to no one. A majority within the cabinet was anxious to enter the collective mind of Monksilver's fellow war criminals so select periodicals dealing with the atrocities were placed before him and his reactions studied. To his hastily assembled psychiatrists, the prisoner was lucid and appeared preternaturally calm. His single element of anxiety centred around his demand to be interviewed by a former pupil, Verity Glasson. Glasson, a fellow countrywoman of Monksilver, had got out before the war began and had come over to our side. This obsession with meeting a representative of the ethnic minority Monksilver's regime had hounded to near-extinction confounded his captors. Sorry wasn't just a word that didn't come easily to Monksilver. It was a word that didn't come at all.

As the final shots of the conflict were fired – and in accordance with an international tribunal – Monksilver was relocated to an abandoned holiday park in the midst of a forest in a remote part of his own nation. The sole inmate, he was provided with a sluggish laptop and a hobbled Internet connection and commenced his memoirs and a beard in short order. Again, the medical people were hoping to glean some insight from these memoirs that would never be published. The prisoner was described as unfailingly courteous. Monksilver found the cook's egg custard especially worthy of celebration and he quickly became plump beneath the burgeoning stubble.

Verity Glasson was unearthed within our Intelligence Section where she had risen to a position of shaky prominence in the translation department. Shaky? Glasson's superiors obviously had to choose their words carefully: let us say her work was superlative, the person herself less so. Lieutenant Glasson had initially refused the summons and a subpoena was issued.

This is where I came in. Although I'd pretty much forgotten that old business myself, it must have set bells ringing in the records department and I had less than two hours to cram my head with all things Monksilver before the Ministry sent a driver for me. I left my ruefully smiling wife in the midnight-dark doorway of our weekend retreat not knowing when I would see her again.

Lieutenant Glasson was already strapped in when I boarded the big transport. Apart from the crew and her rather glossy carer Madison (the woman's first or last name? I'll never know now) we were the only occupants. I took my place next to Verity amidst the tumbled chaos of aero-netted supplies and accepted some warm Liebfraumilch in a plastic tumbler from the co-pilot. After the barest of greetings, any attempt to pre-brief Verity *via* Madison – or to merely enquire as to why Monksilver was so insistent on an interview – came to nothing.

"I understand you're an artist," I finally declared an hour and a half into our journey. I tried to keep it light, aware of the accusatory element of that simple statement. Madison looked blazes but I stared right at Verity even though I knew she couldn't hear me. The old familiar odour – I'd almost forgotten it – filled my nostrils: wood smoke and animal fat.

Verity appeared to be looking up at the bulkhead ceiling. One of her fugue states. I lay my newspaper down and studied her face. I was still intrigued as to why she might have caught Monksilver's eye all those years ago. No great beauty, far from it. The strangely stunted nostrils and ears, vestigial remnants almost; the beakish lips, incapable of speech. A small greyish woman with the arm joints in all the wrong places. Prematurely old, somewhere in the fifties. Must be nearly sixty now. The eyes though: the corneas thick and clouded like a sealion's, a defiant green certainly – but when the tube light caught them they turned the brightest, most blazing yellow. It was as if the light shone outward in compensation. The file stated that Verity was scared of the dark. I'd forgotten that; the fear of something that couldn't be seen or, arguably, imagined.

"I had never encountered art before I entered the class of Dr Monksilver." The tube light flickered a trifle. "As you know all too well, Stephen."

It was Madison who had spoken, of course.

The last words she would ever speak.

The place was more of a military strip than a proper airport. We were bustled through customs at 3.00 am.

We left Madison back on the aircraft: apparently there was a mortuary facility already waiting in the lower hold, the authorities anticipating Verity's desire to communicate and the inevitable consequence. Madison's replacement waited for us by the deserted taxi rank: a slight, muttering man called Klerglas who sported the height of fashion from twenty years ago.

Klerglas was also our driver and after stashing the wheelchair in the boot we spent a further eighteen hours rolling around in the back of a limousine that pre-dated the previous regime. The man – who made no attempt to hide his disdain for Verity and even invoked the sign to ward off the Evil Eye as if he had been coached by Bram Stoker himself – took us higher and higher into the nation's mountain system, the roads ever-more pre-industrial, the villages that flashed by taking on the semblance of crouching trolls. We refuelled from diesel tanks in farmyards. As dawn coloured the snowy peaks, I glanced at the silent woman. I had only seen her in artificial light and now the strange face/non-face was bathed in the early sunshine of her own country. Every mottling teased out, the thick hair triple-crowned like a guinea pig's.

I knew that everything tallied on the genetic level but nevertheless I wondered, almost seriously and not for the first time, if Verity Glasson was entirely human.

When we reached Ligne Claire I was barely human myself. It was teatime now. The car journey had been impossibly long. Surely we had crossed time zones. The continual switchbacks, the gleam and sudden dark of the mountains and the suicidal tendencies of Klerglas. He changed up to round the final bend and the summer camp was suddenly crouching before us in a curious melange of seasoned cinders and barbed wire. A single guard from the international force waved us through and we were immediately shrouded in dense evergreen as the track took us past shuttered booths and badly-parked golf buggies; the air cloyed with the ghosts of gymnasia and young voices. This place had once been vital and now it had delivered itself into the uncaring arms of the eternal forest.

I considered this pithy observation as the basis of a possible re-opening of my dialogue with Verity but caught Klerglas's eye in the rear view mirror. Verity was asleep – appeared to be asleep – anyway, her head against the window, mouth open. We halted at a villa, all wood and glass and carelessly exposed breeze blocks. A cement mixer still stood on the grassless lawn. The house was one of five that bordered a lake, silvered and moving in the larch shadows. The sun would soon be setting. A coffee cup stood on the balcony rail of the villa next door, steam whipping off the top of it in the newly-cold evening. The French windows were closed, the blinds drawn. Was the whole world sleeping today?

Were dreams so much better now?

I surrendered our bags into the arms of a silent housekeeper and returned to the car but Verity had gone. Klerglas was monotoning in the kitchen. The clank of beer bottles.

I padded around the lake's perimeter. No signal on the mobile. Grey sand had been imported and the skeleton of a pedalo was beached next to a pile of mismatched plimsolls. The place was a maze of otter trails. In the seriously fading light, one's eyes strained to fill in the gaps. On the far side I could make out two figures.

But I couldn't be sure.

Flickering imaginos. Like Monksilver's old zoetrope. Why had I suddenly remembered that? The shadows cut across the kitchen with its unfinished wallpapering job. Flick-flicker, flick-flicker: silhouettes scuttling in the low sun of morning, the dark jazzing with the gold. I struggled up. The two-seater settee had seemed comfortable in the dark. And of course Verity – when she had appeared – had been taken upstairs to the only bed in the place. I listened hard but the floor above held only silence. But there *was* sound. As light as a bird on the shingles, lighter even. A crackle like one hears below electrical pylons. The window had no proper curtain, just a gauze blind that caught the shadows and sent them on their furtive way into the farthest corners of the room. I looked up onto the forest path that lay at the back of the building.

Runners. Runners and carts. No, not carts. With their big balloon tyres and rattling parasols these were baby buggies. The runners were dressed in white, like Edwardian Olympians. Or nurses maybe. Yes. ID tags swinging from their necks, red crosses on their breasts, both women and men, maybe a dozen; whippet thin and eyes turned sideways out of forward-facing heads. They seemed to be intent on the house next door.

One of the nurses gazed too long and collided with his fellow. The woman stumbled in turn and lost control of her charge, the buggy careering down the short bank and coming to rest against our kitchen door. I moved – sluggishly, but I moved – to open the window, to offer some helpless remark. But the buggy was empty. Just a tangerine-coloured blanket, slightly soiled. They were all empty. The speeding headlong gait of the runners told me that now. The woman had rescued her buggy and was already hauling it back up the slope. Our eyes briefly locked – puzzlingly one of hers looked just like Verity's – but she was already intent on her journey back into the forest.

The sun, as pale as egg white, somehow less ingenuous, threw its bright coolness about the great bank of primroses above the adventure playground. A pyramid made of ropes; rusting child-sized metal Catherine wheels. I had followed Klerglas as he pushed Verity around the lake and down the wooden ramp and I sat now on the bench next to the apparatus. The bench was formed out of an entire fallen tree trunk, a wellingtonia, and the wood carver had added some flourishes by way of some Disneyesque otters and pine martens. There were several bullet holes.

The wheelchair had been parked by the pyramid. Fascinated, I watched Verity raise her arms, feeling for the ropes. The seemingly boneless fingers made contact and she manoeuvred her strange multi-jointed body upwards, meticulous, the digits splayed and vibrating.

"The trick is only to plant along the top of the bank," I called up, looking directly at Klerglas who promptly spat.

"Plant what?" I answered myself in a sing-song voice.

"Primroses," I replied to myself.

"Primroses?" I sing-songed.

Klerglas snorted, almost caught himself smiling.

I continued: "Primroses. Look how the bank's covered in them. Yellow, pink, roseated hybrids. If the gardeners had planted every inch, the flowers would have choked on each other. But this way the seeds blow naturally down and the effect is more deft."

"He introduced me to darkness," Klerglas said suddenly. His right hand shook but he was holding it together, eyes closed.

Verity swung down in a single movement, one arm cricked over the ropes at the elbow, the fingers of the other reaching to pick one of the flowers. How could she do it? So delicate, so precise. She had some of the furry leaves too, pinched between the digits of her thumbless hand, shivering like the ears of tiny rabbits.

Verity was a mind reader.

"If rabbits grew from the ground, their ears would look like this," said Klerglas.

Stiffly, the driver staggered forward and kicked at a log, revealing the dead yellow grass beneath. Something brown and leathery too. No, only earth.

Klerglas kept kicking.

The darkness.

"Maybe it's something you'd rather forget…" I attempted.

"Why on earth should she want to forget?"

Monksilver stood beside us and his mild eyes locked with mine. He seemed to be curiously alone. But I supposed his guards were somewhere – most likely securing the perimeter against incomers rather than preventing the departure of their solitary prisoner. Dr Monksilver knew all too well what would happen to him beyond these conifered confines.

I tried to equate the figure before me with that Blaze of Glory I had known four decades previously. Not quite as thin – the custard had already got to work – and the lithe elasticity of his limbs seemed to have tightened. He had taken to stillness. The beard against the orange jumpsuit was as suddenly white as snow on cooling lava.

"So. Together again. I'd have dressed more quietly if I knew we had company." He still seemed to be looking at me but his eyes were actually focused on the figure depending from the ropes above the primrose patch. "Part of the charm of this place. Keeping one out of the loop." He closed his eyes, clicked his fingers at Klerglas. "Attend." And then more quietly: "Listen, Verity."

It was an invitation to silence and we took it. Seized it even. The sun was red behind my closed lids. And apart from the chattering of jays high up in the spruces, that silence would have been absolute.

I opened my eyes and turned to Verity but she had disappeared. No. She was here somewhere. I could feel it. Monksilver still stood there, mouth set, his own lids locked, those eyebrows raised in an abruptly remembered aspect of questioning humour.

I stumbled over Klerglas first, perhaps fifty metres distant: bloodied ears staining the leaf litter. Then I found her. Verity had crawled and curled herself around a tree trunk like a snake, the small body somehow elongated, one arm above her head, the other folded into the cleft between body and tree. She had embedded herself into it, had turned her skin the colour of spruce bark. Eyes blank as the yellow irises flipped up inside her head.

The minders were already running towards Monksilver; had him face down spluttering in the sandy soil and tree roots. I reached out to Verity, was only a metre or two away. Watched her eyes finally close as she crumpled down onto the ground as easily as if the trunk was slick with Vaseline.

I discovered Verity's husk at the back of the villa below the forest path that afternoon. I was grateful that I was alone. I wondered if Verity had brought it with her or if the authorities had prepared it prior to our arrival. Perhaps she had crawled outside during the night. It was smaller than the one I remembered from college days but retained what seemed to be key features: the high openings, the curiously taut-yet-untaut construction. Organic. I was aware of a faint odour, the smell of Verity herself.

Doctors had emerged from the woods following Verity's collapse. One of the jogging nurses helped to carry her back then she and Klerglas had slid her into the husk. Klerglas was okay about it, a bloody handkerchief held to his ear. He was in the kitchen now, chuckling quietly. A cable – for all the world like smoked and twisted human flesh – emerged from one of the husk's high openings and disappeared through the trees towards the East. I listened for the crackle, trying to remember what it had truly sounded like.

But all I could hear was the brittle clatter of a ping-pong ball.

*

"Do you know what Ligne Claire means?"

Monksilver and I were playing a brisk game of table tennis in the small courtyard that separated our two houses. The light was fading and he was winning.

"It's an artistic term for clear line. Hergé was a famous exponent." I returned with a slow lazy shot that he easily anticipated, in spite of the limp.

"You're right, of course. But look around. This place is new. It's never been used, never been abandoned. It was built just for me. They were waiting. This place is a clear line between the past and the future."

"It's peaceful."

"Oh yes. They've cleared the countryside. There's a band of landmines that stretches five kilometres out. I have my very own spy plane. You can't see it, it's too far up. They check my toilet seat daily for neurotoxins..." – his volleyed ball shot off the table and nearly shattered against the breeze blocks – "...They want to be seen to be fair. There'll be a trial once they've stopped arguing where to have it. They want to keep it clean, don't want it to be like the Ceauçescus." He stretched and groaned as he reached down for a bottle of water. "And then they'll hang me." He straightened. "At least it'll sort my bloody back out."

As dawn broke, I tried to call my wife from the first floor of the villa but the signal had obviously been jammed. A breeze was up and as I glanced through the rattling windows I noticed the bodies dangling from the branches of the dahurian larches on the other side of the lake. They bumped together like silent wind chimes.

After my second coffee, I went around and checked. Quite good likenesses, the features of real people. Verity's people reduced to painted beanbags. The work of some Eastern protest group who'd managed to break through the perimeter and the guards' ambivalence.

I took the long way back, keenly sensing the eyes all around. I paused on the buggy-trail above the kitchen, bent to retrieve something bright and yellow. A contact lens.

Monksilver was on his balcony when I came around, orange elbows on the rail and relishing the wind. I could make out the lid of the open laptop on a table behind him. He looked down and smiled.

"I'm rather drawn to that primrose business."

Monksilver had never been one for horticulture. I remembered the grandeur of devastation that passed for his garden back in the old days.

"You plant a few seeds and the flowers will spread of their own accord," he continued. It was typical of the man to immediately assume concept proprietorship. "It was the same with The Eastern Question. I didn't need to do much myself. The few seeds I released found fertile ground. They accuse me of genocide. It wasn't like that. It just wasn't like that."

"What *was* it like, Benjamin?" I had spoken so quietly I wasn't sure if he had heard me.

Monksilver snarled: "Those *things*. Those bags of nothing. No more than those bags on the trees over there. Less than that. Can't see, can't hear. Can't speak, most of them. Hack their bloody arms off and they barely know it. Oh yes. We did that. The tabloids were right. But there weren't even two thousand of them. A tiny gene pool interbreeding itself into oblivion. But you would never understand, Stephen. You're a parochial *non-creator*. A real artist knows when to erase, when to wash the canvas clean."

"My God. You see the genocide as a work of art?"

There was a moment. The hum of Verity's cable from behind the villa changing in tone.

Monksilver said in a completely different voice: "Do you remember that funny umbrella she used to carry about with her?"

The sun was still low and I passed into the long shadows leaving the war artist's question unanswered.

*

Mid-morning on the third day and Monksilver and I were deep in the woods, running. What from, I couldn't honestly say – but on the surface we were simply trying to keep fit. They'd found me some tennis shoes and a pair of white shorts from one of the nurses. We'd circled the lake and the villas five times and were now branching off down one of the side trails towards the perimeter.

Running in mutual silence can be comforting. With Monksilver it was merely disconcerting.

Finally: "I've been doing some sculpting, Stephen." It was a relief to realise Monksilver was feeling the burn – although he'd decided to discard the limp for the day.

"Not that bloody Disney bench in the woods. Jesus."

"Beauty through usability. Pure William Morris."

"Well, nobody died –" my stitch was getting worse, I had to stop "– if that's what you mean."

"That's exactly what I mean."

I staggered to a stop, hands on thighs, gasping. We were at the very edge of the camp. There seemed to be no wire here. I could sense the emptiness beyond the trees.

Monksilver continued to run on the spot before doing a couple of star jumps. Bastard. "I've been working on another project too." He abruptly stopped, enveloped in the complete stillness that I'd noticed before. Minutes may have passed. "I've lived too long in darkness, Stephen. And I should never have introduced her to it." He was breathing lightly when he spoke again. "So long."

Monksilver was gone and his words disappeared with him into the silver firs. The branches opened and snapped shut as if he'd never been there.

I blinked the salt out of my eyes. Without looking up, I knew that Verity's cable – musky, sinewy – hummed overhead. He was following it. As far as it would go, out to the farthest East. The ground beneath the brown needles was hot through my rubber soles. In the great murmuring airlessness my breath came in pants, my heartbeat in my head.

An aircraft in the stratosphere made its ice skate trail across the sky. Away to my left a machine-gun opened up.

2

I had my first taste of Verity Glasson at Gavin Beeching's funeral forty years ago. At that point she would have known nothing of Monk-Silver's part in Beeching's demise nor had the slightest inkling – any more than anyone could – of what the following months would bring. Or so I thought.

The coffin had been lowered and the pallbearers had long departed as Monk-Silver (he still affected the hyphen back then) held court by the grave, all collars up against the grey snow. I'd been told that the snow had always been grey in that part of the city.

What one might almost describe as a queue had formed, a flurry of jostling here and there. A handful of female insiders – those that he'd yet to inseminate – were permitted to sit and shiver on the coffin stools in varying attitudes of adoration or concentrated indifference. I was one of Monk-Silver's periphery dwellers, a counsel occasionally engaged, a rollie frequently cadged. By this stage, The Monk-Silver Effect was for me beginning to pall but in the art school hothouse it was difficult to avoid each other.

She stumbled towards the group on a walking frame – her boots a little more hand-stitched than the norm, the Afghan coat closer to its indigenous forebear than the usual boutiquery. That hunch wasn't quite so obvious. She carried a child's umbrella hooked over her forearm that deployed in the shape and colour of a ladybird. And her face. But we were so knowing by then. By this frozen January in the first year of the new decade we knew so much more than we used to. We'd grown up, hadn't we? We all had the Habitat catalogue. We were accepting of the exotic, pretended to shrug it off as the norm.

Nevertheless, could one quite place her provenance?

She was accompanied by a tall woman who introduced herself as Senta. Senta's face and hair held no colour; a hand lying limply on the bar of Verity's walking frame.

Monk-Silver didn't hesitate as he took Verity's hand and staring into the yellow-green eyes, started to ask a question.

"She can't hear you, can't see you. Can't feel –" Senta looked away into the greyness, her free hand beginning to shudder.

"What's your name?" he repeated, his words almost snatched by the traffic from the nearby motorway.

The girl opened her lips a second time but again it was the woman who spoke.

"Her name's Verity."

The three of them had disappeared through the brittle leafless trees of the cemetery, the rest of us forgotten like the grey stones on the grey snow.

Had Verity and he become lovers?

This quickly became a note of common currency within their own circles. Correction: within Monk-Silver's own seething circle. Apart from her colourless companion – who had been encountered quite by chance upon her arrival at the city's railway terminus – Verity had no circle. And she certainly seemed to have no need of one. Verity dwelt in her own imperfect place. That she became a pupil of Benjamin Monk-Silver is a matter of public record. And needless to say the pupils of Dr Monk-Silver had been few and select.

I suppose you know all about Monk-Silver at that time? He had made a career out of wrong-footing his public. Of leading them down a garden path to be confronted not by a green – but by a madhouse. A vegetarian who habitually formed his pea puree into the shape of lamb cutlets. The motoring journalist who did not drive. A throwaway/found object installationist who spent a year deciding on the correct colour to paint his studio walls.

He had begun his career aping the etchings of Pieter Warnock. Yes, the niggling nervy neo-Elizabethan miniature etchings of Pieter Warnock. Pieter Warnock could actually have written that last sentence. "Those trill-trill nothings", as Clive James once opined of Warnock's neurotic output. Was Monk-Silver taking Warnock for a ride? The works of the two artists were at times interchangeable. A cross-hatching versus a shading; an almost but not quite. For Monk-Silver this was art referencing art. Art at its most genuine. Warnock smelled litigation: but how can you police a straight line – or lines – on the waxy ground of an etching plate?

Gavin Beeching was Monk-Silver's next target. Beeching was an obscure happenings artist beloved of the in-in-crowd who frequented book stores more than art schools and thrilled to the thrall so indicative of the era. A master of indeterminacy and tape loops of sham silence (recordings were always made in different spaces and time of day was vital) Beeching at career-peak was considered a very serious jester indeed. But the last joke was on Benjamin Monk-Silver. Much to the chagrin of the Warnock crowd, Monk-Silver succeeded in patenting silence when discoursed through a high-fidelity system thus rendering Beeching a non-player at his own game overnight.

But Monk-Silver could be a charmer back then. A rampant misogynist by today's lights but a warm presence to those of us who knew him. Doing the rounds in his coupé the colour of over-creamed coffee – a rotating guest driver at the wheel of the car of this man who didn't drive. A good mixer at parties, a little too many of which were hosted by himself. He could have lived on *vol-au-vonts* and Asti. He firmly believed that art could not exist by itself. It could only exist in the presence of other art. Warnock never stood a chance and Beeching took the coward's way out.

Yes. A rare artist indeed, this egoist without ego. I'd read those words quite recently in one of the reports from the war crimes tribunal. And I need hardly mention that they were written by Benjamin Monk-Silver himself.

And into this world hobbled a girl from A Different Place. And that she came from a culture without art – that simply did not understand the concept of art – would have left Benjamin breathless, the post-show canapés catching in his craw, his mind and body reeling.

They said she came out of the East. That was the word from Monk-Silver's people. Her mixture of gaucheness and... wisdom, was it? ...seemed to be enough to set the Master's disciples nodding. Ah, the East. The place where the electricity petered out and religion ran rife. Where the snow turned from grey to white. That frontier beyond which the permafrost melted and the old cities tumbled into the dripping ice caverns.

Things were bad in the East.

Perhaps Verity was traumatised. The middle distance would certainly have been her friend – if only she could see; silence her solace if her ears hadn't turned against her.

Shortly after the cemetery business, Monk-Silver had been cornered at a gallery opening by a notorious harpie with lipstuck incisors and an ill-considered Mia Farrow cut who insisted on knowing, darling, just who *was* this little jewel of a savage and who was the teacher and who was the taught? The gathering had drawn in its collective breath, ready for Monk-Silver's acid-tipped rapier but he had barely paused, had even smiled slightly. "She lives in a world without art." Monk-Silver swallowed an olive and its pimiento without chewing. "She's built a little shed in the garden and I've learnt quite a lot from her."

The party wasn't quite the same after that.

A world without art?

I had come to their city, to their country, to study it. A refugee from the benighted suburbs of my own nation, I sought enlightenment in the metropolis of another. It was an extraordinary upheaval – facilitated by an unexpected scholarship and the divorce of my parents. I don't suppose they even noticed I was gone: invisibility was my defining trait back then. And it's become quite an asset in this latter part of my career.

I like to feel I made the most of my newly-discovered freedom, locale and time period. A shared squat with an anarchist events group who despised clothing plus a landlady who brought me hot chocolate every morning with the latest news from the burning streets of Paris. Actually I lived on campus, rarely mixed in those early days and subsisted on egg sandwiches and Marmite flown in from home in quantities that would have done justice to the Berlin Airlift. I was there to study art restoration. I would not be distracted. My tastes were staid, to be sure, with a fatal edging towards the populist. No matter. I understood I was more artisan than artist and perhaps I could be cured of my parochialism.

And then I met Benjamin Monk-Silver.

I wonder whether he mistook me for someone else, sitting as he did with such ease at my canteen table. But perhaps it was merely The Monk-Silver Effect: light bent ever so slightly when he entered a room; you had to wriggle your jaw sideways to counteract the pressure drop. I didn't realise he was one of the tutors. Or was supposed to be. He crunched sugar cubes with his teeth and started to laugh out loud at my mispronunciations. I suppose he adopted me. Not because he wanted his own star to shine all the brighter (I was a one-off in that respect) but because he was intrigued and disgusted by my ambition to become an art restorer.

It was only to be expected. I was a mere repairer of other people's work, a *non-creator*. Apparently, according to the Code of Monk-Silver, I was a man who went against the species ideal of aiming higher. I should still be living in the trees of a pre-Marmite epoch. But to preserve the genius of others, I argued in my stumbling attempts at his language, to become an essentially invisible conduit... The altruism of the restorer/conservator was a rare quality indeed.

And the clear fact that Monk-Silver himself might be seen as a thieving conduit through which flowed the work of others had altogether escaped him.

Monk-Silver had inherited a fading town house in an artistic enclave besieged by business districts. Countless floors; white-washed rooms empty but for a single tuba or an old-fashioned zoetrope or an over-thumbed paperback printed in Tangier; scratchings and scrapings behind the skirting boards; inexplicable mounds of coat hangers in the corridors. And the people... blank-eyed and retreating back into their respective doorways upon our approach. And the back garden was an entire world of its chaotic own: wind sculptures and shattered hothouses; the little Lotus garaged in some sort of bomb shelter.

I was initially taken with the headiness – but was relieved to accept Monk-Silver's invitation to join him on his more relaxed travels around the antique markets and art cinemas. We took to indulging in day-long sessions at the latter: *Ashes and Diamonds, Cul-de-Sac, Women in Love* – the groan-worthy student staples. We seemed to be dwelling in a place of our own. The rest of society like the vortex surrounding the two drowned lovers after they'd loosed the floodgates in the Ken Russell film. Our senses were working on overload.

And then the senseless Verity entered in and two became three.

Two weeks into the relationship thing (his words) with Verity, Monk-Silver had cornered me in the canteen to casually announce he had been into Verity's shed and introduced her to darkness. I stifled a titter. More particularly, he continued with more pomp, the *contrast* between the dark and the light. A slowly flickering zoetrope, black, white, black. In Verity's world of snow, Monk-Silver maintained, true darkness was virtually unknown. But Verity was blind, I pointed out, and virtually senseless in all other respects: the bloodied but uncomplaining knees from the numerous falls, the unheard traffic narrowly avoided...

But I just got The Look and several sugar lumps worth of silence. I – the non-artist – simply didn't understand, that much was clear. Monk-Silver was able to radiate more darkness than Verity had ever dreamed of. If she dreamed. At least that's what Senta told me as she bawled her eyes out in the loo at some happening soon after.

Senta and I actually moved in together for a brief period. We shared the garden flat at Monk-Silver's house. It probably only lasted for days. I've forgotten now. The set-up amused Monk-Silver. He'd completely taken over Verity's care by this stage and Senta's commitment to her own colourless life was rapidly dwindling.

I think Senta wanted to take things further with me. The invisible couple: she may have been attracted by my earnestness. I'd left the revolution in the hands of my brother who'd recently been found blissed-out but dead on a flower bus somewhere in northern India. I owed it to my parents to stay alive, I informed Senta in rather dramatic terms, before striding out into Monk-Silver's vast decrepit garden.

I would never see Senta again. I heard she died detonating a car bomb two years ago.

I stood out in the garden for some time.

The back gardens in the terrace were connected by gateways. Not gates, just gateways. Neighbours came and went with a little wave or a nod. All very communal. When I wasn't doing the films, I spent whole afternoons sitting in a deckchair just waving to people. That's my main memory of this period.

That and Verity's shed.

The shed (or *husk* – Monk-Silver had recently alighted upon the term with some delight) had appeared at the same time as Verity. Nothing much had been said: it was just something we accepted like everything else back then.

The husk appeared to be constructed of a taut material that nevertheless gave slightly to the touch. I'd never been this close before. Organic – like the skin of a drum. Skin. That was it. But it couldn't be, could it? Brown, deeper and lighter in patches. Although the husk possessed a couple of high windows – just openings really – there appeared no obvious means of entry. And looping away from it through the shrubs and continuing on above the other gardens was what appeared to be some sort of cable.

The humming could have been my imagination.

I awoke suddenly a couple of nights later.

By the city-dirty moonlight – in league with the grey snow, no doubt – I padded to the French windows and opened a crack onto the freezing night. Verity was there by the husk, looking right at me. I was somehow certain she could sense me. She wore just a bed-shirt and leant on a single stick, her breath condensing in the blue light; that light silhouetting the bizarre twists of her body against the husk's organic flanks.

And I wasn't imagining it this time. A vibration, a humming from the high-up twisted-skin cable: a melody, a cadence that suddenly filled the world. And it was Verity herself who was singing; who was digging hard now into the husk's surface with her fragmenting fingernails. Creating patterns, darker brown against the lighter. Forms: animal… human… other…

Art from this girl who knew nothing of art.

Song from this girl who could not speak.

I'm not sure when Verity left the city.

When I put it to Monk-Silver the last time I saw him he said she'd left the previous semester.

I'd moved on to a cheap flat beyond the campus soon after I'd seen Verity in the garden that night. Suddenly months were years and Monk-Silver's orbit had spun well out of reach. Even if I had wanted to continue the relationship, he would have flitted on to his next leaf, his next sugar-crunching turn.

He was in the garden on that final visit, sitting out in a deckchair beside the windows of the garden flat. Slug trails crisped on the broken glass houses in the morning warmth. Monk-Silver was currently engaged in a complex civil action involving the colour red.

He was exhausted apparently and didn't get up. He knew I was leaving. My father had suffered his first stroke and mother was being a bit helpless about it all. After Dan's death, I felt I had to seek a surer career path and was considering the civil service. Monk-Silver had laughed – as I knew he would – and declared that this was typical of me. The facilitator of the actions of others.

He, in the meantime, had decided to enter politics.

We left off discussing Verity until the last watch-glancing moment. I'd noticed her husk had gone, a yellowed patch of grass testament to its passing. Mud and sphagnum moss.

Monk-Silver followed my glance. "She took it with her."

I must have looked more of an idiot than usual.

"She sort of rolled it up and took it away with her when she went. Actually she sent a van for it." Monk-Silver seemed amused by this final act of practicality.

I gingerly skirted the broken panes. The traffic throb was quieter here. There were tiny crescent-shaped objects in the mud, stained by the soil's acidity into things of soft waxy rust.

I remembered Verity had bitten her nails.

3

Verity stopped and roll-turned for a second time on the other side of the river but Klerglas and the militaries were already scurrying back to their sleds. They were at war with the new fall of snow. Snow would never be their friend. The men had shaken their heads when we said we would carry on into the white mist; Klerglas had one final spit in the direction of the other-breed woman who had so majestically outpaced them on the glacier: who had drained their sick huskies of blood and discarded the livers before putting the beasts in the pot.

Verity had ditched the chair for the support of ski poles quite soon after leaving Ligne Claire – but she'd been a true revelation as soon as we hit the ice, snapping her skis in half and discarding the nylon anorak in favour of the caribou fat and felt cagoule and leggings of her own people. She slid on her belly now. It was extraordinary, hands and feet paddling like the fins of a sealion, her head raised up like the figurehead of a grey sail-less ship. What new senses were coming into play out here on the great white? Verity had felt the snow flash against the tangerine clouds with a shudder; had steered our course away from a newly-calved ravine and followed the organic moaning cable across the ice sheet. She could sense everything.

Some sort of shaman, I supposed the militaries thought her. That she could hear your heartbeat like wolves can. And this from people – apart from the urban Klerglas – who considered themselves frontiersmen; sneering edge dwellers who still carried purifying tablets and for whom Nature's door would always be barred.

Could Monksilver survive out here? Everything was always on his own terms. He must have a plan. Was the escape some new work of art?

My own mind had slowed right down. The processes that had dominated my life up to this point had no truck on the tundra.

A week beyond Ligne Claire we had rested at some half-town, its buttery foundations already giving way to the warming permafrost. Malnutrition was a way of life and the music was expiring with the electricity. The saloons were silent. I tried to get a call through to my wife without success. Verity had been obliged to call in at the council offices where the local travel committee had grudgingly issued us with internal passports to continue on beyond the glacier. We were to have a military escort. The casual dropping of Benjamin Monksilver into the non-conversation had little effect beyond confirming that he had secured a snowmobile – but didn't appear as if he could survive for more than a few days. Monksilver was a name that could have opened several doors – or assisted a bullet into the backs of our heads.

We dropped off the glacier that morning where its boulders and slag hit a river of real running water. We followed a broken motorway. The grubby remains of an ice fair littered the riverbanks. Shell craters too: I'd never realised the war had reached this far out. We found a ford and Klerglas – with that final spit – and the soldiers struggled up as far as the tree line on the far bank before finally turning back to the West.

Verity did not bother to twist around a third time. Ahead and out of the mist slid the first clutch of husks and she hummed with them and belly-slid up and away into the rolling white vapour.

I'd lost ten kilograms of body fat in a week. Even if Verity had waited I don't suppose her reviving snow senses would have acknowledged The Invisible Man as he collapsed head first into the powder.

But I managed to remain upright, even made some sort of progress. My phone rang as I limped through the husk plantation. The phone was too deep inside my clothes, I couldn't get it. Some husks were occupied, their music louder; others quieter and waiting for life. Oh, this darkless place. The sun kissing the low white hills like shattered sugar cubes. There was no perspective, the eye ran riot and invented.

Verity had caught up with Monksilver. He wasn't in a good way. They were maybe five hundred metres ahead of me. Or fifty. The drone of the snowmobile was seized and taken by the land and air.

My phone rang.

For a moment I thought they were coming back. Monksilver was staring right at me just like Verity that night in the garden. But then he began manhandling the husks around with a new supernatural strength. Shaping and piling them up, the flailing cables slapping and fighting him as he finally forced his way inside. A great rattling filled the misted atmosphere. Verity was already within. I knew that. I was suddenly part of their picture. I was back in the in-crowd. I'd left the Marmite behind. We were on the same cable. The *axon*. We were joined. My phone rang. We were in a deeper, lighter place. The husks were everywhere. I began to run on the crisp, non-giving ice. I could make it in ten minutes.

I'm sure I could.

I am safe in the ganglion. I work slowly on Benjamin; let the frozen limbs thaw gently in their carapace of felt and animal fat. I begin at the shoulders, I squeeze the muscles; feel them ripple past the elbows, a muscle wave easing its way fingerwards. I hum as I work. Deep, bone-buzzingly low. It will be the last thing Benjamin hears. He's sweating now, the beads freezing almost immediately on the snowburnt brow as I knead his eyelids together to keep the light inside. His chemicals are all wrong – he's doused in soap and antiperspirant – but the heat is returning. I nibble Benjamin's fingernails for him. No blackness of dead broken blood. I pluck his ice-brittle eye lashes before I smear them over and slip them between my lips, grateful for the moisture and the salt. I take his eyes and ears and make them mine. The epidermis sloughs off its sensitivity. My fingers catch the skin's fabric like Benjamin's stippling brush testing a new canvas. His face is in my hands. I must be careful what to remove. A real artist knows when to erase, when to wash the canvas clean. Benjamin opens his mouth and begins to speak.

: for Joseph Beuys

THE SENSATIONALISTS

Twenty-one words about their good selves plus an indication of their favourite sense.

Allen Ashley

Writer, editor, poet, writing tutor. Founder of Clockhouse London Writers. Latest book: "Dreaming Spheres" written with Sarah Doyle (PS Publishing/Stanza, 2014)

His favourite sense is touch, just wouldn't want to be without the others.

Tracy Berg

There are words inside
All infected with story
Root withers with bloom.
What else to say? Chronic spewer of thoughts. www.infinity-press.com.

She has never, ever been good at choosing favorites.

David Buchan

David's very short stories have appeared in "Supernatural Tales" and "The Mammoth Book of Best New Horror", amongst other publications.

His favourite sense is sight, probably.

Gary Budgen

Still lives in London. Member of Clockhouse London Writers. A list of published and up and coming work is at: http://garybudgen.wordpress.com/

Favourite sense is touch.

Adam Craig

Writer, photographer, designer. Edits literary imprint "Liquorice Fish" (www. cinnamonpress.com/home/liquorice-fish/). Novel, "Vitus Dreams", published by Cinnamon Press.

Favourite sense: sight.

Kelda Crich

Find Kelda's stories in the "Lovecraft E-zine", "Journal of Unlikely Acceptances", and the Bram Stoker winning "After Death" anthology.

Kelda's favourite sense is smell. She likes nothing better than unsealing a jar and inhaling the sharp smell of formaldehyde and the perfume of cold, preserved flesh. Or kicking though a bed of rotten autumn leaves unveiling the hidden scent of what lies underneath.

Terry Grimwood

Charlatan, con man, mountebank, womansing rogue, claims to be a writer but is patently a fraud, a cad and a bounder.

(Or)

Terry Grimwood

Writer of short stories, novellas, novels, plays and textbooks, publisher at theEXAGGERATEDpress, blues harpist, college tutor, husband, father and granddad.

His favourite sense is most definitely sight.

David Gullen

Fell in love with a mermaid, writing ever since. "Shopocalypse" is his SF novel, "Open Waters" his collection. http://davidgullen.com

His favourite sense is sound.

Rhys Hughes

Author of many works. Lover of other cultures and diversity. Traveller, stargazer, climber, dancer, drummer, mathematician. Founder of Gloomy Seahorse Press.

His favourite sense is sight and capturing photons with his different coloured eyes is one of his main hobbies.

Ian Hunter

Children's author, editor, poet, book reviewer, Director of the Scottish Writers' Collective Read Raw, and poetry editor for the "BFS Journal".

His favourite sense is sight despite having chronic corneal dystrophy in his right eye which occasionally gets "scraped" to let his cornea re-grow, which causes his left eye to close in sympathy, or in fear.

Jon Michael Kelley

Writer. Recent credits include "Qualia Nous", "Chiral Mad 2", "Dark Muses/Spoken Silences", "Miseria's Chorale", and the upcoming "Dead Harvest".

His favorite sense is the one most fickle: The Sixth.

Mark Patrick Lynch

Isn't sure why he writes. Is scared of stopping, though. "Hour of the Black Wolf" (hardcover: Robert Hale; reprint: FA Thorpe).

He tells people his favourite sense is good sense, but anyone who knows him will tell you he hasn't any of that and it's all nonsense.

E. Lillith McDermott

Writer of dark fiction for young adults and adults who think young. Her work can be found on TheColoredLens.com and Metrofiction.net.

Her favorite sense is sight – so much reading to do!

David McGroarty

Scottish writer of strange and fantastic fiction. Stories in "Astrologica", "Rustblind and Silverbright", "Caledonia Dreamin'". Member of Clockhouse London Writers. (www.davidmcgroarty.net)

His favourite sense is taste, particularly if butter is involved.

Ralph Robert Moore

Novelist, short story writer, essayist. His latest book, "Ghosters", a novel in the form of short stories, will appear in 2015.

His favorite sense is taste. You put part of the world inside you.

Christine Morgan

Horror fan. Weird/cool mom. Works nights in a psych facility. Talks to her cats. Reads, writes, reviews, edits.
http://www.christine-morgan.org/
https://www.facebook.com/christinemorganauthor

Her favourite sense is sight; one of her worst fears is blindness.

Richard Mosses

Word shaman, lapsed scientist, economic developer. Unpublished novels looking for a good home. www.khaibit.com

His most developed sense is smell; his Kryptonite is Chanel No 5.

Tim Nickels

Full-time reader, part-time writer. The buggy jogger scene is inspired by a real-life 5.00 am encounter one Autumn morning at Center Parcs.

Other than wonder, his favourite sense is that of hearing.

Douglas Thompson

Director of the Scottish Writers Centre, author of eight books: "Ultrameta", "Sylvow", "Apoidea", "Mechagnosis", "Entanglement", "The Brahan Seer", "The Rhymer", "Volwys".

His favourite sense is smell because it seems to afford time travel.

David Turnbull

Writer of short fiction. Clockhouse London writer. Recent anthologies: "Best British Fantasy 2014", "Horror Uncut", "A Taste of Saccharine". http://www.tumsh.co.uk/

As a former chef, taste has to be up there as his favourite but smell and sight are just as important to a good meal.

Stanley B. Webb

A writer, artist, dreamer, connoisseur of monster movies, handyman, resides near Lake Ontario. Anthologies include "Teeming Terrors" and "Daylight Dims 2".

Vision is his favored sense.

Aliya Whiteley

Her latest book, "The Beauty" is available from Unsung Stories (2014). She writes speculative fiction and tweets most days as @AliyaWhiteley.

Her favourite sense is smell, particularly first thing in the morning.